# DUST TO DUST

EXPERIMENT IN TERROR #9

KARINA HALLE

THE FINAL BOOK IN THE EIT SERIES

Copyright © 2014 by Karina Halle

First edition published by Metal Blonde Books

Second edition published 2020

All rights reserved.

No part of this book may be reproduced in any form or by any electronic or mechanical means, including information storage and retrieval systems, without written permission from the author, except for the use of brief quotations in a book review.

Cover: Hang Le Designs

Edited by: Kara Malinczak

*For Dex and Perry. I hope I did you proud.*

# 1

PERRY

I was walking on the Brooklyn Bridge, the sky above me a black velvet blanket tinged with orange the closer it got to the horizon. There were no stars, not here with the city of New York right in front of me. The buildings acted like stars instead, their lights blurred and out of focus like the Photoshop bokeh effect.

Though it wasn't snowing, the bridge was covered in a light dusting of pure white snow. I was only wearing my jeans and a thin Slayer hoodie and yet wasn't cold at all.

Everything around me was silent. There were no cars and there were no people. The river below didn't lap, and the sounds of the city didn't carry. The snow was a blank sheet of paper except for the one set of tracks that cut down the middle.

I knew those footprints—made by boots—like I knew the back of my hand. They were what I had been searching for all this time. Why I was here.

I walked on, slowly, hearing the snow squeak beneath my Chuck Taylors. Suddenly the footprints veered off to the side of the walkway and stopped. I followed them and looked over the edge to where the cars should have been driving past, heading into the city.

There was a man standing on the shoulder, looking out at the Hudson River. I couldn't see anything but his shadowy back, but I knew it was him.

"Dex!" I yelled. But he didn't move. He didn't turn around.

I yelled again. I knew it was him. Why wasn't he listening? Just how long had we been apart?

I was so tempted to take off my shoe and chuck it at him but decided I'd probably miss. Instead, I took in a deep breath and managed to climb over the edge of the walkway and onto one of the metal beams that spanned above the lanes. Somehow I was able to balance perfectly, like a tightrope walker, as I made my way across. When I was near Dex, I lay down on my stomach and then slid off the edge of the beam, hanging in the air like a child from monkey bars for a few seconds before I let go.

I landed with a soft thud, my knees aching from the impact. It was a long drop, and I was surprised that I had even done it to begin with but there was no time to question anything.

I ran up to him and put my hand on his arm, my fingers wrapping around his elbow, afraid to let him go ever again.

He didn't turn to look at me. He didn't move. He didn't make a sound.

I pulled back at him hard, panic coursing through me. What was going on?

He was immovable, stuck to the cold white ground.

"Dex?" I whispered, and walked around him. He was staring forward at the inky water, his face startlingly handsome with his high cheekbones and strong jaw flanked by light facial hair. But he was pale as snow, and his eyes were so dark they rivaled the sky. His expression was strangely blank, and the wisps of his shaggy black hair swayed lightly in the breeze.

He wouldn't look at me, wouldn't acknowledge me. I wasn't even sure if he was real or a wax figure. I watched him, feeling the horror rising from deep within me, wondering if he was even breathing.

"That's not Declan," a smug voice from behind me said. I jumped and whirled around to see ... no one.

"Up here."

I looked up and saw a man in a business suit standing on the beam above me. The ends of his blazer flapped in the breeze and his face was obscured in shadow.

Still, I knew who he was. Every bone in my body told me who this was. I had met him before.

"What's wrong with him?" I asked the man. I grabbed Dex's hand, squeezing it and staring into his face, trying to get a reaction, to get something out of him. He didn't even blink. He was just still, his eyebrow ring glinting from the city lights. This was Dex, my Dex, my man, my love, my fiancé. This was him. I knew him better than I knew myself.

Then what was wrong with him? I couldn't have traveled all this way to have failed in the end. I was supposed to bring him home.

"There is nothing wrong with him," the man said from above. "He's better now. He's buried down below where he belongs."

I looked up at the man, feeling his hateful eyes upon me. They shone like nickels in the shadows, and my stomach steeled itself in protest. This man evoked nothing but primal fear in me.

"What did you do to him?" I whispered. My eyes flitted

over to Dex again, and I could only shake my head. This *was* Dex.

"The same thing I will do to you and your sister and your mother," he said.

My breath caught in my throat, and when I finally exhaled, it came out painfully cold. Glowing embers began to fall from the sky, turning to ash as soon as they hit my skin. It burned and the snow sizzled.

"What?" I managed to ask, feeling myself slowly being drained of strength.

He grinned at me and his teeth glowed white. "You'll find out soon enough."

Then he turned sharply and strode away along the beam, the metal creaking until he reached the walkway.

"Michael!" I screamed after him. "You can't leave him like this. He's your brother."

He shook his head, and for once I could see the glow of his skin from the light of the city. It was burned and red. I blinked my eyes, trying to see if it was his skin tone or color being reflected onto him.

"No," he said. "He's not my brother. And I haven't been Michael for a very long time."

He climbed onto the walkway and disappeared.

Suddenly the bridge quaked, jerking from side to side and throwing me off balance. I grabbed on to Dex to steady me, and as I did so a terrific crash throttled the air. The bridge deck began to split from the end, a crack racing toward us in one dark, jagged line. Flames began to lick up through the split, and the suspension cables along the bridge began to snap and fly out, whooshing through the air with a metallic noise.

Everything was still shaking, the bridge splitting right in two. It was heading right for us, right for Dex. The flames grew higher as they shot out of the crack, and from the corner of my eye the world was slowly starting to become lighter, the East River turning from inky black water to a living floor of fire.

"Dex!" I yelled, trying to get him out of the way.

But he wouldn't budge.

The damn man wouldn't budge.

And the bridge continued to crack.

I had two choices, and in that I had *no* choice. I was either going to go down with him and be swallowed whole by the inferno that was about to devour us, or I could step aside, save myself, and let him die.

There really was only one choice.

I grabbed on to his stiff body, wrapping my arms around him from behind, and buried my face into the back of his neck.

"I love you," I whimpered. "Always. Beyond death."

My legs started to wobble. The fire got hotter. The crack seemed to split my world.

But before I was sure the ground beneath us would fall, Dex suddenly moved.

He spun around to face me and kissed me, quick and searing on my lips, making my heart flutter and my body ache with need and love. When I opened my eyes, I saw his eyes brimming with intensity. Here he was, right before the end.

Then he pushed me backward. I stumbled and fell back on the deck just as the crack was a split second from taking him away from me.

"Don't let him in, kiddo," he said gravely, his gaze freezing me. "Don't let him in."

I screamed, "No!" and tried vainly to get to my feet. "Dex!"

But the split rocked under him, the ground opening with a deafening crack.

Dex slipped away from view, swallowed by the flames.

He was gone into a fiery hell while the embers continued to fall from the sky.

Turning to ash.

Turning to dust.

Just like my heart.

I AWOKE to something tickling my face. I groaned and moved my head. It felt as if something was inside my brain, pinching at different sections, impeding my ability to think. I couldn't think—it was just all blank. Dull and grey.

I decided to keep my eyes closed and go back to wherever I came from.

Something wet swiped across my cheeks. More tickling.

Finally I opened my eyes, wincing at the bright light from the sky and yellow fur that was in front of my face.

"Kayla!" someone yelled from far away, a woman's voice.

Suddenly the licking stopped. I slowly pushed myself up on my elbows and watched as a shaggy golden retriever ran away and into the bushes.

Where the hell was I? I looked around, feeling stupider than ever, like my mental ability had regressed a few decades. What had happened?

"Oh my goodness," came a voice above me, and I looked up to see a middle-aged woman stop a few feet away, the golden retriever at her side. "Are you okay?"

I blinked and tried to get up but could barely get to my feet. The woman was at my side and helping me the rest of the way.

Her eyes peered at me inquisitively. "Do you need me to call an ambulance?" she asked, her dog sticking its cold nose into my hand.

Though I was dizzy, I knew I was okay. Physically, anyway. "No," I said slowly, trying to step away from her grasp. My mind raced, trying desperately to hold on to the fragments of memory that were whizzing past.

I had gone for a walk by the river.

A man had been here.

He'd talked to me.

He knew my name.

"Are you sure?" the woman was repeating, while telling her dog Kayla to leave me alone.

I stared at her dumbly, absently noting how silver her hair was, as shock hit me with a million pinpricks.

Michael O'Shea, Dex's brother, had been here. He knew my name, he'd mentioned my blood. He said he'd see me in New York.

Then he kissed me and I was out.

He was going after Dex.

"I have to go!" I told the woman, turning on my heel and running down the path that would take me to my street. I couldn't run fast enough. Even though I knew I hadn't been hurt by the altercation, it still felt like a nightmare, like I was trying to lift my feet out of drying cement and I couldn't move fast enough. Even my fingers were slow as I repeatedly tried to call Dex's cell. It rang and rang and rang until it finally started going straight to voicemail.

Somehow I made it to my house. My parents' car was still gone but now so was the Highlander.

Shit.

I couldn't exactly explain what it was that was making me panic; maybe it was the obtuse way Michael had talked to me, maybe it was Pippa's warnings ringing in my ear and forcing me to connect the dots, or maybe it was the fact that when I looked into Michael's eyes I saw the absence of humanity inside their depths. It didn't matter. Every single nerve in my body was telling me to hurry now and ask questions later. The fact that Dex's car was gone was not helping. It seemed like going for a friendly drive with his estranged brother would be the last thing he'd want to do.

The front door to my house was already open, though as I booked it up the driveway, I noted that there weren't any signs of blood or struggle. I burst into the front hall and looked around wildly.

"Dex!" I yelled. "Dex!" I started running for the stairs but heard a slight moan coming from the kitchen. I paused. "Ada!?"

I ran inside and saw her lying on her side on the tile floor, trying to sit up, her blonde hair in her face. I immediately dropped to my knees and put my hands on her shoulders. She was damp to the touch, though it was probably from the workout she had been doing in the living room earlier.

"Ada!" I said, trying not to screech. "What happened?"

"Perry?" she asked weakly. I helped her get into a sitting position.

"What happened?" I asked again, applying slight pressure to her shoulders. "Where is Dex?"

She put a hand to her forehead and slowly shook her head. "I ... I don't know. I ... there was a man here." Suddenly she looked straight at me, fear mixed with sweat on her brow. "Oh my god. He took Dex."

I swallowed hard, trying my hardest not to let the terror take over me. "How do you know that? What happened? Think!"

She rubbed her lips together, her forehead creased as she tried to think. "I was just in the living room ... working out. I heard a knock at the door and went to answer it. There was this guy. At first I thought he was selling something, he had this douchebag kind of smile, you know, and then I realized that there was something seriously wrong with this guy." She took in a deep breath. "I can't explain why I thought that, it was just a feeling or the way he was looking at me, I don't know. He asked if Dex was home. And he was ... I'm sorry, Perry, I didn't know what to say."

I shook my head, trying to get her to continue. I felt like we were losing time by the second.

She went on, sliding her hands down over her face. "I told him to hang on a second, that I would go get him. But Dex was already coming down the stairs, like he knew. And that's when I knew I made a big fucking mistake by answering that door. The look on Dex's face ... I can't describe it. He was angry. And then, then it was like he was fucking terrified, more than I've ever seen him."

She paused. "The guy, he told Dex he'd been looking for him, that he finally needed him for something. And Dex, he didn't say anything. I wasn't even sure if he heard him at first. Then he looked at me, and I knew how much trouble we were in. He yelled at me to run and get you." She exhaled shakily, and in her eyes I saw as much helplessness as I felt. "I was going to, I started to run. Then the guy reached out and touched my shoulder, and that's the last thing I remember. I guess he dragged me to the kitchen, I don't know."

I couldn't even process it, and yet my brain was attempting to. Dex was gone. Michael had him. He had managed to knock both Ada and I out with either a touch or some way of getting inside of our heads. What did he want with Dex? Did Dex go willingly? Where were they headed?

*I'll see you in New York, Perry*. That's what Michael had said to me.

"What is it?" Ada asked. "Who was that guy? What happened to me?"

I took in a deep breath, trying to hold it together in whatever way I could. "That was Dex's brother."

She frowned. "Huh?"

I slowly got to my feet and helped her to hers. "Michael O'Shea," I told her. "I met him on my walk. Whatever he did to you, he did to me. He was able to get in my head and he was able to get in yours. And whatever he wants with Dex … it's not good."

"I figured as much."

"Ada," I said slowly, wishing she could feel my panic, know what Pippa had said to me. "Listen to me. As dramatic and batshit crazy as this all is and all sounds, we have to get Dex back."

She pursed her lips, perhaps weighing just how crazy it did all sound. "How?"

I paced across the kitchen, wringing my hands, trying to go through the options. There weren't many.

"I don't know. He's gone with Michael, in his car. I doubt it was voluntary, and even if it was … I have to go to New York."

She stared at me blankly. "Sorry, what?"

I bit my lip and nodded to myself. "Yeah. I have to go to New York. Manhattan. That's where Michael is taking him."

"And how do you happen to know this?"

Splices of a dream came back to me. One with Pippa just a week ago, a dream of warnings on the Brooklyn Bridge. The other dream more recent, punctuated by raining embers in snow. A dream of death and Dex.

Now that I knew what had to happen, I was filled with

an even greater sense of urgency. All signs were pointing to this.

I tried to explain to her as quickly as I could and as best I could, starting with what little I knew about Michael, about the Pippa in my dreams warning me about imminent danger, about what Michael had said to me. The more I talked, the crazier it all sounded, but Ada, bless her soul, was able to put that aside and just listen. She was able to believe me.

"You can't just fly to New York, Perry," she said after I felt absolutely breathless from the truth. "Where will you go? Wander the streets shouting for Dex like a nutter butter? You have nothing to go on."

"No," I said. "I have something to go on." I brought out my phone, and in vain tried Dex's cell again. I hung up at his familiar message, ignoring the pang of hurt that threatened to rip through me at the mere sound of his voice.

This couldn't be happening. Not like this. Not now when everything in our lives was finally coming together.

"Perry?" Ada asked, and I realized I was standing there, hand to my chest, my grip nearly breaking my phone.

I quickly nodded and dialed a number. My first thought was to call Rebecca, but as much as I needed her help, she also wasn't like me, like *us*—she didn't know how to deal with this sort of thing, despite what we had just gone through at the asylum. Also, she was still on the I-5, riding Putt-Putt toward her final destination, and time wasn't on my side.

So I called the only other person who not only would understand but could possibly help me and help Dex. The only person who knew a thing about Dex's life in New York.

I called Maximus.

But, naturally, life was a sick bitch and he didn't answer

his phone. I started to wonder if perhaps Michael's reach was farther than I thought and he too had been compromised. So I left a frantic voice message for the ginger to call me back and then ran upstairs to pack an overnight bag.

"What are you doing?" Ada yelled at me, hot on my heels.

"I told you!" I raced into my room and started throwing shit around. I crammed a few pairs of underwear and a bra into a small carry-on along with a pair of jeans and a few shirts.

"Perry, seriously!" she screeched, grabbing my arm and making me stop. I'd never seen such worry in her eyes before. "Don't just go and do this. You don't know anything for sure."

"I know that if he just wanted to talk to Dex, he wouldn't have sought me out. He wouldn't have done what he did to us. You saw his eyes, that ... that emptiness. You know he's bad news."

"But he *wants* you to come to New York," she said. "He's baiting you."

I stood up straight and looked her dead in the eye. "Then I'm taking the bait. But I can't stay here and hope that he'll come back, hope that I'll get a hold of him. We both know that's not going to happen. It's this or it's nothing, and I'm supposed to marry the fucking guy! If there is anything I know about me and Dex it's that nothing is never an option. I'm going to New York. And you're letting me go."

"Fuck that," she swore, a strange gleam coming over her eyes. "I'm not letting you go. I'm coming with you."

"Ada," I said incredulously. "No way."

"Yes," she said. "You're my sister, and I'm not going to let you do this by yourself."

"You've got school," I said feebly. Truth was, I wanted her

to come. More than that, I needed her to come. I could feel it in my gut, like I was stronger with her by my side. But I wouldn't be a good sister if I didn't insist she stay out of it. She was too young to get wrapped up in something that neither of us understood.

"You can't stop me," she said full of fiery conviction. "If you do this without me, I'll be right behind you. You have money on your credit card? I have money on mine."

"You're too young to travel alone," I countered.

She smiled coyly. "I have ways."

"Mom and Dad will never let it happen."

"You let me worry about them."

"Ada."

"Perry," she answered, and for once I saw how damn serious she was. "If you're going after him, I'm going with you. End of story. Now, would you rather me go with you now or trail your ass through the city trying to catch up? Though perhaps I'll meet some nice New York men who'll be willing to help me."

I grimaced at the thought of my little sister alone in the Big Apple trying to duplicate scenes from Sex and the City. Throw in some blood and gore, and it would be pretty accurate.

*Don't think like that,* I told myself. *Don't think at all. Just go there. Keep calling, keep trying. And go.*

And so I did. There was no way I was able to prevent Ada from going with me, and from the conviction in her face, I know she'd be stupid enough to try it alone. She was better off with me, even if I had no clue what I was about to do.

While she packed in a whirlwind—I think, despite the dire circumstances, she was excited about going to New York for the first time—I called a cab and sent texts to Maximus,

Rebecca, and Dex. I knew the Dex one wouldn't go through —normally I could tell when he read them, and it wasn't the case. I still watched with my breath held, hoping that he'd read my words.

When I realized he wouldn't, I put down the phone and closed my eyes.

*Dex!* I yelled inside my head. It was a long shot, but I was still going to take it. *Dex, can you hear me? I don't know where you are or what's going on but I know you need me. Michael, your brother, he's not a good person and I'm scared for you. I'm coming to New York, hoping you're there.* I paused. *I love you.*

Even in my head, it came out more like a whisper.

I waited again, not knowing if he could hear me wherever he was, and if he could, if he would respond. But there was a void. There was nothing but the prickly grey behind my eyes and the sound of Ada running down the stairs.

My heart never felt so empty.

Ada put her hand on my shoulder and squeezed it. "Hey. We're gonna get him back. He's gonna be fine."

I looked at her and tried to draw in her strength. I nodded. "Cab will be here. Let's go wait outside."

I'D NEVER JUST SHOWN up at an airport before and tried to buy a ticket for a plane. In fact, I don't think I'd ever really bought a ticket for a plane in general. In the past, whenever I'd travel, it was always my parents who made the arrangements.

Or Dex.

I thought back to the first time I'd flown alone, when I was going down to meet him in Red Fox, New Mexico. It felt so long ago, not only with the passing of time but the passing of character. I was no longer that shy, insecure girl who stared adoringly at Dex and prayed that he felt the same thing for me as I did for him. Granted, I was still flawed, deeply and terribly, but when I looked back at how far I'd come, sometimes it was almost unbelievable.

It wouldn't have happened without him. I wouldn't have become the person I was without him.

I couldn't lose him. I wouldn't.

I tried to keep those feelings at bay while the cab took us to the airport. Every moment I thought about Dex, every time I felt that rush of anxiety and pain, it was a moment taking me out of the game. I had to stay focused.

Turns out though, that you can't just hop on a plane to New York. Well, you can—they took my money, after all. But we were put on standby, which didn't help with my anxiety. While Ada took her time perusing the airport gift shops and snapping up bags of junk food and high fashion magazines, I started texting the crap out of Rebecca, Maximus, and Dex again. I also started waiting for the dreaded phone call from my parents, the one they'd make once they realized everyone had suddenly disappeared. It probably would have helped to leave a note, but what the hell would it have said anyway? Be right back, we've gone to New York because Dex was kidnapped by his long lost brother whom we think is in cahoots with Satan? Not that my parents would be terribly surprised at this rate.

I thought back to my mom, about the medication I'd taken from her. I hadn't meant to take it, just switch out a few pills and see what happened. But the pills were in the bottom of my purse, and they were coming with me. I could no longer monitor her and see if she was experiencing anything, to see if she saw ghosts like I did. I could only hope that what I did would make her realize that I knew and that she needed to fess up to being just like Ada and me.

Thankfully it didn't take too long for us to get on standby, even though Ada had to occupy another seat further back in the plane. She wasn't too happy about that, but at least she was seated next to a thin, anti-social looking woman. I was seated next to some fat businessman who kept jabbing his elbows into me, taking up far more space than what was politely possible.

It was just when everyone had boarded and the flight attendants started their safety demonstration that Rebecca called me. Even though the nearest attendant had just made a point about putting all phones in airplane mode, I quickly answered it.

"Thank god," I said into the phone.

"Perry?" Rebecca asked. "I just got your text. What happened?"

"I don't know," I said, my voice shaking all over again. I was aware that bacon in a suit was looking at me with interest. I moved closer to the window, until I was smooshed up against it. "Dex ... he's gone. His brother appeared out of nowhere and I think he took him," I whispered frantically into the phone.

"Miss, you're going to have to turn off your phone, please," I heard the flight attendant say.

I looked over my shoulder at her and nodded. "Okay," I said to her before I addressed Rebecca. "Rebecca, I have to go. I'm heading to New York with Ada."

"What?" she screeched.

"I think that's where Michael is taking Dex," I said. "I'll call you when we land, okay?"

"Bloody hell, Perry," she said. "What the hell is going on?"

I bit my lip. "I wish I knew."

I quickly hung up just as the attendant came back up the aisle again, her narrow eagle eyes on me.

And my phone rang again.

"Shit," I said, fishing it out of the seat pocket and fumbling in the contained space. It was from Maximus.

"Max!' I cried out into the phone.

"Perry, what's wrong?" Strange to say, but it felt good to hear that familiar drawl of his.

"It's Dex. He's in trouble," I said, now totally aware that not only was the guy next to me staring at me but the person on the aisle too. And the flight attendant was back.

She pointed to the phone, her lips pinched together. "Miss, please, you must—"

I actually shushed her and went back to listening to Maximus who was saying, "You said Michael has him. Are you sure? How is that possible?"

"Yes, I'm sure," I said quickly. "We're on a plane to New York, me and Ada. Please, you've got to help us. I know you're busy and all but I'm really fucking worried, and I feel like this is much bigger than it seems."

"Miss," the attendant snapped.

"This is a matter of life or death!" I snapped right back, glaring at her. Every head on the plane turned to look at me. I heard Ada groan in the background, obviously embarrassed. I sounded like a crazy person, but for once I knew I wasn't.

"Then it won't make a difference if you're removed from the plane or not," she said. "Please shut down your phone or that's exactly what will happen."

I sighed, knowing it was a losing battle. "I'll call you when we land," I told him before I hung up.

I sat back in my seat in a huff as I put the phone in

airplane mode. There had to be nothing worse than being out of contact for five hours when you were in the middle of telling someone something important. Actually, the only thing worse was having to sit there and wait five hours until you could do anything to try and save the man you loved.

That and having elbows jabbed into your boobs every five seconds.

## 2

PERRY

We got to New York late, as was expected when you were on standby and flying from West to East. Luckily, NYC was the city that never sleeps and we were still running on time from three hours earlier. The minute Ada and I stepped off the plane and into JFK, we were jumping from nerves. After being accosted by several wannabe rapists that were pretending to be cab drivers, we got into a legit taxi and headed to the Big Apple, Ada practically hanging her head out the window in awe.

It was odd to finally see the landmarks of the city up close and personal for the first time. Though I found myself marveling at the fact that I was here, I wasn't enjoying any of it. How could I? I always imagined I'd see New York with Dex by my side, not going after Dex because I believed he was in danger.

*Oh Dex, where are you?* I thought as I rested my head against the window and watched the landscape slide past into a mess of twinkling lights. *How could everything have changed so quickly?*

"Where are we going, by the way?" Ada asked, turning to face me, half of her hidden in the passing shadows.

Before we left Portland, I quickly found a hotel for us to stay at for a few nights. It seemed clean and safe (and, like all other hotels in the city, expensive), which is all I needed at a time like this, but even though I gave the cabbie an address, I had no idea where in New York it was.

"I don't know," I said.

I caught the cabbie eying me in the rearview mirror. "Uptown, Westside," he said in his thick accent.

Normally I would have pretended to know where that was, just to save face, but I didn't have it in me. Instead, Ada leaned forward in her seat and started talking the cabbie's face off, seemingly delighted by our first "real" New Yorker. It should have annoyed me that she was acting like Dex's life wasn't at stake, but it didn't. She was keeping me calm and sane, which in turn was keeping me focused.

The thing was, there was no game plan. Once off the plane, I called Maximus but again it went to voicemail. I had a few voicemails of my own, but they were from my parents. I checked, just in case they were from Dex or Max, but the minute I heard my mother's shrill voice, I erased it. I knew I had to deal with it, but I just couldn't, not until I had a plan.

Now that I was in Manhattan, I was feeling rather stupid and unprepared. I had acted on impulse and impulse had brought me here with no plan at all, and because of that, I had no idea whatsoever how we were going to find Dex.

On the plus side, I knew we were in the right place. Whether Dex was here or not, I knew we were where we were supposed to be. I could feel it, deep inside my bones, like there was some truth at the center of my marrow. Underneath the flashy lights and the slick streets and the throngs of people passing in the warm night, there was an undertone to the city that reeked of madness.

I'm sure it had nothing to do with New York itself. It was because I was here and so was something else. Something malicious and sinister, something black and oozing and hateful that clung to the legs of passerby and on the side of the buildings and permeated the air. I couldn't quite see it, but I could sense it, and whether it was a trick of the eye or the glare of the window, I could catch glimpses of this evil sticking in patches around me.

Ada didn't seem to notice at all. She was all wrapped up in the glitz and glamor, as any girl her age should be. But it didn't stay that way for long.

It turned out our hotel was located just off Broadway and a bit north of all the shows. If memory served me correctly, this was the neighborhood Jerry Seinfeld lived in. The hotel was smaller and more posh than I had imagined; then again I was used to staying in motels with Dex, so what did I know?

After checking in, Ada and I got into the empty elevator. The hotel was quiet at this time of night. Our room was on the ninth floor, and though it wasn't the speediest elevator, it started to slow down around floor five.

Then it slowly came to a stop on floor six.

Ada and I exchanged a glance. All the fine hairs at the back of my neck stood on end, and it wasn't because I was afraid of an elevator malfunction.

Something was on the other side of the elevator doors. Something I didn't want to see.

I swallowed hard and tried to calm my heart which started jumping about in my chest. My mouth was suddenly dry, and I opened it, wanting to say something to Ada but not sure what to say. I wanted to warn her.

But about *what*?

The elevator doors groaned and slowly began to open, one two-inch crack at a time. At first I saw someone passing on the other side—a tall shadow, the white gleam of an all-seeing eye as it looked right at me, but as the doors opened wider, there was nothing there but the empty hallway.

A shiver rocked through me. This was only the beginning.

"That's weird," Ada said, but her voice was nothing more than a ragged whisper.

"Yeah," I agreed, knowing that nothing was just weird when it came to me. Weird was what you called abnormal things when you were normal. Weird you could write off. We couldn't write off any of this. There were no such things as strange occurrences—everything had a purpose. Everything was very real and very dangerous. There was no way any of this was going to be easy.

Thankfully, the elevator doors began to close, and we were whisked up to our floor. Ada seemed to forget the weird incident the moment she saw our room. While it wasn't very big—just a desk, a chair, and two twin beds off a tiny bathroom—it was very sleek and modern, the kind of pink and white scheme you'd see on any trendy show or in a magazine.

My phone was dead so I started charging it while I tried to figure out what to do. I was just wondering what Maximus would suggest, when Ada started to strip down, her thin back to me in a rare show of modesty, putting on her pajamas.

"What are you doing?" I asked her.

"Going to bed?" she said questioningly.

I threw out my arms in an exaggerated motion. "Now?"

She frowned. "It's one o'clock."

"Yeah, east coast time. It's only ten o'clock for us."

She went to her bed and threw back the fluffy covers. "And I go to bed at ten anyway. Beauty sleep, hello? What's your deal? Do you really think we're going to go searching through the streets of New York fucking City past midnight, just the two of us? I don't think so."

That made me pause. I took in a deep breath. "Stop being the voice of reason."

"Someone has to," she said as she crawled under the covers and gave me a dry look. "I know you want to find Dex, and we will. I believe you and Pippa and everything that was said. But we don't even know if he's here right now. Did they fly? Did they take a road trip? We don't know."

"He's here," I muttered to myself.

"Maybe," she said. "But there is seriously nothing we can do right now, am I right? Right. So let's just chill out and go to sleep. I'm tired, you're tired, and this bed is really fucking comfy."

I sighed, staring at my phone that was still dead but charging. I did tell Maximus what hotel we were staying at, so at least he could call us that way.

I reluctantly wiped my makeup off my face and then went to bed too.

I expected to stay awake the whole night, just tossing and turning, but I didn't have to do so for long. I was out in a few minutes.

Ada was right. The bed really was comfy.

∼

I DREAMED ABOUT DEX. We were back on the Brooklyn Bridge, but it was a glorious, warm sunny day. We were holding hands, his strong, familiar fingers laced with mine, and swinging our arms like little kids. There were people milling around us on the walkway, but it felt like we were the only people alive.

At some point we stopped to stare at the buildings of Manhattan, and he pulled me to him, kissing my temple. I felt flooded with the warmth of his touch, of his love, and with the sunshine that beat down on us from above.

Even though nothing unusual was happening, I knew it was a dream and that this moment of peace and clarity wouldn't last.

And yet it did. The dream continued on so seamlessly, so real, that I couldn't believe my luck. No burning embers fell from the sky, no Satanic creatures came crawling out of the sea. People were happy.

We were happy.

I leaned into Dex and admired the sparkle of my ring in the light. It looked brighter here, with him. Better. Everything was better with him by my side.

But the dream didn't last forever. Just as I was laughing over something he said—because when wasn't I laughing with Dex—and melting at the sight of his smile, everything started to fade and get fuzzy. He was slipping from my grasp, from my view.

The dream was ending.

And suddenly I was in a hotel room in New York, Ada snoring softly beside me. It was dark, though a sliver of orange light slid in through the blackout curtains. Outside the city hummed with constant noise and it was impossible to tell whether the city was winding down or waking up.

My face was wet with tears and my fingers were gripped firmly around my engagement ring, the stones cutting deep into my skin.

My chest was utterly bereft. I felt like I'd left my heart in the dream.

And real life, now this was the nightmare.

When I woke up again, the light in the room was a hazy grey and my head throbbed with a dull ache, the kind you get from crying all night. I spent a few moments there, pulling my thoughts from sleep, before there was a knock at the door that made me jump.

Ada immediately turned over, her hair in her face as she struggled to sit up.

"Who is it?" I asked loudly, my mouth dry from sleep.

"Room Service," a familiar voice said from the other side of the door.

I got out of bed and crept over to the peephole. Through it I saw a tall ginger.

I sighed with relief and quickly opened it, not caring that I was just in my Dream Theatre concert tee and underwear.

"Hey," I exclaimed as the door opened up to reveal Maximus. I heard Ada squeal behind me and pull the sheets up to cover her pajama top, but I was so exhausted that I just fell forward and collapsed into his arms.

Thankfully, Maximus was always the gentleman and held me for a few moments with no questions. He had a strong hold and it gave me a bit of strength just to know that I had someone who really had the power to help me and help Dex, at least more so than I did. It also didn't hurt that he was a big, strong man, and we were two young girls in a scary, unknown city.

"How are you holding up?" he asked in his drawl.

I pulled away and stared up at him. "I think you're the only thing holding me up right now."

He gave me a quick smile that didn't quite reach his eyes. Maximus was usually quite easygoing, and to see the worry on his brow made my heart kick up a notch again.

"Mornin', little lady," he said over my head, nodding at Ada.

She held her sheets to her chest and nodded gravely in return. "Mornin', big dude."

"So now that I'm here," he said, walking over to the edge of my bed and sitting down, hands clasped together, "why don't you fill me in on everything, from the start."

His eyes briefly trailed to my underwear, and I quickly grabbed a robe out of the closet and covered myself up before I launched into the events of the last twenty-four hours. Maximus listened patiently as I went on, his brow furrowing even deeper.

When I finished, breathless, he ran a freckled hand through his thick hair and sighed.

"What?" I asked. "What is it?"

He shot me an apologetic look. "Sorry, Perry. It's a lot to take in, and to be honest with you, I'm not sure where to start."

My face fell. "What do you mean? You knew Dex back then, when you both lived here."

He nodded. "It was a long time ago, too, don't forget that. Dex was living in an apartment. I can take you there, but he rarely talked about his childhood, about where he lived with Michael. I don't know where that is."

"But," I said, stepping closer to him and staring hard at his green eyes, "you do know something, you have to."

He gave me a sympathetic smile. "New York wasn't the best of times, Perry. I'm sure you know the story by now."

I crossed my arms. "How you were best buds and then Abby died and then he slept with your girlfriend and went insane all while you turned a blind eye? Yeah, I heard the story."

His eyes narrowed briefly, a flash of hurt and warning. "Hey, I reckon it's not as black and white as it seems. But either way, many mistakes were made, and I gotta be honest with ya, it's not easy for me to be here."

"Well, what the fuck are we supposed to do?" I yelled, throwing my hands up in the air.

"Perry," Ada said gently, about to tell me to take a chill pill.

"Sorry," I mumbled, turning away from them. Then I turned back, fueled by desperation. "No, you know what? I'm not sorry. Not one bit. I'm mad. I'm freaking the fuck out. I'm panicking. You guys don't seem to fucking understand what's happening. Dex is my best friend, my fiancé, my future husband." I pointed my finger at Ada. "Your future brother-in-law. He's everything to all of us, and I am not joking, I am not exaggerating, when I say that we have to get to him now. We have to or we will never, ever see him again."

Maximus studied me for a few moments, and a wave of fear trickled down my shoulders. *He thinks I'm crazy. He's regretting coming here. He's not going to help me. He's going to turn around and go home. He doesn't believe me.*

"Okay," he said after a minute. "I'll do what I can."

I raised my brow. "So you believe me, you believe everything I said."

He gave me a lopsided smile. "More than you know."

I had no idea what that meant and it didn't assuage my fears. Though Max saw a lot of the supernatural stuff when we were in Red Fox and New Orleans, I could never really forget that this was the guy that watched me become possessed in front of his eyes and still denied it.

Just then my phone started ringing, now that it was fully charged. I looked over at it and at Ada. We knew who it was.

"I've got it," Ada said, snatching it up from the bedside table. Before I could tell her not to answer it, before we could come up with a plan of what to do, what to say, she did.

"Hi, Mom," she said lightly, as if everything was just peachy.

She immediately winced, and the hotel room filled with the tinny sound of my mother yelling over the airwaves. I watched as Ada tried to get a few words in before she suddenly blurted out, "We're in New York City."

You could feel the silence as the truth soaked in.

Then the yelling started all over again. I let it continue for another minute until I pulled out the older sister card and took responsibility.

Naturally, it didn't matter what I told my mother. Or my father, once he came on the line. They obviously didn't believe a word when I said Dex's brother was trouble and we had reason to believe he'd been taken against his will.

In the end, it was all my fault, and I was to bring Ada back to Portland. I promised them I would when we got Dex. I told them they could reach us if they were worried and gave them the hotel name too, but that this was our call, and we'd come back when we could.

Obviously that didn't go over very well, and I was quickly forced to put my phone on silent, knowing they would call again and again and again. I couldn't be distracted by that, not now.

"All righty," I said, fighting the urge to clap my hands

together, as if this could be trivial. "Let's get started. Let's find him."

"I reckon you may want to put pants on," Maximus said. "I know anything goes in New York but that might be pushing it." He added with a smirk, "Not that I'm complaining."

I gave him a look but quickly got changed in the bathroom. While I was in there, staring at the retro medicine cabinet above the sink, I was reminded of what I had done to my mother. How I had taken the pills. I wondered if she was starting to unravel a bit without them, if she'd already made an appointment to have them replaced, if she knew it was me.

I wondered if she was going to start feeling like her daughters any time soon.

But, like all thoughts that weren't related to Dex, I couldn't even let myself think about it. Each moment I was away from him was a moment that my heart sank deeper into my chest. I felt there would be nothing left of me if we didn't find him soon.

It was too bad then, that even with Maximus there, we still had no idea where to start looking.

Somewhere a clock was counting down to something none of us wanted to understand.

## 3

DEX

I've woken up in some fucked up places before. Once, on a bench in some park in Bellevue, a ritzy Seattle suburb, with happy squirrels bouncing all around me like over-caffeinated rats. Still not sure how I ended up there. Another time I was on the roof of a Vancouver hotel, rain pelting me on the face and an empty bottle of Jack Daniels beside me. I remember how I ended up there—damn stripper led me astray and stole all my money. At least I had Jack for company.

But I have never woken up in my old bedroom of my childhood home, a home I tried to erase from my memory until I was certain it no longer existed.

And yet it did exist. More than that, I was lying on my puny old bed, legs hanging off the weak frame, and the room was exactly the same as I had remembered it as a child.

Which was, you know, pretty much fucking impossible. But there you had it.

I lay back on the bed for a few drawn-out moments, blinking at the stick-on stars on the ceiling that I put there back when I was a little shit. My eyes slowly trailed down the walls, pausing on the Alice in Chains and Nirvana posters and cut-outs from Spin and Rolling Stone magazine I had placed haphazardly on the greying wallpaper. I bet if I peeled back the corners, I would see the Blu-tack I used to put them up. God forbid I put a pin or thumbtack into the wall without my father slaughtering me.

Suddenly memories flooded my mind and I could barely contain them, feeling like a thirsty alcoholic with an undersized bladder. Holy shit. This wasn't some crazy fucking dream. I really was here, in my old room. Everything was the same, everything except me. I was Dex Foray, not Declan O'Shea, yet the essence of who I was clung to the carpet like mildew, just as the fear used to.

But there was nothing to fear now, was there?

I slowly sat up and stared at my feet, at the toes of my boots, tapping them together loudly. The sound was hollow, peculiar. It didn't quite feel real. But this was real. Right? Every breath I took in made me second guess it; every breath I exhaled told me the truth.

I reached up and pinched the tip of my ear. It hurt like hell. It had healed since it was sliced off in New Orleans, but it was currently the most sensitive part of my body (other than my dick, but that seemed unnecessarily cruel). Anyway, point is, I was alive and well, and this was no nightmare manifested of unresolved issues from my childhood. This was real.

I was motherfucking *Dr. Who*.

Outside the window, the light was starting to fade. I eased myself out of bed and peered through it. The view was the same as I remembered. The neighbor was so close you could touch their brick wall—well, I couldn't because I was never tall enough, but my friend Joey once did. He nearly fell out the window and crashed into the garbage cans below, which would have really ruined his drumming skills. After that, I made a rope ladder for emergencies.

Craning my neck, I could see the street out front. 78$^{th}$ or 88$^{th}$ or 98$^{th}$, I couldn't remember. It was framed by leafy trees and busy with passerby going about their business. The Upper West Side. A place completely and totally removed from my life and everything that I was.

So why was I here?

I racked my brain, surprised at how sluggish it was, how slow the other memories came to me. My life before I was here.

Perry.

My chest clenched at the thought of her and then the novelty of where I was vanished in an instant.

I had been at Perry's parents' house in Portland, editing the video we shot at the sanatorium. Perry had decided to go for a walk. Her parents were out somewhere. Her sister, Ada, was downstairs doing some annoying workout video by that angry chick who yells at everyone.

I wasn't sure how much time had passed before I heard a knock at the door. I remember I was staring at an image of Perry on the computer screen, her face beautiful even in the grainy green light of the night vision. For some reason the sight of her, combined with the knock at the door, brought this whisk to my gut, turned me inside out.

Without thinking, I got up and looked out the window. There was no car outside except for my Highlander, something that inexplicably made the feeling worsen. I opened the door and poked my head out into the hall and heard a voice that made my spine stiffen.

A voice that should never have brought such fear into me.

Yet it did. And before I knew what I was doing, I was walking down the stairs, feeling almost pulled toward my brother.

I told Ada to run, to get Perry, to get out of there. But that was all I could do.

I don't remember the rest. I have no fucking clue how I ended up in New York, in my old house, if it was even in this plane of existence.

And—shit your pants scarier than all of that—I had no idea where Perry was and if she was okay. Because, god help me, if Michael had done something to her, I had no problem getting blood on my hands.

At that thought, I went for the door and cautiously opened it. Now that my brain was in high gear, all my senses were following suit. I refused to submit to fear.

The hallway looked different, was different. Though my bedroom remained trapped in the past, a clean, pleasant version of all my years in the house combined, the hallway that led to the other bedrooms and bathrooms was blackened, as if there were a fire recently that scorched the walls and tinged the dingy carpet.

But on closer inspection, the walls weren't charred. They were coated with a black substance that oozed and wriggled on the wall. I had a feeling if I looked even closer than that I'd see creatures in it moving, as if it were a wall of pulsing insects.

Luckily the light in the hallway, coming in only from the foyer's wide windows at the end, didn't allow for much detail. I stepped out and was met with a wash of frigid air that cut deep, momentarily stealing my breath.

The hall resounded with a creak and I slowly turned my head to see the door to Michael's room swinging open. Purplish smoke followed, wafting out then disappearing.

Wanting to leave but knowing I couldn't without answers, I turned and went toward it. The carpet was wet under my feet, sticking to the soles of my boots, smelling like an old drunk: mold and alcohol.

At his door, I stopped and peered inside. Michael's room didn't look anything like mine, or like his back in the day. I mean, he was an annoying, straight-laced kid but there wasn't anything about him as a child that made me think he was Damien from *The Omen*. But now, now was a different story.

Here, his room was a black cave, the doorway framed by hanging stalactites that looked as heavy and dense as iron. Inside, the cave looked as if it went on forever, a tunnel of cold, dripping walls that led to a dancing flame, as if there was a fire at the end, raging far away.

"Declan," my brother said, his voice impossibly low, almost guttural. He was sitting on the floor, staring at nothing.

"Where's Perry?" I asked. I hoped I came across as commanding but it felt like I wasn't speaking over a whisper.

He looked up and I was struck by how much he looked like my mother. Our mother. But it was hard to think that way, to think we both came from her, because he lacked something that I had, or at least I hoped I had. His eyes were dark pools that had no depth, no sign that the man had any empathy at all—or that he was even a man.

I thought back to my mother, the last time I had a vision of her before she stopped haunting me. What had she said about him? What was it that I didn't understand?

Michael laughed, empty and cold. "You ask where Perry is? Not where you are, how you got here, what is going to happen to you. But you ask where *she* is."

I feigned strength. "Where is Perry?" I repeated.

He cocked his head like a bird. Like a raptor. "She's fine."

"*Where* is she?"

"Here, of course," he said. "Manhattan. She's come looking for you."

My heart sank. How the hell did Perry know to come here?

"I told her," he said smugly, reading my face, or my thoughts.

My fists clenched and unclenched. "Why?"

"You don't seem to be surprised to be here. I thought you'd appreciate it."

I frowned at him, feeling rage and frustration begin to bubble up inside. He was changing the subject and I was walking right into it. "Appreciate it? Being here? How the fuck can I appreciate that? This place is hell."

He grinned at me like a shark. "I know. It always was, wasn't it? That's the whole beauty of it, don't you see, Declan? This has always been hell."

I narrowed my eyes. "I'm pretty fucking sure your hell was never as bad as mine."

He slowly got to his feet and dusted off the suit he was wearing. "You're right. It wasn't. But you had one thing that I didn't."

"And what was that?" Somewhere in the distance, down the low tunnel of the cave, I heard faint screams that faded as quickly as they started.

"You had love," he said simply.

I nearly laughed. Love was the one thing I didn't have growing up. My mother was an abusive, alcoholic trainwreck, my father was a man devoid of feeling, except the pride he vested only in Michael.

"We were both different," he continued, taking a step

toward me. His footfalls echoed off the dank walls. "Did you know that? That they were afraid of *both* of us?"

"Why? Why were they afraid?" I'd always known that my parents recoiled from me, as if I were covered in a layer of dirt that would never wash off, though I never knew why. I always figured it was just because I wasn't as good enough as Michael, their golden boy. I was scrawny, weird, artistic—second best.

But to hear that they were afraid of both of us, that made absolutely no sense.

"You really don't know," he mused. Then he grinned to himself and shook his head. "No, I suppose you don't. Otherwise you wouldn't have lived your life the way you did. You would have embraced the change. Just like I did."

"Look," I told him, "if you're going to start spouting *Changeling* shit with me, you're talking to the wrong guy."

"And I used to think you were so open-minded. Oh, that's right," he said with a snap of his fingers. "I forgot you used to medicate yourself. Talk about closing one's mind off." I stared at him with hard eyes and he continued, "No, there is no *Changeling* shit, as you so eloquently stated. You knew our mother was sick, didn't you?"

I sighed noisily and my breath froze in the air. "In more ways than one."

"She was mentally weak ... mentally curious. She strived for answers to her sorry life, she wanted ways to cope with what she saw—the horrors, the ghosts. I truly believe she wanted what was best for herself and marrying our father should have provided that. It at least provided money. But then again, I'm done with trying to figure out the shallow depths that lie inside each human."

I cocked my brow warily. Human?

He noted my look and came even closer to me. The air

filled with the smell of sour milk, rotted meat, and I did what I could to breathe through my mouth. He stopped a foot away, and again I was struck with a fuckton of fear, like it was just being dumped from above. Maybe I didn't want to know what he was going to tell me.

"Regine, your mother, was ... not herself when she had you. Not that she had any real idea of who she was, but she was better, you know, before we were born. I obviously did a number on her, so she tried to fix that. She asked for help. Like before, she got help, in what she perceived as the wrong form. She was possessed when she got pregnant, possessed while she carried you."

He let that sink in for a moment. It took more than a moment. My mother was possessed when she had me? Sadly, it didn't shock me. She acted like a wild creature throughout my childhood, until her death, until I accidently killed her. It almost made sense—almost.

"If you ask me," I said, trying to keep my voice level, to project an air of nonchalance that I didn't feel, "I don't think there was a moment when she wasn't possessed. You saw her, the way she was."

He nodded. "It's true. That is enough to make you go crazy, to know that you've had someone else inside you, pulling the strings, controlling the ride. To fear that your child may not be as totally human as you had hoped."

There was that word again. Human.

"Are you saying I'm *not* human?" I asked, wincing at how incredibly stupid the words sounded coming out of my mouth. The fact was though, if he told me I wasn't, I wouldn't have been surprised about that either. It would explain at least some of the bogus shit I'd been putting up with.

My brother gave me an uncharacteristically shy smile.

"You're human, Declan. You have some abilities, as you know, that make you *special*." He snorted at his choice of words, as if I could ever be that. "But you're still a product of your mother and father, no matter what residue remains." His smile now turned pitiful. "You are nothing like me at all. I'm not sure why you thought *you* were the one they were afraid of."

I didn't understand. But I felt it. The malevolence, the evil. It slinked off of him just as it did from the fiery pit at the end of the cave, or from the oozing black walls in our old hallway.

I was afraid of him. I always had been. Not because he was better than me. No, I was quickly figuring that out now. But because he was worse.

"Who are you?" I asked him, my voice rough and ragged, caught in my throat.

Another smile with dead eyes. "I used to be your brother. A very long time ago."

"What happened to Michael?" His name sounded strange on my lips.

He shrugged. "He was phased out. He wasn't very strong. He wasn't like you, you see. You had some inner strength that he didn't have. Wasn't his fault, of course. You had your parents. He did not."

"He had them too," I said, knowing it was going to be refuted. It was strange talking about my brother in the third person to my brother. But I knew that wasn't him. I should have always known, but I was too fucking self-absorbed to even notice he had changed over the years, distancing himself from me, my mother, and Pippa. We had never been close, so it was nearly impossible to tell when the rift had started. But it had and now I was feeling the first emotions of loss over him.

"He did, at first," he said. "But I think your father always knew that he wasn't his. He revered him out of fear, not pride."

"What the hell do you mean he wasn't his?" I asked incredulously, trying not to look at this man (who looked like Michael but wasn't Michael) in the eyes. Those fathomless, oily eyes.

"Your mother wasn't you when she had you. But you still had a father, your father. Michael had neither."

I shook my head slowly, unable to understand. My thoughts felt like they were trying to form through molasses. "How is that possible?"

"Anything is possible, Declan," he said smoothly, adjusting his tie. "Your mother was possessed during her first pregnancy. Nearly all the way. She still had a shred of humanity in her, but it wasn't enough. Not then. She was able to ... consort with something she ought to have not. It wasn't your father."

I blinked. Now we were going from *The Changeling* to some *Rosemary's Baby* shit. I couldn't even begin to wrap my head around it. I was open-minded but what I was hearing was too fucking much. My brother was the product of my possessed mother and a demon? My family had just turned into every seventies horror movie cliché. Why didn't I just start running around with a chainsaw and call myself Leatherface?

And yet for how fucking ridiculous and unbelievable it all sounded, I knew deep down that this was the truth. That made it worse, somehow, to have your gut tell you that all this crazy shit was as real as the balls between your legs.

All this damn time I had been living with a brother who wasn't really mine. All this time I thought my parents had been afraid of me, when it was Michael they had feared. No wonder my father took off when he did. No wonder my mother drank herself into the abyss. No wonder I had turned out so utterly fucked up.

But in the end I was still human. I was still me, no matter what "residue" he said had stayed behind. I was no demon child. Not like him.

"It's a lot to take," he said, eying me carefully. The air around us snapped, growing colder, screams starting again, wailing from along the tunnel.

"I'm an old pro," I said cautiously. All the chit chat and the revelations, they weren't for nothing. All of this was going somewhere, and as the seconds ticked by in this cave, in this house, in this world I wasn't even sure existed, I was getting closer to some reveal I wasn't going to like. Something worse than, "Your brother is a demon."

So I bit the bullet. "Why did you come for me now? Why am I here, wherever this is?" I took in a deep, icy breath. "What do you want from me?"

He put his hand out in front of him and lifted one finger. "Why did I come for you now? Because things in your life are starting to align. The company you keep is becoming more and more like you." I opened my mouth to question that but he lifted another finger. "Why are you here? Because this was where hell began for you, for Michael..." He looked down the tunnel, to the fire. "Where the walls are weakest." He studied me carefully. "You've been close to it, you know."

"To what?"

He grinned. "To Hell. You nearly went there once to bring back your dear beloved Perry. Your nanny called it the Thin Veil and it *is* thin. It's growing thinner. And you're able to punch holes into it. You can step into the Veil, and from there you can step into Hell. And those like me, we will be able to do the same." His eyes flitted over to the flames. "We've been waiting a long time to come over. Not everyone is as lucky as I am."

Clarity came over me with a kick of nausea. I knew where this was going. Every stretched nerve in my body was telling me to run far away from the truth. But of course, I was a dumb fuck who wasn't going anywhere.

He lifted up the third finger. "And finally, what do I want from you? Declan, you're special, so fucking special, as you would say. But I ... we," he gestured down the tunnel, "we don't want just you. Alone, you're not as good as you think you are. Together, though, that is a different story."

I swallowed hard, unable to feel my feet. "Perry," I whispered.

He nodded with ease. "Yes. Perry. She makes everything you do ... better. But it's not just her. It's what she's brought with her." He took another step and rested his hand on my shoulder. It felt like the weight of the world. "All of them, in this place, will cause a rift you'll never be able to piece back together."

He leaned in, so he was whispering in my ear. His voice was no longer human. It conjured up images of beasts and death. "And with my help, you're going to lead them straight back here, to the house that life and love forgot. Aren't you, Declan?"

I found myself nodding as he pulled back.

Flames danced in his dirty eyes until the orange glow was all I could see.

## 4

PERRY

Heat rippled above the pavement and the air stunk like garbage. Though it was the end of May, New York City was going through an early heatwave and we were feeling the brunt of it.

Ada, Maximus, and I had been walking up and down the city streets, searching for answers in a city that wasn't providing anything but stink and hot air. Maximus was insistent on us taking the Subway, but for whatever reason, Ada wasn't too keen on the idea. In fact, every time he brought it up, her face paled a little. I'd never known her to have a fear of the underground, but she seemed to believe that being in the unrelenting sunshine, walking on tired feet, was much better.

As we walked, Maximus went over the ways we could possibly track him down. We did internet searches for Regine Foray but they were coming up blank, as if his mother had never existed. The same went for Declan and Michael. Still, Maximus thought New York's City Clerk could help us with records.

I felt a bit like an investigative reporter. I knew we could have probably holed up at a coffee shop and done most of this over the web, but there was something more proactive and productive about treading pavement and searching for answers face-to-face. It didn't seem right to just whittle the day away on the internet while Dex was out there somewhere.

I tried really hard not to think about him, about what might be happening, whether he was in any pain, about why he was taken. But I wasn't made of stone. I slipped up often, and my body nearly crumbled each time. The thought of losing Dex was far too much to bear.

Luckily, Maximus, with his determination, kept me moving, and Ada, with her sweet, subtle displays of affection, let me know I wasn't alone. And with them, we kept walking, block after Manhattan block, searching for something, anything.

After a visit to the city clerk turned up nothing, we ended up checking out the New York Public Library. When I remembered the lions coming to life in Ghostbusters, I laughed to myself and then was immediately met with sorrow when I realized how badly I wanted to make a joke to Dex about it. We had been the Ghostbusters. Now there was no Experiment in Terror and no Dex.

We grabbed a quick sandwich at a kiosk and found a bench to sit on in Bryant Park. I stared up at the buildings towering over us, trying to find respite in their strange familiarity. It was weird being in a place you'd never been to but had seen so many times that you could trick yourself into thinking you had. Ada was having a ball people watching and muttering about how all the fashionistas are spotted in Bryant Park during fashion week.

It was then that a trick of the eye, the light hitting the

door of a taxi cab as it swung open, causing the air to warp and shimmer, struck me with a terrible idea.

I had been getting no more visits from Pippa, but it was she who held all the answers. Even though she had been weak, ill, and brutally vague during our last correspondence, she could go anywhere, see anything from inside the Veil. She would know where Dex was. And if she wasn't going to come to me, I was going to have to go to her.

"Perry," Maximus said, his low voice drawing me out of my thoughts.

I snapped my eyes to him with renewed verve. "What?"

He shook his head ever so gently. "Don't even think about it."

I frowned. "What are you talking about?" He couldn't have just heard my thoughts, could he? He wasn't like *us*.

He slowly licked his lips and turned away, his gaze resting on the people passing by, hurrying, going about their busy but normal lives. He seemed to have an internal debate with himself. He sighed and then leaned back against the bench, his wide frame nearly knocking Ada over the side. She gave a little grunt of annoyance at his intrusion into her personal space.

"I know what you're thinking," he finally said, his words measured, as if he wasn't sure how much each one was worth.

"You can hear my thoughts?" I asked loudly, then quickly lowered my voice when I realized we were in public. Ada stopped eating, mid-chew, and craned her neck to give him a look.

He gave me a quick smile. "Sometimes. You're right. I'm not like you. But I still pick up on things, and I know enough to tell you not to go into the Thin Veil. I don't think you'll find what you're looking for."

"And what's that?" I asked.

"Pippa."

"Hold up," Ada said, raising a finger in the air. "Let me get this straight. You, Ginger Rogers, you know about the Thin Veil. About our grandma. You can hear Perry's thoughts."

He nodded, not seeming to appreciate another nickname.

"And how do you know all this?" I asked. "For how long?" I thought back to my possession and was hit with anger. "And for God's sake, don't tell me you knew back when I was possessed!"

"Perry," Maximus said gently, "I couldn't hear your thoughts back then. It wasn't until after you went into the Veil that I was able to pick up on you. You do remember the Veil, right? How Dex had to go in there and pull you out. You do not want to go back in there. If Pippa wanted you to—"

"Oh, fuck off," I sneered. "What the hell do you know about her? How dare you keep all of this to yourself!"

"I didn't," he said quickly. "Dex knows."

My eyes widened then turned hard. "What?" I roared, getting to my feet, my iced coffee splashing out of the cup. "Dex knows?! Since when?"

He looked momentarily frightened but answered with conviction. "Since New Orleans."

Before I had a chance to stew on that, to simmer on the fact that Dex had kept something from me, Ada spoke up.

"And what exactly does Dex know?" Ada asked. "You can hear Perry's thoughts? You know about the Veil? What else?" She narrowed her eyes at him and leaned in closer. "Just who are you, you ginger freak?"

A wash of shame came over his brow. "I am Maximus Jacobs. A mere mortal like you both."

"Mortal?" I repeated, finding it an odd word choice. Everything about this was odd.

He nodded. "Yes. But, as I'm sure you're guessing, it wasn't always that way."

"That's totally *not* what I was guessing," Ada commented.

Maximus looked to me. "You remember your Jacob, right?"

*My* Jacob. Spikey-haired, damaged, totally inhuman. He led me astray when I was fifteen and put the rest of my life into turbulent action. "How could I forget?" Wait. How did *he* know about them?

He raised his brows expectantly but I was too slow to piece it together. "Well," he said, "I was Dex's Jacob. Before that, I was someone else's. And after that I was Rose's."

"Rose?" This was crazy. I almost laughed. "So Dex ... wait. Did Dex know? He must have."

"No," he said, shaking his head. "He didn't. Which is why he, well, floundered through life I reckon."

"He was in a mental asylum," I said, feeling that anger build again. "You put him there."

"No," he said sharply. "I did not. I tried to help Dex, really I did. But I just couldn't handle it. Handle him. You weren't there, you don't understand."

"Oh, I understand. He slept with your girlfriend and suddenly you didn't want to help him anymore. Is that it?"

"Perry, please, it's in the past."

I rolled my eyes. "No wonder Dex hated you."

He flinched as if hurt. "He didn't know."

"I bet on some level he did. That you were there to help

him and then you *abandoned* him." I tried to slice him with that word.

"I went to help someone else that I could," he said. "Rose needed me."

I felt a pang of guilt at her name and wanted to ask how she was doing. She was nearly comatose after New Orleans and our incident with the Voodoo queen. But that was a concern for another time. Now, I had something so big on my plate that I could barely handle it.

"All this time," I said slowly. "From the start. You knew, you believed. And you lied."

"I did what I had to do," he said. "To protect you, myself, Dex. To protect the way things work."

"You knew I was possessed and you sided with my parents," I seethed. "You made it seem like I was crazy."

"I had no choice. Your parents would not have believed me," he said, raising his hands. "Not then, anyway."

I shook my head, unable to take it in. So all this time, he'd always known, always believed. Suddenly everything seemed to slide and click into place. I looked down at my hands, realizing I was tearing at my cuticles so hard they were drawing blood. "So now what? You're mortal?"

"That's right," he said. "I went rogue. For Rose. I gave it all up."

"Now?"

"Years and years ago. *Before* it all went sour and we broke up."

"And so you knew this would happen to Dex."

His mouth settled in a firm line before he said, "No, I never imagined this. I'm telling you the truth when I say I'm as confused as you are. I don't know where Dex grew up, I never had that information, and whatever ways I had to find out are now gone. I'm just like you, I know about as much as you. And believe it or not, I want to find him as much as you do. I care about the damn fool."

The three of us lapsed into a silence that seemed to stretch over the whole city. Finally Ada clasped her hands together and said, "Some people give up their virginity to stay in a relationship. You gave up immortality. That's pretty rough, dude."

He shrugged and rubbed a hand across his chin. "Yeah, well I reckon it was worth it in the end. I still have Rose. She is doing better, she remembers who I am. We've had to fight against a lot in the last two months; believe me it was pretty scary there for a while, but we're both where we need to be. We're each other's home. And Perry, I know Dex is yours and you are his. That's why we'll find him. Things just won't be right in this damn universe until we do."

"Then let me go into the Veil," I said, bolstered even more now.

He tilted his head to study me. "Your bravery is admirable, little lady, but your stupidity is not." I opened my mouth to attempt to zing him with something but he said, "It's not my place to tell you what to do; just as a friend who knows some things, I know it would be a mistake. Every time you go in there, you come back with something. Either you're weakening the Veil or yourself. In some cases you strengthen. But strengths that you don't know how to use only end up being a weakness."

I mulled over that. It was true that when Dex and I were in the Veil, we came back changed. He was stronger, physically, and I came back with the ability to project my thoughts and, on occasion, have other people hear them. But having that kind of "gift" was still a challenge to navigate. It only seemed to work half the time, and when it did work, it was burdensome.

Not to say it hadn't saved our lives every now and then. But it was hard to rely on something if you didn't know how it worked.

Dex, though. Dex was unbelievable. He healed faster, possessed amazing strength and agility, and fought against certain death, coming out a winner. There was no weakness with him, not with his body anyway.

His mind, though, that was a different story. I swallowed a terrible thought, the idea that he could be corrupted. Dex, as funny, loving, smart, and sexual as he was, always seemed to be battling himself—his inner workings. His childhood and "mental illness" were nemeses of his, chipping away at his self-esteem and encouraging his self-loathing.

Dex was many wonderful things, but he wasn't perfect—he was his own greatest enemy. I had hoped that I could help him over time—with the two of us together, he finally seemed to put many of his demons to rest. But I knew he had a lot of work in front of him. We both did.

Of course, none of that meant shit if I couldn't find him, help him. In fact, just recognizing that, despite all his strength, Michael could exploit Dex's flaws, made everything that more urgent.

Fuck Ginger Balls, as Dex would say. If I had a chance to get him back, I was taking it.

I started scanning the area, wondering how to go about doing this supernatural, insanely improbable thing that I had never done before.

"Perry," Maximus warned again, reading me. "Don't do it. I can't go in there and get you out if something goes wrong."

"Maybe I can," Ada spoke up. We both looked at her sternly.

"Don't even think about it," I told her. "You won't be able to handle it."

"And you can?" she shot back.

I ignored her, hoping that if anything did go wrong, Maximus wouldn't let her. That was the thing about the Veil. While it seemed you could use your mind to open doors and create portals (shimmering holes in the air), you actually needed to step in with your body. Usually, anyway. Even if I created or found a passage in the air here in Bryant Park, hundreds of New Yorkers would watch me step through and vanish into thin air. Not exactly a subtle practice.

And it's not that Maximus and Ada would physically let me.

"Fine, fair enough." I stretched my arms above my head and eyed the paid toilets in the corner of the park. I thrust my iced coffee into Ada's hands and said, "Hold this for me. Just going to use the washroom."

She frowned, as if she was trying to scan my mind, but I willed myself to be as blank as possible. It seemed to work and she nodded lightly. Perhaps I could learn to control these gifts after all.

I didn't even bother looking at Maximus. Who knows what the lumberjack could pick up on?

I walked across the park, utterly conscious of their eyes on me, and disappeared into the toilet. It wasn't as gross as I had expected; perhaps because you did have to spend a quarter to get in. I went pee anyway, and after I washed up, I tried to figure out what to do next.

Usually it was Pippa who either pulled me into the Veil or to some other limbo-like place, somewhere between reality and dreaming. Other times, it was my possessed soul that was banished there while my body stayed behind.

Truthfully, I had no idea what to do or how to do it. I

remember Pippa explaining how it worked for her, how she had to concentrate and imagine the air bending before she could physically step through, but perhaps that wasn't the same for everyone.

I stared blankly at the toilet for a few moments until it began to feel like a smelly tomb, then closed my eyes and decided to try creating the Veil from inside myself. At first I called for Pippa, asking for her in my head over and over again, willing her to help me, for her to appear. Then, when nothing happened, I moved on to Dex, asking the same. I pleaded with all my heart and soul.

Just like the many times I had tried since his disappearance, I heard and felt nothing. Sweat formed on my skin and stuck my t-shirt to my back. The washroom was growing hotter and my head was starting to hurt.

But I wouldn't give up.

I took in a deep breath through my mouth and tried to steady my heart, which was thumping hard from exertion and nerves and the mounting feeling of helplessness. Maybe I just had to imagine it, create it, focus my thoughts like I did when I was trying to project onto people.

I stared at a blank spot right in front of the door, using the sight as a means to visualize and focus. I imagined the air starting to shimmer, like a mirage inside of the bathroom, but though I could see it clearly in my mind's eye, I couldn't actually see it happen.

I kept at it, sweat pouring down my arms, my face growing hot, trying so, so hard to make this happen. I had almost given up when it happened. As it was, I looked away from the area I was concentrating on for just a moment, enough time to see a small bug crawling up the wall, when the area around the door, just in my peripheral, started to move. I looked back at it quickly and it was still again.

Rubbing my lips together, I tried to both concentrate on the area and look away from it at the same time. I focused but let the focus blur.

And when I did just that, the air started to warp and shift. I slowly brought that into focus, and now I could see it clearly. There was a hazy shimmer in the air, like I was looking at the washroom door through clear, moving water.

Cautiously, I raised my hand and put it through the projection. Once it passed into the shimmer, my arm turned a desaturated shade of grey and was instantly chilled. My skin started prickling, all the hairs standing straight up like I was being electrocuted. Every part of my body was telling me to withdraw my arm, to take it back, to stay in this world, this dimension, this universe where the living belonged.

Every instinct told me to not cross over.

But Dex could be on the other side. Answers could hang from trees, ripe for the picking.

Sometimes your instincts were wrong. Your body wants you to survive but sometimes there are more important things than just surviving.

I took in a deep breath and stepped through the shimmer.

My body instantly froze from the intense chill and my limbs grew stiff and rigid as waves of electricity coursed through my body, and the pressure inside my head built to a boiling point.

I shut my eyes hard and cried out, not sure where my screams would end up.

I walked another step and suddenly the world was sucked away from me, violently removed, like it was being vacuumed.

I was no longer in the washroom.

I was no longer in this world.

## 5

PERRY

When I opened my eyes on the other side, I was in Bryant Park. But there were no people about. There was no sound. There was no real smell, except for a stale, musty odor, like the inside of an old, upholstered car on a hot day. Except it was no longer hot, like the hazy sun above Manhattan. It was cold enough to make my breath turn to cloud and my lungs to burn with each breath.

That was to say, of course, that I was even breathing air.

I turned around, wondering if I could find my way back to the other side. The air shimmered right behind me, though it looked like it was growing fainter by the second. I could barely see the toilet on the other side, and I wondered how long I had before Ada or Maximus, or some New Yorker who really had to piss, would start banging on it. I couldn't remember if time stood still while you were in the Veil or if it went on as usual. I couldn't remember if there were any rules.

Fear pricked at the back of my neck, but I straightened my shoulders, refusing it. I couldn't start panicking now at what I had done. I had to follow through. I would do whatever it took in order to find him or Pippa.

But where the fuck did I even start? This world was grey and devoid of life. Where were the lost souls, the reluctant dead? Hell, I'd even welcome the giant woodbugs and earthworms that I had seen once before.

*Maybe no one knows you're here*, I thought quickly to myself. *Maybe that's a very good thing.*

I made a mental note to keep quiet and stop wishing. I began to walk across the park and to the street, past the bench where Ada and Maximus would be sitting on the other side of things. I wondered if they could sense me, hovering behind their existence. Part of me wanted to stay there, feeling safe and tethered to them, but the other, more desperate part, needed to go on.

I walked up and down the streets, keeping quiet and sticking to the walls of buildings, hiding in the shadows that formed despite there being no sun in the sky, just this grimy dead light that hung above me.

For blocks there was nothing. The chill in the air lessened its hold on me, but my footfalls still had only a whisper of sound. I felt as if I was walking inside a miniature city kept inside a jar, with only a few holes poked at the top.

I didn't know where I was going—my feet were not being consciously moved, but considering I had no other ideas, I just went with it and walked and walked.

Finally, I saw something.

Or, should I say, it saw me.

There was a grandiose building—a bank, I think—with a row of wide, dusty steps leading up to stately looking pillars, Grecian-style. At the top of the steps was a man, pacing back and forth.

At least I thought it was a man. As I came closer, my pace slowing, I could see some things were off about him. He moved with jerks, like a marionette puppet, and his pants seemed too thin, too flexible, like he didn't actually have any legs under there at all.

He also had no eyes and no nose—just black, crusted over cavities that I imagined would be bright red in another world.

I swallowed my revulsion. Then he turned his bald head toward me, and I knew he saw me. Revulsion turned to fear.

*Who are you?* he asked quietly in my head. To my surprise, there was a note of fear in his voice too. *I know you're there.*

I kept my mouth closed, wondering if maybe he couldn't see me after all.

He reached into his suit pocket then bent down and placed something on the ground. Two black and white creatures—insects—skittered down the stairs toward me. When they got closer, I realized they were giant cockroaches. But that wasn't all there was to them.

The insects stopped a few feet away, and my mouth dropped open. I took a step back, my hand flying to my lips to keep the bile inside.

The cockroaches didn't have heads. Instead they had an eyeball each. Human eyeballs, staring right at me from skewed angles, their optic nerves forged onto the legs of the insects, like veiny armor.

*Who are you?* The voice repeated, and now I knew he could see me. *Where did you come from?*

It took a moment to gather my words. *I'm looking for someone. Can you help me?*

The cockroaches skittered closer to each other, their legs

making a *scritch-scritch* sound on the pavement that seemed impossibly loud in this airless world.

The voice laughed, but when I looked up at the man who was still standing on the steps of the bank, he was motionless.

*I can help you*, he said, *no more than you can help me. You are here where I don't wish to be.* He paused, and my gaze darted down to the cockroach eyeballs that were beginning to dance excitedly. *You could get me out of here. There are so many people I wish to see.*

Was he starting to go all Dr. Seuss on my ass?

I ignored his plea. Like hell I was going to help him cross over to my world so he could start haunting people. *I'm looking for a woman*, I told him. *She used to live in here.*

*Here is a large world*, the man said, and the cockroaches scampered right up to my feet. I fought the violent urge to step on them and squish the eyeballs into the ground. But who knew what ire I'd draw if I did that. I needed to stay calm and play it safe.

*Her name is Pippa*, I said. Or *was* Pippa. The last image I had of her was that she was skin and bone and she was dying. I could only hope she was still around, but if she wasn't, then I prayed she was somewhere where she was finally at rest. If the man with the detached eyeballs was any indication, the Thin Veil was not a world where you found rest or peace.

*She said things would happen here in New York*, I told him. To be more precise, she had said, "That's where I saw you, Perry, when I first used the Veil to look into your life. It's where Dex and Michael were born, brought into this world. Where both Dex and I were put away. It's the beginning of so many horrors. And I believe it will be the end."

*This is not New York*, the man said, even though I could

see a glimpse of the Chrysler building through the glass office building opposite us. *This is not anywhere. You will find no one here except poor souls like me.*

Suddenly the man started walking down the stairs toward me, and while my attention was on his body, the cockroaches began to crawl up my legs. I shuddered and shrieked, swatting at them in automatic horror.

The man was sprinting now, yelling out in pain as I managed to knock the cockroaches to the ground and leap backwards out of the way. They reared up on their back legs and waved sharp incisors at me, ready to take a bite.

I screamed again and turned quickly on my heel as they came for me. I ran as fast as I could through the grey streets, hearing his footsteps after me and the scratching sound of the insect legs as they scraped over the concrete.

Thankfully I didn't have to run for too long before the man and his eyeballs seemed to give up the chase. It didn't make me feel any better—if something like him was here, then what else was? But at least I was out of immediate danger.

Unfortunately, I was no better off than before. The man had never heard of Pippa, and even if he had, he wasn't about to help me find her. Perhaps I should have struck some kind of bargain with him—you help me and I'll help you. But who knew what would happen if I brought that monstrosity back to the other side with me. Probably nothing good.

I stopped and looked around. Something about the place was familiar, though I didn't know how. Just a feeling I had. I looked around at the buildings, down the empty street, wondering why buildings were here but cars were not.

Out of the corner of my eye something was moving. I

cautiously turned my head and saw a black, hairy spider the size of a fucking cat crawl behind a row of stairs, its solid body and foot-long legs disappearing one by one.

Holy *shit*. Forget the noseless man with the eyeball roaches—a spider the size of a cat was another thing entirely. My whole body immediately went numb with terror, and I stood there for a long time, waiting for it to come back out, debating whether I should turn around and head the other way.

But something was compelling me to keep walking forward, and when I noticed the air starting to fill with fluttering snowflakes, I knew what it was. Where I was.

The Brooklyn Bridge was just around the corner.

I gathered up what strength I had and tried to shake the cold flakes off my shoulders. Taking in a deep breath, I walked as briskly and as quietly as possible past the area where the spider had disappeared.

I had to look, of course, as I walked past. I only saw shadows, and in those shadows, the sickly gleam of hundreds of eyes clumped together, shining like quarters as they watched me pass.

My heart skipped a nervous beat but I kept going, feeling those spider eyes trail up and down my back like I was being poked by spindly legs. Now I was shivering nonstop, from the falling snow and that icky sense of doom you get when you walk through a spider web. Just multiply that feeling by, oh, a million.

I don't know why I was drawn to the bridge, other than the fact I'd seen it a million times in my dreams. Maybe, in the real world, we should have gone there right away. I wasn't sure what I'd find here, in the Veil.

Unless Dex was in here with me.

At that thought, my pace quickened, and soon I was

jogging. As I passed by the lamp posts, they all started turning on, as if they were leading the way to him. I started to feel that dangerous notion of hope grow in the pit of my stomach, and I ran faster and faster. I ignored the things that could have been hiding in the shadows. I kept my focus dead ahead.

As I passed by City Hall, I could see the bridge was deserted and the pedestrian walkway was covered with a thin layer of snow. I slid a little as the path turned from pavement to wood slats but kept on going.

I was about halfway across the bridge, Brooklyn looming in the distance, when the air in front of me began to shift. I stopped in my tracks, the hair on my arms standing up, my nerves popping from waves of electricity.

And there he was.

Dex.

My Dex.

He was standing a few feet in front of me, seeming to materialize out of thin air. He had his grey newsboy cap on his head, and was dressed in a black t-shirt and black jeans and boots. The same thing he was wearing when Michael took him. But despite his monochrome clothing, *he* was in color. His eyes were mahogany brown and squinting against the sun as he scoured his gaze over the river, looking utterly confused, his skin tone flawless and lightly tanned. His features were warped by the moving air, which meant he was not in the Veil at all, but in our world.

I wasn't sure why I was being shown this, why there was a rip between the worlds right here in front of me. But I'd be stupid not to take it.

My heart swelled. I had found him. I was his again, and he was mine.

"Dex!" I said, my voice sounding weak and metallic despite the joy that was flooding through me.

But he seemed to hear it. He turned his head and looked in my direction, though not at me.

It didn't matter. I took quick steps toward the shimmer, preparing myself to walk through, not caring how it would look to people on the other side, a girl materializing out of thin air. I waited for the cold to intensify, for the pressure in my head to build, to feel like I was being sucked away.

Nothing happened.

I opened my eyes. I was still in the Veil. The shimmer was gone.

Dex was gone.

I was all alone.

But at least now, I knew where he was. I knew he was alive and out there, in New York City, and he was by himself. That was more than I could have hoped for.

Now I had to think of how the hell I was going to get back. I couldn't count on another window opening up like that. Perhaps that was all it had been, a window to the other side, not a door.

I waved my hands in the air in vain hope that I would strike something, make something happen. I was frantic, panic coursing through me, and the idea that I couldn't get to him fast enough was setting my nerves on fire.

*Ada!* I yelled in my head, hoping she could hear me on the other side. I didn't know how long I'd been in the bathroom in Bryant Park, but they no doubt would be worried about me by now. I hoped she and Maximus were tuned in, listening, figuring out what happened and how to get me back.

*Ada! Maximus!* I yelled again, looking around me. It wouldn't do, not here. I had to head back to the park, back to the washrooms. Otherwise they'd have no idea where I was.

I turned around and headed back along the bridge. I hated to leave Dex; even though I couldn't see him I still knew he was there, but there was no way I could get to him this way. I'd have to get through to Ada and Maximus first, then all of us would have to hightail it to the bridge and hope to track him down.

Time didn't feel like it was on my side. I started running again, and this time my movement brought things out of the shadows.

I heard a hard, scratching sound behind me and looked over my shoulder to see a giant spider—and by giant, again, the size of a cat—come crawling down the side of a brick building. It leaped onto the ground and started for me.

A similar sound came from my right. I shot a furtive glance in that direction and saw two more spiders emerge, one from underneath a bench, the other out of a sewer drain, their foot-long legs straining toward me like blackened fingers.

Oh shit.

Now I was booking it, running through the dead streets as fast as I could move, my hair whipping behind me. I praised God for Manhattan's grid setup as I was easily able to zigzag my way toward the park. The city was a piece of cake when there were no taxi cabs and rushing pedestrians around.

I was only a block away when something came out of nowhere and flew at my chest.

I shrieked and looked down to see the cockroach eyeball dig its pincers into my skin, the eye staring up at me with mad clarity.

*Take me with you*, the man's voice said, though in my

panic and confusion I couldn't tell where it was coming from. *I'll ward them off if you take me with you.*

"Get off of me!" I screamed, and the roach only dug its claws in deeper, filling my chest with shards of pain. Grimacing, I had no choice but to put my hand around the jagged, hard-backed shell, my fingers sliding along the pulsing veins of the optic nerve.

I yanked it off and threw it far away just as his other eye came crawling toward me. Without thinking, I raised my foot and smashed the creature beneath my Chucks. The eyeball was resistant for a second before the pressure caused it to splatter into slimy goo beneath my sole. Somewhere, the man was screaming.

I went back to running, slipping slightly on the eyeball residue. Whether he could stop the oversized spiders, with their hundreds of one-inch eyes and forearm sized legs, I didn't know. I didn't want to chance it. The dead were known to lie.

Finally I found myself at Bryant Park and whipped past the bench that Maximus and Ada would have been sitting on. I knew they weren't there though, I knew they had moved on. The question was where?

The toilets didn't exist on the Veil side of the world, for one reason or another, so I had to kind of guess where they would be. I looked around, up and down, for any signs of weakness in the air, any shimmers or ripples, but couldn't see anything.

*Don't panic*, I told myself, though the reminder was ridiculous. Of course I was panicking. I used to have panic attacks over making phone calls to Pizza Hut.

And I wasn't alone. The man was still screaming over his loss of eyes and was out there—sightless but angry. And the spiders, well it seemed I had lost them for the moment, but I knew it was a matter of time before they caught up. They too wished to come to the other side. Or to eat me. I had a feeling they wouldn't be too fussy about it.

"Ada!" I yelled, knowing I'd attracted enough attention already. "Ada, I'm here, I'm going to come through."

But try as I might, I could not get the air to shift. I closed my eyes, concentrating until my head felt as if it was going to explode. I focused off and on, pretending I was looking at one of those Magic Eye paintings that were everywhere in the nineties, but even that didn't work.

Shit, shit, shit. Why wasn't it working? Was I just not trying hard enough?

I took in a deep breath and attempted to count backward from ten. When I came through from the other side earlier, I felt I had time on my side. Here I didn't. I needed to relax and trust that it would happen. I needed to calm the fuck down.

I only got as far as four though when I heard the scratching sound of overgrown spider legs, a sound I'd hoped to never hear again. I looked over my shoulder to see five of them coming around the corner, heading straight for me, all their eyes on their prize, their pincers clicking against each other as if they were imagining eating me already.

Fuck this shit. I let out a small cry, knowing that it would be impossible now for me to escape. I swatted at the air, tears threatening to spill down my face. I was so close to Dex, so close to my world, our life, and I was going to get stuck here.

The spiders began to give off a low, guttural growl, like a drooling dog on the attack. I looked over my shoulder at them again. At their current pace, they'd be on me in ten seconds. I glanced around for plan B—did I even have enough time to find a weapon to fight them off?—when I saw yet another problem.

A creature emerged from the side of one of the buildings. She might have been a woman in another life, but here she could barely be called that. She pulled herself along the sidewalk, the lower part of her severed off, guts trailing behind her like a flowing tail.

Her head was on backward. I could see bald patches through her ratty, dark hair, as she crawled toward me, skeletal arms and fingers reaching my way, worn down to the bone.

I would have probably thrown up at the sight of her if it wasn't for the fact that I was about to be eviscerated by giant spiders in a few seconds.

"Perry!"

I whirled around in time to see Ada emerging from the shimmering air, across the park, near the coffee kiosk where we had gotten our lunch.

I couldn't afford to be mad at her for coming through, not now. She was saving my ass.

I yelled back and quickly ran past the spiders, trying to avoid them. One leaped straight for me, tackling me from behind. Hairy legs tangled in my hair, and the sheer weight of it threatened to pull me down.

Screaming, I whipped around, stumbling wildly in an attempt to get it off. Somehow it did, painfully taking out strands of my hair as it let go, and let out a high-pitched whine as it fell to the ground. There was no time to dwell on it—I kept running and running, keenly aware that the spiders were in hot pursuit, coming faster now.

Just when I thought Ada was about to disappear—she was growing fainter before my eyes—she ran forward and grabbed my hand. I could barely feel her grip in mine, her body somewhere between solid and liquid. Her eyes darted over my shoulder and widened. I didn't dare turn around again.

She yanked me toward her with all her might, and in an instant I was being sucked into the shimmer, the familiar pressure kicking out from the inside of my brain.

My ears popped, and there was a moment of blinding light and screams, before I found myself tumbling forward and falling down into the dirt.

Dirt. Brown, smelly, earthy dirt under my hands and knees. I breathed it in deep, taking a moment to be grateful for this world.

Then I looked up, remembering what this world was willing to accept. There was an old lady on the bench across from me, reading a book and staring at me with her mouth open. I quickly looked around. Ada was standing beside me, offering her hand, her face both worried and sheepish. Behind us was the coffee kiosk, blocking our view from most of the park. It seemed that only the lady had seen me materialize out of thin air.

I let Ada help me to my feet, her grip solid again, and I dusted off my jeans before I gave the stunned lady my most winning smile.

"Magic trick," I explained to her with a slight shrug. "Looks like we got it right this time."

Then I led Ada away from her and to the other side of the kiosk. In seconds we were joined by Maximus, breathing hard from running across the park.

"What the hell did you do, Perry?" he asked, though he put his hand on my shoulder and squeezed it affectionately. "I told you."

"I know you did," I said. "But it worked! I found Dex! Quick, we have to hurry."

He didn't smile at that, nor did he remove his hand. "Ada had to go after you. I couldn't stop her. If she hadn't, you might have been lost in there forever."

I swallowed hard and looked them both in the eye. "I know. I wish you wouldn't have," I said to Ada. "But you got me out and you seem fine too. You feel fine, right?" Good lord, I hope she felt fine.

She nodded and gave me a crooked smile, though I noticed she was being more quiet than normal. I forgot that a trip to the Veil can leave you slightly shell-shocked for a while.

"Did you really find Dex?" Maximus asked, turning my attention back to him.

"Yes!" I cried out, feeling the hourglass tipping over again. "I saw him and I think he heard me. It was like a window opened up, and I was able to see into this world, but not cross over. He was on the Brooklyn Bridge. Alone."

"Just like your dreams," Ada mused blankly, still sounding a bit out of it. "Or whatever they were."

"Exactly. I should have known to go there, but it didn't occur to me. But he's there. And he's alive. If we hurry, maybe we can catch up with him. At the very least, at least we know he's in the city, and he's got to be looking for us."

Maximus sighed, though he was relaxing a bit. "All right. If you ladies are both feeling okay to hightail it to the bridge, I reckon it's worth a shot."

He could barely finish his sentence. I was already on the run, heading to Dex.

# 6

DEX

"Excuse me, sir. Are you all right?"

The quiet but concerned voice brought everything into focus. I found myself staring into the eyes of a hipster. That was my first thought anyway. She was wearing a plaid, short-sleeved collared shirt, had close-cropped hair, and lime green glasses that didn't seem to have lenses. Oh, and a septum nose ring.

I blinked at her a few times, stupidly. Behind her the brown buildings of Brooklyn gradually appeared, like the whole world was being painted into place. Well, Brooklyn certainly explained the hipster.

It did not explain why I was standing on the middle of the Brooklyn Bridge, hands gripped to the railing of the pedestrian walkway like a fucking loon.

"Are you tripping?" she asked.

The polite, earnest way she said that made me laugh.

I most certainly was tripping. I had no fucking idea why I was in New York City. In fact, I think I finally, *finally* had lost my damn mind. I'd been waiting for this moment for a very long time.

"Doctor put me on new meds," I lied. "Can't seem to figure out how I got here."

She smiled at me, a lot warmer now. I'd wrongly assumed she was a lesbian; now she seemed to be into me. "Where are you from?" she asked slyly, which only cemented the suspicion.

"Seattle," I said. "I'm on vacation with my girlfriend," I added quickly as I felt the blood drain out of me. Jesus crackers, where the fuck *was* Perry? How the hell did I get here? I had way too many questions to keep inside my brain, and I was afraid that if I spent another minute with this woman, I was going to say something that would get me committed. Unless being tits-up crazy was suddenly cool. It wasn't when I was young.

Shot down, she still smiled, though not as open as before,.. "Cool. Well, hope you enjoy the city. And I hope your new meds work out."

She gave me a wave and continued on her way toward Brooklyn, lost in the stream of people walking to and fro.

Now that she was gone, I could breathe. AKA, not breathe, AKA freak the fuck out.

*Think, you idiot*, I told myself, adjusting my cap against the glare of the sun. Why the hell was it so warm here?

And, once again, why the hell was I in New York?

I tried to think back and couldn't remember anything except being in Portland at Perry's parents' house.

A flash of a familiar face came into my mind, but my instincts couldn't be correct.

Why did I have the feeling that I saw my brother Michael at some point? That was as likely as Kim Kardashian's ass being real. I hadn't seen him since, well, since we were teenagers.

And yet I kept seeing him, as he would be today. A tall,

dark, handsome asshole in a suit. Not as handsome as me, but close enough. And with the thought of him came this feeling that maybe I really was tripping out. Being alone in NYC with no memory of how I got there was bad enough, but it had nothing on the wash of dread that was sinking into my pores.

I shivered to myself and shook my head a few times, trying to shake it off, trying to shake some sense in. Nothing doing. The feeling intensified like it was just taking root and finding sunlight.

Before I really started to panic, I searched my pocket for my phone.

It was gone.

Shitballs.

I was alone in NYC, I kept feeling like the world was going to end at any moment, and I didn't even have my phone or a wallet. I only had my wits, and I was starting to think those were in short supply.

"Dex!"

It was Perry's voice, soft as satin sheets. I turned around, my eyes scanning the aloof people walking past, but I didn't see her anywhere.

Had I even heard her? I looked again, harder, searching each person, my ears trained for her voice. Suddenly I was hit with an overwhelming sense of urgency. It wasn't that my situation wasn't scary—it was. Ask any drunk the next morning when they didn't know where they were.

But in the back of my mind, I'd already begun rationalizing everything. I must have blacked out for one reason or another, but I had to have come to New York with Perry. I don't know why we came here or when, but we would have come together.

We would have had to. The girl just agreed to marry me

—the crazy fucking girl—and I know I wouldn't have let her out of my sight for a second. She was more precious to me than life itself.

And yet, she wasn't here. I felt her presence, heard her voice, but it was about as substantial as the air in front of my face. She was nowhere to be seen just as I probably was for her.

My heart decided to take a nose dive.

What if I couldn't find her?

What if something horrible had happened to her? To us? With every second that ticked past on that bridge, I was getting the feeling that some horrible *had* happened and the world was just waiting for me to catch on.

I put my hand to my chest and kneaded my knuckles along it, hoping to dispel the nervous energy that was building up. I needed a cigarette to clear my head. I needed a drink to calm my nerves.

I needed Perry just to get by.

I breathed in deeply through my nose, willing the pain in my ribs to go away. I had to have a plan of some sort if I was going to get anywhere. Staring at the throngs of people as they walked past, their attention utterly focused on the space in front of them, I wondered if anyone would be nice enough to let me borrow their phone to call Perry. I contemplated running after the lime green glasses girl but she was long gone.

Lady luck was smiling at me, however. I asked two twenty-something girls in sundresses with cigarettes dangling from their lips if I could bum a smoke. After one of them did, rather begrudgingly, I turned my charms onto the nicer, plumper one, and asked if she wouldn't mind me borrowing her phone for a minute.

This time, mentioning a girlfriend came in handy, and

once she realized the guy with the 'stache wasn't getting potentially rapey on her, she gave me her Samsung. I actually had to correct myself and tell her my girlfriend was actually my fiancé now. Man, did that sound both weird and awesome to say that out loud, but it seemed to win me a few points, which I hoped would turn into a few extra minutes on the phone.

Turns out I needed them. Perry didn't answer her phone, even when I called three times in a row. The girl was starting to sigh and look put out, the subtle way to say "Dude, get the fuck off the phone," and I grinned nervously at her. "Just one more person to try."

Actually, I had more than a few people to try but since the last place I remembered was the Palominos, I figured that was my best bet. I hated having to ring her parents, but hey, I guess they were going to be my parents too one day. They better get used to it. And so should I.

But there was no answer at their house either, which struck me as odd. Usually her mother was home, if not Ada. I left a long, yelling message on the machine.

"Hey, so it's Dex, and sorry to bother you, but if Perry is there I would love to speak to her. I'm in New York City. Not sure how that happened. Anyhoo, I would be much obliged if someone, anyone ... Ada ... Mr. Palomino ... Dad? I guess I have to call you Dad soon, right? Maybe not. Anyone really, if you would pick up the phone because I think this will be my last call for a while, and I can't seem to find my phone. Or my wallet. Or know what's going on or how I got here. So yeah. Answering the phone would be great. Hello? Bueller?" Pause. Waiting for them to pick up. "But you won't do that because you're not home. That's fine. I'm busy too. I'm on the Brooklyn Bridge. It's awesome. There are two young ladies here, one I'm sure has something against mustaches, and the other who is giving me a look like she's sorry she lent me her phone. Well, if I don't hear from you guys, it's because I don't have my cell. I told you that, right? Anyway, I'll call back. When I can. I might not be able to." Another pause, and this is when I noticed both girls looked like they were ten seconds away from blowing their rape whistle and bringing out the pepper spray. "Okay, bye."

I hung up and gave the phone back to the girl, shooting her an apologetic smile. "Sorry. I thought maybe they'd pick up if I started rambling nonsense."

She stared at me while she tucked the phone in her purse. Then, without saying anything, she and the other girl walked away in a hurry, shooting me anxious glances over their shoulders, as if they'd never left a message like that on a machine before.

I exhaled and watched them go. Well, that was a bust. I decided to start walking to Manhattan, give it a few minutes, then try someone else for a phone. Perry had to pick up at some point; I left her more than enough voicemails.

*Not if she's not okay*, the thought shot through my head like a bullet. *Maybe that's why you can't get a hold of her.*

Fuck. I clenched and unclenched my fists. What if something had happened to her?

I refused to entertain the thought. I needed to hold it together, not fall apart. As long as I found out she was okay, just to hear her voice, more than anything, then I'd deal with the rest.

But refusing to think about it didn't mean I didn't *feel* it. That sickness, black and sticky like tar, clinging to the inside of my lungs.

Before I knew what I was doing, I was sprinting down the bridge, urgency pressing through my legs. I was bumping into people, knocking commuters off balance, their cries of anger and annoyance the soundtrack to my pumping limbs, but I couldn't give any fucks. There were no fucks to give. It was like the faster I went, the more I was aware that something horrible was about to go down and all the speed in the world wouldn't help me.

Or her.

Or anyone.

I was nearly at the place where the bridge promenade swooped into City Hall Park, thinking about one of the last times I was in the area, paying a parking ticket with Maximus back in the wayback days, when I felt like my nonexistent drug trip just intensified.

There was Maximus, stepping out from the grandiose pillars of the Manhattan Municipal Building, his floppy ginger coif standing out like a red beacon on the end of a flannel stick. He wasn't even wearing flannel, but that wasn't the point.

I came to a halt, making sure I was seeing this right. Did I run right into the past? Déjà vu swept over me, momentarily washing that feeling of doom aside. How could I just think about him and make him appear? Was I Gandalf?

But it wasn't just him. It was also Ada. Fucking Little Fifteen Ada Palomino throwing change at a hotdog vendor and trying to catch up with Maximus, all long limbs and bad eye makeup.

What the actual fuck?

Before I could even contemplate just what sort of wizardry was at work here I heard my name.

"Dex!"

It was more of a panicked shriek, but to say it didn't immediately fill my heart with gold would be lying.

I turned my head toward the park and saw Perry, beautiful, crazy Perry, running toward me, about to head straight into traffic.

I let out a yelp, my body frozen from the impending disaster, but she managed to skirt in front of the cars which were slowing down as they turned onto the bridge, and soon she was on my side of the road, unscathed except for a few people laying on their horns in her wake.

There's a moment in the movie *10* when Dudley Moore sees Bo Derek running down the beach in slow motion. Most people don't know what I'm talking about because most people don't educate themselves with the classics, particularly Blake Edwards, but anyway, this moment rivaled that one.

And that doesn't trivialize it, believe me, because seeing Perry run toward me, her face scrunched in the sheer desire to reach me, did something to my soul. It grabbed at me, clawed at me, made me realize just how damn empty I'd been without her by my side, even if for a short while. It made me realize I needed to do everything I could to ensure that would never happen again.

"Dex!" she cried out again, and in an instant she was in my arms and she was safe and I was safe, and the rest of the world could go to hell for all I cared.

I held her close to me as she sobbed into my chest. I wanted to calm her down, but at the same time I wasn't doing so well either. The more she shook in my arms, the more worried I became.

"Hey, baby," I whispered into the top of her head. "You're here, I'm here."

Right?

She half mumbled, half cried something into my chest, and I had to pull back to give her some room to talk. I smoothed the hair behind her ears, imploring her to look at me. She eventually did even though the tears wouldn't stop running down her face.

"What's wrong?" I asked her softly. I hated seeing her cry more than anything.

She grimaced and wiped the tears off her cheeks. "You don't know?"

"I'm afraid I don't know much, kiddo. Last thing I remember is being in Portland, upstairs, editing. Next thing I know I'm on the Brooklyn Bridge, talking to a hipster. Apparently, I've missed some shit between points A and B."

She frowned, studying my face, and squeezed my hand hard. "That's really all you remember? You don't remember your brother?"

Michael. Again, his face flashed through my mind, as clear as day. Why it struck the fear of god in me, I don't know.

I paused. "I don't think so?"

"Lord, Dex, aren't you a sight for sore eyes," Maximus said as he walked over to us.

"Good, cuz the sight of *you* makes my eyes sore," I said right back but I couldn't help but grin at him. I looked at Ada who had somehow already devoured the hot dog and was staring at me with questioning eyes. "Little Fifteen. Fancy meeting you in the Big Apple. Can one of you jokers please inform me of what the fuck is going on here?"

"He says he doesn't remember anything," Perry said to them.

I wrapped my arm protectively around her waist and pulled her closer to me. "I'm assuming some major shit went down, or somehow the teleporter was invented without me knowing it."

I don't know why I thought they'd find that amusing but all three of them stared at me gravely, and my hackles went up. "Okay, seriously. I don't know what happened. Can one of you please indulge me?"

Surprisingly, it was Ada who spoke up. "You were upstairs. I was working out. Do you remember that?"

"Yeah," I said slowly, the sound of that scary athletic chick's voice pounding into my head. "A workout video with the hot but crazy girl with the big jaw."

"Yes," she said with a raise of her brow. I just then noticed how tired Ada looked. She'd always bordered on that because of her fascination with a metric ton of eyeliner, but there was something different about her. The exhaustion made her seems eons older than she was, like she'd seen a lot recently.

She continued, "Then there was a knock at the front door. Do you remember that?"

I tugged at my hat while I tried to think, my other arm tightening around the small of Perry's waist. I thought she'd relax into me, but she felt just as tense as I did. "I don't think so." Did I remember a knock at the door? It was hard to say if my memory was true or I was just conjuring up what it would have sounded like.

"Do you know who it was?" she asked.

I shook my head even though every part of me wanted to say it was Michael.

"It was your brother."

I nodded. Hearing it didn't make it seem more real but it also didn't feel like a lie. It just didn't make any sense—that was the real problem I was having with it. Why would my brother show up now after all these years? How did he know where to find me?

"What did he want?" I asked.

She glared off into the distance and crossed her arms.

"You, obviously. He did some weird shit to my head, and the next thing I remember, Perry was shaking me awake."

"And you were gone," Perry filled in quietly. "You left in the Highlander with him."

"Willingly?" I asked.

She shrugged. "We don't know. We've been trying to figure that out. But Ada said you knew something was wrong. That once you saw him, you told her to run, to get out of there, to go and get me. You knew he was bad news."

I scratched at my chin, unsure how to take any of this. "My brother and I may have had our differences back in the day, but I don't think his appearance would have made me freak out."

"Well you did," Ada said. "And now you're here."

It was then that I noticed Maximus had been awfully silent. I glanced at him and was met with a suspicious gaze, green eyes appraising me as if I was spewing bullshit. I was close to delivering another barb to him, just to put him in his fucking place, when Perry said, "You really don't remember anything? Anything at all?"

I'm sure if I went into a psychotherapist's office and subjected myself to some hypnosis, I could conjure up some hidden memories, as well as stop my on-and-off-again affair with smoking and badly-lit porn. "I don't remember anything, but the moment I do, I'll let you know." I licked my lips and eyed them all. "So, if I'm here, how did you know where to find me?"

Perry sighed as if she'd been asked this question a million times already. Perhaps she had.

"I ran into your brother when I was off on my walk," she said carefully, her eyes flitting to the pavement. "Before all this happened."

My heart felt chipped. This didn't sound like it was

going in a good direction. As much as I didn't like my brother, I also didn't want to know what she was going to say next.

She continued, "He told me some things, about who he was and where you'd be going. So I knew." She nervously wiped the back of her hand across her lips. "And Pippa told me too. Back when we were on the coast, at the school. The visions I'd had."

And that was fucking news to me. But as much as I wanted to be in the loop over any visions or Pippa encounters that Perry had—and kept from me—what she said about Michael was far more troubling.

I stared down at her until her eyes met mine. "What happened after that? With Michael?"

I could see her inhaling through her nose, but to her credit she didn't break my gaze, even though I saw pity in her eyes, maybe even fear. "He did something to me."

My heart banged angrily in my ribcage. "What?" I asked, my voice low and hard. Fire licked at my guts.

"I don't know," she said helplessly. "He ... he made it so I was powerless. At first anyway. I couldn't move. And then, then I just fell to the ground, I guess, and passed out."

"What did he say to you?"

She exhaled sharply then said, "He said, 'You really are pretty, you know that. And young. Young blood is the best. My brother has excellent taste.' Then he said..." She paused.

"What?" I asked, my fingers gripping her tightly.

She looked away from me. "'He doesn't know I'm here,'" she said, her voice lowering to mimic his. "'And I wanted to keep it that way. I was rather a jerk to him after our mother died. And yet, now I need him. And I'm sure I'll need you, Perry.' Then he added, 'See you soon,' and I already knew he mentioned New York to me. Pippa mentioned it too. So we came as soon as we could. It was a hunch, in a way. I mean, we had nothing to go on. But somehow we found you."

Maximus snorted. I managed to tear my eyes off of her and glance at him, though I was still seething and grappling with what my brother had said and done to Perry and what the hell it all meant.

"Not somehow, little lady," Maximus said with an unamused roll of his eyes. He looked to me. "She went into the Veil to find you. I reckon it worked, but it was mighty stupid of her."

It *was* stupid of her. "Perry," I said, hating the idea that she would even entertain that thought, hating all of this.

"Figured you wouldn't like it either," Maximus said.

"I had no choice," she said defensively. "Dex would have done the same for me."

And that was definitely the truth. I would have scoured the ends of this world and many others if I were in her shoes and she in mine.

Suddenly I was hit with a wave of dizziness and that strange, creeping feeling again, almost like something was watching me. I quickly glanced around, half-expecting to see my fabled brother, but only saw the cityscape of New York instead. To say it was all overwhelming was being facetious.

"Are you okay?" Perry asked quickly, running her fingertips along my cheek.

I closed my eyes at her touch and nodded slowly. "It's a lot to take in. I need a beer and a cigarette and some time to wrap my head around things. All the things."

"I know just the place to cure what ails ya," Maximus said, forced levity in his voice. I was certain he was going to take me to a dive bar a few blocks from here, one we used to get cheap fish tacos at in college.

I nodded, and with my hand gripped firmly around Perry's, the four of us made our way down the street. The crazy thing was, even with my beloved and my friends at my side, even though all I had wanted to do was find Perry and now I had her in my arms, it didn't make everything right.

It should have.

But it didn't.

That horrible feeling, like something tragic was about to go down, and all the speed in the world wouldn't help me? That had only gotten worse since I found them.

And I had no damn clue what that meant.

# 7

PERRY

My heart pumped forcefully in my ears. It was whole again. Happy. I could breathe.

I sat, chin resting on my hands, and watched Dex drain the glass of amber beer that had been poured for him moments ago. To anyone else Dex may have seemed calm and cool, his usual cocky self.

But his hands were shaking ever so slightly, and his knee wouldn't stop jumping beneath the table. His dark eyes kept flitting to different corners of the room, waiting or watching or just trying to make sense of things. I didn't know.

It was Dex though, I knew that much. He was alive and well and in my grasp, and I wasn't going to let him go after this. Not just because I could barely survive the twenty-four hours without him, but because we still didn't know what happened to him, and because of that, it was impossible to know whether it would happen again.

All I did know is that if Michael dared show his smug face again, I was ready to fight to the death. I would steel my mind. I would not let him succeed this time.

"Are you all right?" Maximus asked, but the question

seemed to be for everyone, not just me. While I realized my fingernails were clawing into the palm of my hand, Dex continued to look sketchy, and Ada was still a bit dazed and blank.

"Fine," I said quickly. I was the last person anyone should worry about. I reached across the table, laid my hand on top of Dex's, and gave him a gentle look. "How about you, baby?"

He flipped my hand over and laced his fingers into mine, giving it a warm, strong squeeze. He smiled, close-lipped. "Well, I'd be lying if I said I haven't been better. I'm just not sure how to make sense of anything. It's kind of weird that the three of you know more about where I've been for the last while than I do."

"It *is* weird," Maximus said. His tone was light but there was a stiffness to his jaw that I wasn't too fond of, almost as if he were questioning whether Dex was telling the truth. But as excellent a liar as Dex was, I almost always knew when he was lying. He was being honest—he had no reason not to be—and was vulnerable as a result. Vulnerability was always something he tried his hardest to avoid.

Dex stared back at him, though I didn't really see the animosity I'd come to expect from him. It was almost as if he was trying to figure out if Maximus had a right to be suspicious. Either way, he knew what Maximus was getting at, and he didn't question it.

I wanted to say something to Maximus, admonish him, but before I could, Dex said, "So I guess the best thing would be to fly home. Only problem is, I don't have my wallet—I don't have ID. Can't fly without that. I'd have to drive or take a bus."

Ugh. The idea of driving from New York to Portland used

to be on my bucket list, but now I wanted more than anything to just go home. I wanted to feel the Seattle rain on my shoulders, I wanted to hole up in cozy cafés with Dex and plan the rest of our lives together, I wanted to cuddle with Fat Rabbit and go shopping with Rebecca, and get back to the life we'd set in motion. I wanted to enjoy being engaged.

This was not how I imagined our engagement would start off. Then again, we were Dex and Perry, and our relationship seemed to thrive on the universe being out of order. Either that or our relationship actually caused the world to turn upside down. It was hard to say.

Ada's phone started to ring. She glanced at it and then quickly excused herself to go stand outside by the door. I twisted in my seat to keep a close eye on her. We were lucky she hadn't been carded once we sat down at the bar, not that she was drinking more than Sprite anyway, but she was still nearly sixteen, and this was a big bad city.

"I guess," I said absently, "we could get Rebecca to send your passport over here on overnight. We could fly out tomorrow or the next day after that." I didn't want to stay here a day longer than we had to, but it seemed that was the only choice.

"Well, I guess there are worse places to be stuck in," Dex said, but I could tell he didn't like the idea either. At any other time, New York would have been a dream vacation—especially since I was here with Dex and my sister. But now, it felt like the entire city was plotting against us. I was probably overdosing on paranoia, but still.

And for Dex and Maximus, I was sure the city was bringing about a whole flood of memories that neither one of them wanted to deal with.

Ada came back into the bar and slid into her seat with a

sigh, looking like your quintessential disaffected youth. "Bad news, guys."

My pulse sped up, and I was certain Dex could feel it against his hand. "What?" What *now*?

She raised her eyes to me and gave me a dry half-smile. "Our parents are coming."

I let go of Dex's hand and let my own fly up into the air like a stereotypical Italian. "What? Why the hell are they coming here? They can't do that."

"They can, and they are," she said, repeatedly stabbing the ice cubes in her drink with her straw. "They just called, said they'd booked a red-eye flight tonight, and will be here in the morning."

"That's insane," I cried out. "Why would they do that?'

"I don't mean to play devil's advocate here," Dex said, drumming his fingers on the table. "But you can't really blame them, Perry."

I shot him a look. "What?"

He shrugged. "You came after me. It's only fair they'd come after you. I mean, maybe not if it was just you..." I glared at him but he continued quickly, "because they trust you and all. But you have their teenage daughter. And she does have things like school and stuff. Parents are big on school and stuff."

I put my head into my hands and groaned, then looked at Ada. "You did tell them that we found Dex and are about to head home, right?"

She nodded. "I did. Didn't make a lick of difference. So I guess we have to stay right here."

"We don't really have a choice," Dex said. "No wallet, no ID. Rebecca will have to mail out my passport if I want to fly anywhere."

I looked over at Maximus. "What about you? Going to head on home to the Big Easy? I bet Rose is worried."

Dex raised his brow, not entirely caught up on the Rose and Maximus situation. Maximus shook his head. "I'm sure you'd all love that, but actually, I'm going to hang around here for a few days until you leave."

"I don't believe I requested a chaperone from District Ginger," Dex pointed out warily.

"I know you didn't," he said. "But I'm going to hang around all the same, if that's okay."

"Is there something you're not telling us?" I asked. I briefly slid my knowing gaze over to Dex and back. "Along with all those other things you didn't tell us?"

Maximus exchanged a look with Dex. The look said, *she knows I'm an ex-supernatural babysitter man, sorry.* He said to me, "No, there isn't. But we all know that what just happened was a little too easy. One minute you're certain you'll never see Dex here again, the next he's walking along the bridge in a daze, unsure of how he got there. Now, you can sweep all that under the rug and pretend that this shit is all over, and believe me, I want to, too. But for everyone's sake, I'm just going to stick around and make sure you guys are all right before you fly home."

"That's thoughtful," Ada spoke up. She actually sounded relieved. Or maybe she didn't want to end up being the third wheel until our parents got here.

"Just one thing though," he said, now looking a bit sheepish. "I didn't book a room, and funds are a little tight since I flew out here and all. Think you guys could help spring for a hotel room?"

I rolled my eyes and sighed loudly. "Fine, you can stay with Ada."

"What?" she cried out. "No way am I sleeping with Ginger Rogers."

Dex snorted, appreciating that.

"You will sleep in separate beds, Ada," I admonished her. "Ew." I looked to Maximus. "No offense. But obviously Dex and I will be in the other room."

"We'll be just like Lucy and Ricky, and Fred and Ethel," Dex said, wagging his finger at Ada and Maximus. "Of course, like Fred and Ethel, I'm going to assume you won't be touching each other."

Both Ada and Maximus grimaced simultaneously. "Lordy," Maximus said, exasperated. "Forget I said anything."

"It's fine," I said, whether it was fine to Ada or not. The truth was, even though Maximus seemed to have put on his detective hat, I was a bit relieved he'd be here with Ada. I knew he looked at her like a sister and that he'd keep her safe. Though he may no longer have any cosmic ties to Dex, I also knew he was acting in his best interests, the best interests of all of us.

I was just happy to have Dex back. I didn't dare think about what else could be lurking around the bend.

"THIS IS SOME SWANKY PLACE," Dex commented, looking mildly around the hotel room as I closed the door behind us. "Where's the bottles of Cristal?"

"Actually," I told him, throwing my duffel bag on a pink leather chair, "the closest thing to Cristal is sparkling wine. It's in the mini-fridge and costs forty dollars for a mouthful."

"Forty dollars for a mouthful? You could get more from a cheap hooker."

I gave him a look but he just grinned at me playfully. I didn't want to know, but his comment meant he was feeling better, and that made my shoulders relax a little.

He walked over to the window and peered outside, at the roar of upper Broadway traffic below. He seemed to lapse into deep thought. I could only imagine what he was thinking.

"It must be strange," I said. "To be here."

He nodded slowly, biting his lip for a moment. "Uh huh. You could say that."

I came up behind him, placing my head on his shoulder, my gaze following his down to the passing cars, metal garbage cans on the sidewalk glinting in the sun.

We stood there for a few moments in silence. I expected his arm to go around me, but it didn't. He stood like a statue, immovable, untouchable.

After a while he said, "I'm sorry."

I tilted my head toward him, my cheek on his shoulder. "About what?"

"About this," he said. "About you being here. I don't know why I walked off with Michael, why I wouldn't have checked with you first, why I just left with Ada unconscious. That's not like me. You know that."

I straightened up, squeezing his forearm. "Dex. I know that. We all know that. That's why it was so fucking scary. You obviously were going either against your will or under false pretenses."

He didn't react. "Or I was just so happy to see my brother again, I would have done anything he said."

I frowned, studying him. I hated how blank and mask-like his face was looking all of a sudden. "I thought things with your brother didn't end very well."

"Yeah, well," he said, going back to biting his lip. "They

didn't." He closed his eyes, almost wincing. "Perry," he said gently. "I don't know what any of this means. Why would my brother bring me here? Why would he do that to you, to Ada? What's the point of all this?"

I didn't say anything. He knew everything that Pippa had told me. That, and Michael's actions were all there really was to go on.

Finally he looked at me, his eyes watering. "Baby."

And that's all he said. That's all he needed to say. I placed my hands on either side of his face and leaned over to kiss him lightly on the lips. I wanted more, but more than that, he needed comfort.

He kissed me back and pulled away slightly, staring at my eyes, my nose, my lips. He looked so lost, so desolate, but his carnality leaked back into his features. He placed his hands at the back of my head, holding me steady.

"Perry, I love you," he said, voice gruff and full of conviction. "I love you absolutely, resolutely. There is no question, no doubt. This love just is. It exists, and because it exists, I exist." He brought his face closer so that the tip of his nose grazed mine. "When you're my wife, I know I'll be a good husband so as long as I never let you forget that, that you, only you, just as you are, are my reason for being."

I swallowed hard, my heart tumbling over itself at his beautiful words. Why was he telling me this? It sounded like he was about to go off to war; it sounded like we were parting, not coming together.

But before I could say anything, his lips were on mine, and he was kissing me, hard. His passion surprised me, stole my breath straight from my lungs. His tongue didn't need to coax me for long. Soon my surprise was melting away into want and need and feverish lust.

I had almost lost this man. I wanted, needed, to fuck him

hard enough to make up for that. I knew he was planning on doing the same to me.

In seconds he was pushing me back onto the bed, and my shirt was being ripped over my head. He deftly got my bra off with what felt like just a snap of his fingers, his mouth and tongue knowing just how to tease and lick my nipples to make my thighs squeeze together in beautiful agony.

We made love as we always did, but there was more urgency and desperation than there was tenderness. I didn't mind. I felt like I couldn't get him close enough. I brought him in so deep, my nails sinking into the hard curve of his ass, that I was sure he'd never be able to pull away.

He seemed to feel the same. He thrust into me, hard enough that the back of my head bounced against the mattress, and he moaned, long and rich. In and out he slid, his cock feeling like hard velvet inside of me. His tongue was in a frenzy, fucking the inside of my mouth with wild intensity. I closed my eyes as he licked and kissed down my neck, indulging in the feeling of him wanting me, of his carnal desire and masculine strength.

"Don't ever leave me again, baby," I groaned as his fingers rubbed at my clit, causing the heat to build in my core like water brought to a rolling boil.

"I won't," he murmured, taking my hard nipple into his teeth and tugging. God, I wasn't going to last much longer. "I can't. You feel so fucking good all the time, all the fucking time."

I stared up at his hard chest, the strain of his sculpted muscles as he continued to drive into me, bringing us both home. We came at the same time, as we usually did thanks to his stamina and patient fingers, and my eyes rolled back as my body was carried away, somewhere warm and beautiful. I didn't want it to end. I never wanted him to leave me.

Eventually though, he did, and we both rolled over on our backs, breathless and sweaty in the hot Manhattan evening. While my body rode the softening waves of orgasm, I felt that warmth tingle within my chest, the one that made me feel like everything was going to be all right now. It's funny how so much strife and distance could disintegrate after sex. It was cliché to say I always felt closer to Dex after he had been inside of me, but of course it was true.

We lay there for some time, his strong, muscled arm around my shoulders, my head buried into his chest. His heartbeat was steady, telling me I was safe and that I was his.

"Perry," he whispered, his voice throaty.

"Mmhmmm," I said, my fingers dancing over the *And With Madness* tattoo on his chest.

"I'm also sorry I didn't tell you about Maximus."

My fingers paused for a moment then resumed their dance, tracing the cursive road.

"That's okay," I said. I wasn't lying. It wasn't quite okay, but I also understood that Maximus's secrets weren't necessarily his to share.

"It isn't," he said. "I don't like keeping things from you. When I found out in New Orleans, it blew my mind. At the same time, I wasn't surprised. Maryse, you remember the haggard voodoo lady, she had called me the exception."

I rolled over on my stomach and rested my chin on his chest, staring up at him. "The exception?" He certainly was exceptional to me, but I had a feeling that in the sack wasn't counting for this one.

He nodded sharply. "That's what she said. I can tell you

that neither Maximus nor I agreed with that statement. What I got out of the whole deal was that Maximus turned into a petty douchebag. But also my sleeping with his girl might have helped to soil the whole thing. But what I'm an exception for, I don't know."

I didn't want to think about this stuff. I wanted my brain to remain floaty and sluggish on endorphins. I was partly tempted to put my hand under the soft sheets and bring Dex back to life again, but I could also tell he wanted to talk, even though I couldn't do anything but listen.

"Maybe that's why your brother sought you out," I offered quietly. "If you're an exception, then I guess that means you're special in a way."

I thought he'd laugh at the word but he seemed to mull it over. "Special," he repeated slowly, as if he was weighing it on his tongue. "But what does that mean? And what did Michael want?"

"Maybe we'll never find out. Perhaps he wanted something with you, and he's already taken it or figured out that you're not as special as he thought. Maybe he just wanted to talk to you, discuss family matters, I don't know. If he thought you wouldn't go with him willingly, if he thought maybe we would have interfered, maybe that's why he acted the way he did."

He crooked his head and peered down at me through his long lashes. "Is that what you believe? That he just wanted to talk?"

I gave him an uneasy smile. "No. I looked into his eyes, Dex. He meant me harm. He meant you harm. And why you're here in this bed with me, I don't know. In some ways..."

"What?"

I moved my gaze to the window, where the light was

turning purple and gold. "In some ways I wished I could have, I don't know, fought for you. Brought you back. Faced him, you know? Then maybe I could figure out what this was all about. Maybe I'd know it was over instead of still going." I carefully brought my eyes back to his. "You feel that, right?"

"That it's not over?"

"Yeah."

He eased himself up, leaning back on his elbows. I sat up, bringing the sheet over my hips and stomach, still self-conscious at times despite everything.

He pursed his lips. "I know Ginger Balls is sticking around for a reason. I may not agree with his mere existence on this planet, but I have to admit his intuition is pretty spot-on sometimes."

"And your intuition? What is it saying?"

He raised his brow. "That I'm supposed to remember something really fucking important, and the fact that I can't recall anything except this vague idea of his face and voice is making me feel like I've fallen down the shitter and I can't get out. It's dark and it smells and I want to scream, but I can't, because if I do, I'm getting shit in my mouth."

"That's a hell of analogy."

He shrugged. "It's a hell of a feeling."

I couldn't help but smile. He grinned right back, and I felt a rush down my spine, that butterfly feeling that I still got when he smiled at me. I couldn't love this guy more.

Then his smile fell a bit and something dark came across his face. "Perry," he said.

I stiffened, wondering what was next. "Yeah?"

"You know I didn't keep all that Maximus stuff from you because I was ashamed or I didn't want you to be in the loop. I always want you in the loop, kiddo. You are my loop."

"I know, I get it."

"It was more that I couldn't think of the right time," he continued. "And I couldn't imagine it would ever be relevant. Sometimes ... the heavier and more crazy the subject, the harder it is to bring up. You know how that is."

I frowned at him. What was he getting out now? "I do..."

He swallowed, his Adam's apple bobbing up and down. "So, it's not a matter of keeping stuff from you. It's a matter of deciding how and when to talk about it. In this exact case, I just didn't know when it would be a good time."

"And I'm sure it didn't help that it wasn't your secret to tell," I said, trying to alleviate some of the burden he suddenly seemed to bring upon himself. "It didn't really involve me. It was about you guys."

"Yeah," he said, but his voice wavered. I stared at him for a moment, wondering what else was on his mind, until I noticed a trickle a blood coming out of his nose.

I jerked back. "Oh god, Dex, your nose."

He sat up straighter and ran his fingers underneath it. He stared down at them, shiny and red with blood. "Huh," he said, staring at it in awe. "That's weird."

I scrunched up my face. "Totally weird. You don't normally get them, do you?"

He shook his head and the blood poured out harder, spraying onto the sheets. He let out a gruff cry, and I shot out of bed, grabbing the nearest box of tissue and bringing it over to him.

I scrunched up a wad and shoved it under his nose. "Easy now," he said, his voice nasally. "I'm all for you playing nurse and all, but you know you have to wear the uniform."

"I'm naked, what more do you want?"

He grinned, and I put my hand behind his head, holding him in place as I tried to stop the bleeding. He eyed me.

"You know, if you had told me that Michael was an alien, this would make a lot more sense. Alien abduction victims are always complaining about nosebleeds and lost time."

"Don't you dare even mention aliens," I warned him.

He smiled and I only pressed the tissue harder. "Aliens? You have a problem with them, Scully?"

"Yes, Fox Mulder," I told him earnestly. "I do. They freak the hell out of me. I can't even."

"So all this time, you brush off ghosts and demons and sasquatch but it's aliens that really get under your skin, huh?" When I didn't say anything, he clicked his tongue. "Well, you learn something new every day."

"And I'm learning that you have an awful lot of blood up your nose," I told him, tossing the blood-soaked wad aside and applying fresh new ones. "Good thing you don't seem to be squeamish, or I'd say when I get pregnant, you should definitely avoid the delivery room."

The air around us seemed to still. Dex sucked in a breath through his teeth, and his eyes immediately left mine, focusing on a bloody spot on the sheets. I immediately felt a bit stupid for mentioning the pregnancy thing. I wasn't sure why. I mean, we were getting married. It was pretty much a given that at some point in our marriage, I would be pregnant, or would at least be trying to be. Maybe not in the immediate future—I was still young and my biological clock wasn't really kicking me yet—but it wasn't unreasonable to start planning on it.

"Sorry," I said awkwardly. "Aliens and babies are touchy subjects for us. They even look the same."

At that, there was a knock at our door. Normally I would have been annoyed considering I was naked and Dex's blood was on my hands, but I was eager to leave that conversation behind.

"Just a minute," I said loudly, and placed Dex's hand over the tissues, motioning for him to keep applying pressure. I quickly grabbed a cushy robe from the closet and wrapped it around me before answering the door.

Ada was standing on the other side. She looked a bit wary, but the minute she saw my blood-stained hands, her eyes widened maniacally. "Oh my god," she said. "Are you okay?"

"Yeah, yeah," I told her, looking over my shoulder to make sure Dex was decent before inviting her inside. He tugged the sheets higher over himself and gave Ada a wave. "He just has a nosebleed."

"Ew," she said, looking totally disgusted. "There was this kid in grade school who kept getting nosebleeds all the time. Aynsley, I think her name was. Totally gross. They said she couldn't keep her finger out of there."

"I don't think this has anything to do with Dex's finger," I told her.

"It's true!" Dex shouted. "My finger prefers other holes."

Now Ada really looked like she wanted to vomit. "Ugh, okay I'm going to go."

I reached out and grabbed her arm before she could turn away. "Seriously, what's up? How are you feeling? I know you must be all sorts of messed up because of the Veil."

She stared down at her fingernails, seeming to examine them, something she tended to do when she was trying to appear blasé. "Yeah, I definitely don't feel one hundred percent. I feel really spacey, like I'm drunk or high, but it's not as comforting."

"It will pass," I told her, though I honestly didn't know if or when it would. I could only hope.

She cocked her head to the side. "Will it? Because it's not

just feeling like I'm walking on the frigging moon without moonboots."

"What do you mean?"

She sighed and looked over my shoulder. "Should I come back at some other time? I don't want to interrupt your bloodplay."

"Ada," I reproached her. "He has a bloody nose. And how do you know about bloodplay?"

"I read kinkier books than you do," she said simply. "Actually, I'm just going to go back up to my room. I want to hit the hay before Maximus starts snoring."

I squeezed her arm harder, my eyes searching her face. She'd already taken off her makeup, which normally made her look more innocent, but that wasn't the case here. There was a weighty quality behind her eyes, like she was beyond tired. Maybe sleep would be best for everyone, even though it was still early and we were in Manhattan of all places.

"What did you want to talk about?" I asked her.

She shook her head. "It can wait." She shot me a quick smile, and when I wouldn't let go of her, she rolled her eyes and gave out a heavy sigh. There was the Ada I knew. I released her, and she started down the hallway toward the elevators and stairwell.

She paused a few steps away and looked over her shoulder at me. "I'll talk to you in the morning. Oh, and by the way, stay away from the sixth floor. There seems to be a demon down there. I'd take the stairs from now on, if I were you."

And then she disappeared around the corner.

I stared at the empty hallway and shivered. Okay, there was definitely something to talk about. I turned back to the room, and Dex was now standing by the window and looking out of it, completely naked. While I spent a second admiring his ass, there was something about the sight that brought the shiver back down my spine.

"Are you okay?" I asked, stepping back into the room and closing the door behind me.

He didn't say anything, didn't move. His hands were down at his side, and the tissues were still on the bed. A drop of blood fell to the floor.

I breathed in deeply, trying to shake off the unease, and walked over to him.

"Dex," I said gently, afraid to touch him, as if he were a sleepwalker.

I stood behind him for a moment. Finally he seemed to notice my presence and turned around. A congealed river of blood had formed beneath his nose. His eyes were dark as coal and strangely blank. He blinked a few times and then said, "Sorry, were you saying something?"

"Not really," I told him with a nervous smile. "I was just talking to Ada. What are you doing, trying to give the neighbors a peep show?"

He looked down at his dick and then let out a laugh. It sounded hollow. "I guess so, huh," he said. He then stretched, his arms above his head, and let out a yawn. "I think I'm going to turn in."

"Your nose is still a bit bloody, by the way," I said to him as he brushed past me and headed right for the bed.

"I'll deal," he said, getting under the sheets. "I'm sure it's nothing."

Didn't you hear what Ada and I were talking about? I wanted to ask him. Demons on the sixth floor? That doesn't interest you at all?

But then again, this wasn't Experiment in Terror. That baby had been put to sleep, and bringing up demons and weird shit at a time like this probably wasn't the best idea.

Tomorrow I'd talk to Ada properly and get Dex checked out, and hopefully this whole maddening event could be put behind us.

Besides, my parents were coming in the morning. Every single one of us needed our strength for that. Oh, the horror, the horror.

I crawled into bed beside Dex and turned out the lights. The sky outside the window was now the darkest indigo, lit by orange neon lampposts. It was more comforting to have that light from the inside seeping in, to know that the world outside was carrying on as usual, even if our lives were anything but.

Still, I didn't fall asleep for the longest time, and when I finally did, my dreams were filled with things that would make the lightest nights seem black.

I dreamed that the man I was lying beside, the man I was set to marry, the love of my life, was not that man at all.

But I didn't know who he was.

## 8

DEX

I woke up feeling like a nun's ass—all dried out and tight as a rubber band, my head absolutely pounding from a headache that wouldn't go away. I must have pressed snooze a million times before I got out of bed, and by snooze, I mean I swatted at Perry every time she tried to shake me awake. I could have slept forever.

But she did remind me each time that her parents would be showing up at the hotel soon with pitchforks, and since I was to be their future son-in-law, I needed to show them some respect. Those weren't exactly her words, of course. She just didn't want me to get frozen by the Swedish Queen of Planet Frigid.

Eventually I pulled myself out of bed and staggered right over to the shower. One look in the mirror, and I was certain Perry would be calling off the wedding. My cheekbones were sticking out like Ziggy Stardust, and my face had taken on this pasty shade of grey. The dried blood beneath my nose didn't help, but at least it matched the red in my bloodshot eyes.

I felt a little more alive with hot water flowing on my

face, but my mind kept wanting to float to things that I wasn't sure I could afford to entertain. It wanted to think about Michael. It wanted to think about the sixth floor of this hotel. It wanted to think about the beginning of the end.

*Dude, I need an IV drip of coffee*, I thought to myself, trying to rip that last thought from my head. The beginning of the end? What the hell was wrong with me? When did I turn into such a fatalistic douche?

Since my brother apparently abducted me, I guess. I still couldn't wrap my head around it. The facts just made no sense, even though they were the facts, and the only things we had to go on.

"Dex!" Perry cried out, pounding on the bathroom door.

The frantic sound of her voice surprised me. I blinked a few times, realizing I was staring at myself in the bathroom mirror, water slowly dripping off of me and pooling at my feet.

I tore my eyes away from my reflection to answer her, but as I did so, the reflection in the mirror changed. Even though it was out of the corner of my eye, I could see the face in the mirror. My reflection opened its eyes, its mouth wide in a distorted scream.

My breath froze in my chest, and I immediately looked at the mirror dead on. It was just me, staring at myself with a look of shock on my face.

I willed my pulse to return to normal and quickly opened the door, no longer wanting to look at myself.

"What is it?" I asked, my voice cracking a bit.

Perry was totally dressed, her hair and makeup done. "What are you doing in there?" she asked, sounding more concerned than annoyed.

"I don't know, showering?"

"I've been knocking on your door and yelling your

name. Didn't you hear me? You've been in there for like forty-five minutes."

I tried to not let the shock register on my face, but there was no way I was in there for that long. Oh god, please don't let those quantum leap time jumps start up for me because that's the last thing I need.

"Well, I'm done now," I said. I grabbed a towel off the rack and quickly wrapped it around my waist. Like a car wreck, I couldn't help but let my eyes drift over to the mirror again.

This time my reflection was staring right at me and grinning like a madman.

I knew I wasn't.

I whipped my head around to look at Perry. She was staring at me in mild horror, though I wasn't sure why. Did she see it too?

"I'm worried about you," she said, and that's when I knew the whole thing must have been in my head. If she had seen my reflection move independently from my body, she wouldn't just be worried. She would be freaking the fuck out times a million.

Kind of like how I was feeling. And I know I should have told her what I was seeing, but I didn't see why giving her another reason to worry about me would have helped.

"Don't be worried," I said, but that wasn't going to change her mind at all. I stepped out into the hallway and made a mental note to avoid all mirrors. "So when do your parents get here?"

"They're already here," she said sternly. I sat down on the bed and looked at her. She really was all dressed and ready to go, and more than that, she had her battle face on,. To my admiration she looked less afraid and more combative. She'd changed a hell of a lot this year, especially when it came to standing up to her parents. I didn't think they were necessarily bad people, but they certainly didn't make things easy for either of us.

"Okay," I told her, wishing I had other clothes to put on besides those I had been found in yesterday. "I'll be ready in a second."

I quickly pulled on my pants and shirt and wondered how Perry would feel about a shopping spree this afternoon. She usually liked that kind of shit, and what better place to do it than New York? I'd pay her back, of course, so long as I didn't have to keep wearing the same pair of briefs for days.

I got ready fast and thought she'd be impressed, but instead she just came over to me and put her hand on my chest. I automatically put my hand over hers.

"What were you doing in there?" she asked, unwilling to let it go.

My mind immediately conjured up the image of me screaming at myself. I swallowed the bubble of fear and put a smile on my face. "Jacking off, naturally."

She narrowed her eyes but seemed to be happy with that answer. Good to know. She was going to make a fabulous wife.

I grabbed her hand, and together we went out into the hall, about to take the elevator to the lobby where she said her parents already were. But as soon as she pressed the button, she seemed to think twice about it and said, "Come on, let's take the stairs."

Just then the elevator doors opened, empty and beckoning. "Are you sure, cuz it's kind of here and everything…"

For whatever reason, fear came over her eyes, her pupils becoming tiny pinpricks, but she composed herself and seemed to brush it off like she did to her hair as she pushed it behind her shoulders.

"All right," I conceded, following her to the stairwell and heading down the echoing stairs. It didn't matter what building you were in, all stairwells had this impersonal, institutional, and cold feeling to them, the doors shutting you in like you're being locked into prison. I didn't know why this was preferable to the elevator, and I was just about to ask when we rounded the sixth floor and she nodded to it.

"Remember the demon."

Again, the image of me in the mirror, me but not me, grinning like I was going to eat myself alive, burned behind my eyes, and my skin immediately erupted into goose bumps.

At any other time I would have brought up the fact that it could make a great EIT episode, that we should explore it and film it, but now, even though EIT no longer existed, there was nothing I wanted less. I wanted to stay as far away from anything supernatural as possible. I was way too fucking weirded out to take on any extracurricular scary shenanigans.

"That's just fucking great," I said.

Soon, though, we were out of the concrete prison of the stairwell and into the lobby that toed the line between classy and try-too-hard trendy. I mean, a carafe of cucumber water is a nice touch, but does anyone need house music piped over the speakers or neon pink fringe pillows? I think not.

And, over there, on the white leather couches adorned by the aforementioned pillows was Mr. and Mrs. Palomino. They did not look happy.

That said, they didn't look like they wanted to kill us either, which I thought was progress. Usually they looked at me as if I'd just talked about slaughtering puppies, even when I was just waving hello. Of course it could all have something to do with the fact that I dared to open my mouth around them, and well, I knew from life experience that my mouth got me into trouble more often than not.

"Perry," her mother, Ingrid, said, holding out her arms and getting to her feet. She looked great—I hoped one day I liked the woman enough to admit that she was a total babe—even though she looked utterly drained, the same kind of look in her blue eyes that I'd seen in Ada's the other day.

I watched as she pulled Perry into an awkward embrace. Perry stiffened, unsure of what to do, and I silently encouraged her to just suck it up and enjoy her mother's affection while it lasted.

Perry, however, for all her telekinetic abilities, didn't seem to pick up on that thought. Her mother embraced her and then let her go. Her sharp Nordic features instantly became severe, perhaps because Perry didn't give in when she wanted her to. For the first time I was acutely aware that their relationship was more of a two-way street than Perry made it out to be.

Of course, the affection and concern didn't last for very long. Suddenly her mother launched into near hysterics, about how irresponsible she was for jetting off here, for the money she wasted, for the danger she put her sister in. All the while, her father, Daniel, was staring me down with that Mafia-look he sometimes had. I'd learned not to be intimidated by it over time, but now he was especially Pacino-esque.

I mean, it was all my fault they were here, wasn't it?

"You know," her father said, stepping toward me, "if you just wanted to go to New York, we wouldn't have cared. You're both free to do what you want, and Dex, you're a man of your own will—you can do what you want as well. But to involve Ada..." He shook his head, disappointed, and looked away, jamming his hands in his pockets. "I just don't know what you were thinking."

Obviously Perry had tried to explain to them what really happened, but the truth never settled very well with her parents. Actually, it never settled well with anyone, even with us. So we let them think what they were going to think anyway. Eventually, they'd get over it.

When Ingrid calmed down a bit, she shot me a nervous glance. I thought that was kind of strange since her looks usually consisted of the glacial variety. I wasn't used to her acting anxious around me. I had to wonder if I still had blood on my face. Maybe I smelled. I subtly pressed my nose to my shoulders and breathed in. Yeah. Time to buy new clothes.

I smiled at them. "Now that you're here, have you been checked in? Why don't we all go out for lunch, do some shopping?"

"Our room isn't ready yet," Daniel said sternly.

The door from the stairwell swung open, saving my ass. It was Ada, and she ran right into her mother's arms with a big smile on her face.

Her mother hugged her tight, then pulled back and held her stiffly by the shoulders, and the whole lecture she gave Perry came out once more. At least this time Ada was seen to be at fault almost as much as the rest of us were.

When all was said and done though, Ada offered her room for her parents to store their bags in until their room was ready. I noticed that she didn't mention Maximus, which was probably a good thing. I know the burly redhead had been a favorite of theirs back when Perry was possessed, but I wasn't sure if this was going to go over too well with them. A nearly sixteen-year-old sharing a room with a man who might have been thousands of years old?

Well, they didn't have to know about the thousands of years/ex-immortal/supernatural guide part. Thirty-two-year-old ginger was bad enough.

Her parents brought their luggage over to the elevator, but Ada flinched and immediately headed to the stairs. "I'll catch up with you, I'm on floor eleven. I need the exercise." She shot Perry an *'are you coming?'* look but Perry only shook her head. It would look weird if all of us decided to walk up eleven floors when the elevator was right there.

Though I wasn't feeling much trepidation about this so-called demon on the sixth floor. After all, her parents were far scarier and relevant. Perry seemed to shudder and then resign herself. She caught me staring at her and attempted a reassuring smile that didn't quite work.

We got into the elevator with her parents and watched the floor numbers as we slowly ascended. It was more than a tad awkward, squished in there with them. I could feel the animosity coming off of them, just fumes at first, then building to smoke of pure hatred.

At least, I thought the hate was from them. But when the elevator unexpectedly stopped at the sixth floor, and I felt the feeling intensify, practically wrapping itself around my neck and choking me, I knew it hadn't been coming from her parents.

It was coming from what was on the other side of the elevator doors.

It was waiting for me.

"Oh, what now?" her father said, jabbing his finger on the elevator button repeatedly. I could feel Perry glance at me in worry, but I couldn't take my eyes way from the door.

The doors slowly parted with a metallic groan.

At the end of the hallway opposite us was a tall, muscular figure, standing with its side to us, absolutely still. It was about seven feet tall, with cow-like horns on top of its head that nearly grazed the ceiling. It was naked, resembling a mixture of human and bull, all hard and sinewy, and black as sin. I wasn't sure if there was skin or short fur, but it was so dark and dense that it felt as if you were looking into something rather than at something.

It deliberately turned its head until it was looking our way. White slits for eyes bore into my own. I couldn't move, couldn't breathe, couldn't think.

We were going to die.

*I* was going to die.

That's all I knew, and I knew it like I knew the sun rose in the east and set in the west.

*You need answers.*

I wasn't sure if I thought it or the phrase just was plucked from the air. It was a voice with no voice.

*You need to find the answers.*

*Start with your past.*

"I thought this was a nice hotel," Perry's dad grumbled, his disgruntled tone bringing me back to reality. The beast at the end of the hall was still standing there, but black red blood began to flow from its bull nose, creating a river of crimson tar that sluggishly moved down the hall toward us.

I could barely bring my eyes away from it to look at her father. He was jabbing the button again, and for a moment I thought maybe he just needed to look up, maybe he needed to look up and he'd see it.

And then he did. He glanced right down the hall and his face never changed. He went back to the button, hitting it harder this time. To him, there was no beast, just a hotel that was getting on his nerves.

Now, the elevator doors finally began to close, shutting off the creature and the blood from reaching us. But it didn't erase the image from my mind. It didn't take away that blanket of evil that I felt settle around my feet like blackened dust.

I looked down at Perry, my mouth open slightly, trying to take in air, like I'd forgotten how to even breathe. She was dead still and staring at her mom.

Ingrid had her hand on her chest, a look of utter horror on her face.

Daniel looked at her. "What's wrong, dear?"

Her mother slowly turned to look at him, blinking fast, her mouth opening and closing, trying to find the words. "You didn't see..."

He frowned. "What? That the health code in this building probably isn't up to par? Damn New Yorkers, always cutting corners. You remember that building we used to live in on 32$^{nd}$, right? My goodness, that was a cause for concern."

Though it was hard to forget what I saw, I was watching Ingrid very closely now, as was Perry. She had seen something. She had seen *it*. The demon on the sixth floor.

I knew Perry must have been losing her shit inside her head. This was big fucking news, the fact that her mother saw the very supernatural thing that her daughter did. It meant so many things.

And yet, I was going to have to let Perry deal with that. I had other things I had to deal with. Mainly, the voice in my head that told me to find answers, to go back to the past. It was like everything was clicking into place, the satisfying snap of puzzle pieces being fit together.

I needed to go find my childhood home.

Then everything, everything, would make sense.

AFTER PERRY'S parents put their bags away in Ada's room and got over the fact that she had to share a room with Maximus last night (naturally, Max would have his own room going forward), we all headed out to lunch like one big fucking happy family.

Understandably, Perry and her mother were on the quiet side, while Ada was overjoyed at my suggestion we hit up H&M. It's not that I enjoyed shopping at a store that catered to European metrosexuals with prepubescent chests, but I needed to get something.

Luckily, I found jeans that didn't show off every curve of my dick or taper into my toes, and a few plain t-shirts that didn't have a cat wearing sunglasses on them. If I hadn't already seen a beast from Hell that morning, I would have sworn I was in Hell itself. Hell & Metrosexuals, that's what H&M stood for, right?

It was hard to keep my mood up, however, because every single time I caught my reflection, whether it was in the changing room mirror or the gleam of the floors or the glass on the buildings, I saw the same fucking thing.

My face, frozen in a scream, eyes open in horror. It got to be so unnerving that I started flinching every time I saw a reflective object.

"What's wrong?" Perry asked as we strolled down Fifth Avenue, Ada scampering into every single high-end designer store. She grabbed my hand and held it tight, pulling me back a bit. Maximus was up ahead, talking to her father, while Ada was trying to convince her mom of something.

I ran my tongue over the tip of my teeth. "Well, I think I might be going crazy."

"You're not," she said, keeping her voice low. "I saw the beast too. And you know what, I think my mom did also. She's acting like she hasn't, but I know it, I *know* it."

I nodded. "Yeah, I picked up on that. But that isn't why I think I'm going crazy."

Her brows furrowed. "That isn't? Dex, I'm pretty sure we just saw Satan on the sixth floor. What else could be more than that?"

I cleared my throat. "Uh, well, every time I see my reflection, it's not matching up with my face." Her frown deepened. "It's screaming," I explained. "And earlier this morning when I was in the bathroom, it was grinning at me, like it was about to fucking tear my head off and piss in it."

"When you say *it*, you mean…"

"Me. My reflection is me and yet it has a mind of its own."

Her grip on my hand tightened, and she sucked in her lip for a moment. "That isn't good."

"No shit. Hence the main reason why I think I'm going crazy."

She exhaled and looked down the sidewalk at Maximus who was getting lost in the crowd. "We should let him know. Maybe it means something."

I shrugged, kind of annoyed that she would be going to him for counsel. I hated thinking that the man knew some shit that I didn't. "I don't know. But I do think I know what will help." She looked at me expectantly and I continued, "I think we need to find the house I grew up in. Where Pippa was me and Michael's nanny. Where we lived before my father fucked off."

Perry didn't say anything. For a second I thought maybe she didn't hear me, but she carefully said, "Are you sure that's a good idea?"

"What's a good idea?" Ada's voice interrupted us.

We looked over to see Ada and her mother standing close by.

"I want to go visit my childhood home, where I grew up," I told them, even though I could tell Perry wanted me to shut it.

"That sounds like a great idea," Perry's mother said.

I shot her a curious look, studying her. I met her eyes and suddenly I understood something that I'd been ignoring before. "Of course you would want to," I conceded.

She gave me a slight nod. Though we never really discussed it, it was common knowledge between all of us that we were connected in more ways than just an upcoming marriage. When she and Daniel lived in New York City, her mother, Pippa, was there too, working as my nanny.

"I was there once," she said to me, her accent gentle. "A very long time ago. My mother ... she brought me over to show me where she worked. I met you, but you were very small. I met your brother, too."

I raised my brow. I had no idea that she'd actually been there, actually met me and my brother as a kid. This was officially getting weirder than cum on a cracker.

"I hope I wasn't a little shit, running around and kicking shins," I said, trying to lighten the mood.

She shook her head. "No, you weren't. You were very quiet."

"Never trust the quiet ones."

"No," she said, adjusting her purse on her shoulder, "I never do."

Ada looked between the two of us. "So, like, this is kinda weird, right? Mom, you actually remember meeting Dex when he was a kid?"

"His brother, too," she said, and then cocked her head at me. "How is your brother? Do you keep in touch?"

I raised my brow and could feel Ada and Perry's eyes on me. I guess she really didn't believe my brother was the reason I was out here. "He's reached out to me a few times. But we're not close."

She seemed to understand that, and before we get into it further, Maximus and Daniel were at our side, looking hot and in need of a beer. "What is the hold up?" Daniel asked.

"Dex wants us to go visit the house he grew up in," she said to her husband. I watched Maximus's eyebrows raise up to the heavens. "You remember where Mama used to work, right? It's close to the hotel. It would be neat to see the place again. I remember she was so happy working there."

Maximus was shooting me a look that was telling me I was crazy, but he didn't even know the half of it. I couldn't explain it myself, just that I felt if I saw the house, I would be able to figure something out—why Michael had brought me here in the first place. It was as if every instinct in my body was being pulled in that direction, and the more I entertained the idea, the more I knew it was something I had to do. And if everyone was going to come with me, then all the better.

Daniel groaned. "Can we do that tomorrow? We've only got a few days here before we head back, and I thought we could at least have dinner in the theatre district tonight, maybe catch a show. You guys all like the Lion King?"

He was met with blank faces. Watching Broadway shows seemed terribly out of place at a time like this, but I had to remember that Perry's parents were there only to get Ada and bring her back to Portland, and were trying to sneak in a mini-vacation at the same time. They didn't have to deal with our reality.

At least, Daniel didn't. Now I wasn't too sure about her mother.

"Sure, a show sounds great," Maximus spoke up, smiling at them. "Might as well see something good while we're here."

Then he and Daniel started discussing the other plays in town, and we all resumed our journey down the street.

The whole time, Perry didn't loosen her grip on my hand. It was almost as if she was holding on to me for dear life.

*I'm not going anywhere*, I wanted to tell her. But the truth was, I couldn't be so sure.

# 9

PERRY

To say I was concerned about Dex was a total understatement. First it was the nosebleed, then it was the time he spent in the bathroom that morning, time I knew he couldn't explain. Then it was seeing the demon thing, and the fact that he said his reflection was always screaming at him. Now, he wanted to visit his childhood home, something I knew was an extremely bad idea.

Something was happening to him, something I didn't understand. I waited until we were all getting ready for dinner when I chanced leaving him alone and went up to Maximus's room. I took the stairs, just in case. No way did I want to get stuck on the sixth floor again and see that terrible beast that made my limbs feel like lead.

My mom had seen it too, which meant my experiment was working. She wasn't on her pills, and the world that eluded her for so long was slowly seeping in.

I rapped on Maximus's door. He answered it, buttoning up a green cowboy shirt with a pointy collar.

"I thought it would be you," he said, his tone hushed. He quickly ushered me inside. "We need to talk."

"Yes, we do," I said, sitting on the end of his bed. "I'm worried about Dex."

He nodded and walked over to the mini bar, bringing out two mini bottles of vodka. He shook them at me. "Care for a drink?"

"You know those are like twenty bucks each."

He shrugged and smiled. "You're paying, aren't you?"

I rolled my eyes but held out my hand. "Yes, give me one. Forget the mix. Cheaper that way."

He sat down beside me and handed me the bottle of Absolut. "I'm worried about him too. I reckon I'm having a right case of déjà vu, don't you?"

*Now that you mention it*, I thought. A trickle of ice went down my spine. Dex was acting a bit like I had been acting when I was possessed. Of course it was nearly impossible to know what I looked like to the outside eye, but Maximus, he had seen me. And now he was seeing him.

But that didn't seem likely. How could his brother possess him? He was human.

"I don't know what I think," I said as I unscrewed the cap and dumped the contents into my mouth. It burned so good as it went down. I hoped it would cauterize my heart.

"Then tell me why you're here. Tell me everything, even if you think it's nothing," he said. "It won't do any good to keep your concerns inside, darlin'."

I breathed in deep through my nose and gathered my thoughts. I started with the nosebleed and ended with him thinking that going to his old house would give him all the answers.

"And just now," I said, "before I came up here, he was just standing by the window and staring at nothing. But it was like he was listening to something I couldn't hear. Occasionally he would smile but I don't know at what. It was ... creepy."

He finished his bottle and ran the back of his hand across his lips. "It could be nothing. He's been through a traumatic event, and even if he can't remember it, perhaps his subconscious does. Maybe he's just catching up."

"But it has to mean something that he wants to go to that place, the very place we were looking for when we first got here."

Maximus nodded. "It does mean something, I just don't know what. But you know, Perry, I don't think there is anything we can do about it. He's going to go, whether or not we go with him. And now, it seems like your mother has the same idea."

I chewed on my lip. "Do you think Michael will be there?"

He sighed and got up. "Lord, I hope not."

"Maybe it will all work out for the best," I said feebly, looking down at my hands. "It could put an end to everything, and we can just go home and never have to look back."

He put his hand on my shoulder and stooped over, raising his brows as he looked at me closely. "Have you ever known something like this to work out for the best?"

He had a point.

"Just keep an eye on him," he said, straightening up. "We all will. And while you're at it, keep an eye on your mother, too."

I stiffened. "What do you mean?"

He gave me a wry smile. "I may no longer be a Jacob, but that doesn't mean I don't pick up on things. She's seeing things—finally. She's going to need you when she finally comes to term with it."

*Until then*, I finished in my head, *she's going to deny, deny, deny.*

But that didn't mean I was going to try. When I went back to our room, Maximus in tow, I discovered Dex talking to my mother and father, looking freshly shaven and bright-eyed. My mother seemed calmer too.

Maybe this was going to go okay. Besides, we didn't even have to think about the house until tomorrow. Now, I was in Manhattan with my fiancé, friend, and family and the night was ours. It couldn't get much better than that. For all the doom and gloom and my tendency to blow shit out of proportion, I could at least try and enjoy the evening.

We went out to a delightful little Italian joint that my parents used to frequent when they were first dating in the city. Even though I didn't have much of an appetite, I enjoyed the Carpaccio and copious glasses of red wine that were splashing around the place.

But most of the time, my attention was on Dex. He was sitting next to me, and I kept my hand on his knee, just to feel him, just to let him know I was there. He was quiet, but when he did talk, he was his usual smartass self. He kept on turning slightly in his chair, looking over his shoulder for someone or something. When I asked him what it was, he just brushed it off, saying he felt like he was being stared at.

I couldn't see anyone in the restaurant who was paying us any attention. And maybe because of that, I was started to get a little more creeped out. Soon *I* was paranoid that we were being watched, but I resisted the urge to keep looking over my shoulder every five seconds. Dex was doing that enough for the both of us.

After dinner, we ended up not seeing the Lion King like my dad had wanted but caught this small off Broadway play with John Lithgow. It was really good, albeit a little too dark for our moods, but the acting and direction was compelling enough to steal my attention for a few hours.

When it was over and night had settled over the city, all of us decided to walk back up to the hotel instead of trying to catch a bunch of cabs. It was about a half an hour walk, but I didn't mind. I was going to use this time wisely.

While Maximus was talking to Dex and seeming to keep an eye on him, I decided to approach my mother. I pulled back on her silk shawl.

"Mom," I said, "can I speak to you? Privately?"

She looked at me in surprise. Or maybe that was fear. Maybe she knew what was coming.

"Sure, pumpkin," she said, and in a rare act of affection, smoothed back my hair from my face. "What is it?"

Even though she sounded casual, there was a tremor to her voice that told me she was anything but. I hated to ruin a moment that had us bonding in such a way, but…

"It's nothing," I said, looping my arm around hers. "It's just that … I know what you saw."

She flinched. I wouldn't have caught it if I wasn't watching her so closely.

"What are you talking about?" she asked lightly. *Too* lightly.

"In the elevator," I said, not wanting to do this dance. "We stopped on the sixth floor. I was watching you. You looked as if you saw the devil himself." Or one of his minions.

She gave me a look. "Oh, honey. I can barely remember a few hours ago. I didn't sleep on the plane, and then there's the jetlag. I was so worried about you and Ada."

Ah, classic diversion. So I only nodded and smiled and let her sweep it under the rug. But just this time. Next time

—and I knew there would be a next time—she was going to be called out on it. Of course, she'd be in total denial.

I patted her arm and then we caught up with the roving band of delinquents I called friends and family. I found myself under the security of Dex's arm as we weaved through the crowded streets, all the way back to the hotel.

If I could have just ignored every frightful thing that had happened over the last couple of days, this would have been the most perfect evening ever.

But it wasn't.

As soon as we were inside the room, Dex picked me up by the shoulders and turned me around, slamming me back against the door so it shut. "I've never needed your cunt more," he growled, pushing me harder into the door.

My mouth dropped open, caught off-guard. Dex was always a dirty talker, but he didn't use the "C-word" all that often. Nor was he usually quite this rough with me.

As if to emphasize that point, he brought me off the door slightly and then slammed me back harder, my head banging against it, forcing me to cry out from pain.

But Dex took no notice. He was completely insatiable, ripping off my jeans, the edges of his nails catching my skin as he did so. I was certain he had drawn blood.

"Dex," I said breathless, but he'd already managed to part my legs as far as they would go, his head buried between them. His fingers pushed aside my underwear and somehow I felt his tongue sinking deep inside me. It scared me, actually, because while Dex had a great tongue and knew how to use it, it seriously wasn't *that* long.

The thought seemed to float away from my head as he licked me to new heights that made my knees want to give out. I didn't know how he was doing it, but at the same time I didn't want him to stop.

Suddenly he pulled back, and before I knew what was happening, he put his arm around my waist and threw me to the floor. I landed on my ass with a painful thud and was just about to tell him off when he put a hand on my chest and shoved me back down, his head returning to the place it was before.

"Dex!" I snapped at him, annoyed. "Take it fucking easy."

"I want to do terrible, horrible things to you," he said with a grunt. "I want to make you scream."

As adventurous as I was, I wasn't sure if I wanted terrible, horrible things done to me, but my protest never left my lips. He started licking me with renewed frenzy, his grunts becoming louder and louder until he started to sound like a lion tearing into its kill.

Somehow it was still a turn on, and I felt my hips lifting toward his mouth as he brought me to near orgasm again. A sharp lance of pain shot through me.

What the fuck? Did he just bite my clit?

Before I could even process the pain, it melted into pleasure, and soon I was coming, my hands curling into fists in his hair and pulling at him, profanities leaving my mouth as I rode a wave far and long. He growled in response, still going at me, like he couldn't get his fill.

Now, though, I was too sensitive and I tried to get him to stop. I pulled harder at his head, and when that didn't work, I propped myself up on my elbows and scooted back and away from his mouth.

I gasped when he looked up at me. With his hair in his face and his skin wet with sweat, he was smiling, his lips bloody.

Jesus, that was way more disturbing than it was hot.

"Dex," I said, trying to find my breath. "Please, I'm too sensitive, you gotta give me a break. You know this."

His grin spread and I noticed this strange emptiness in his eyes. A feeling of dread came over me.

"I'm not done," he said, and his voice was lower than I'd ever heard it. "You're not done."

I gave him an uneasy smile and swallowed. He wiped his fingers along his mouth and stared at the blood, then smiled at it. "Whoops. Guess I got a bit carried away there."

I nodded quickly. "Yeah, you did." But my heart rate was slowing a bit. He seemed to be composing himself. "So, how do you want to —"

He was on me in a second, his bloody mouth smothering my words. One hand squeezed at my breasts while I could tell he was taking his cock out with the other. "You didn't scream before," he whispered harshly against my lips. "I want you to scream this time. I want you to try."

Part of me was still a bit turned on by the out-of-character roughness, the other part was unnerved by him. Was this role playing or was this something else? Because this certainly wasn't Dex at the moment.

I pulled my head back just as he thrust himself into me in one hard motion. I gasped a little and put my hand on his chest, trying to keep some of his weight off of me, but he was impossible to move. Just like that, he suddenly weighed a ton.

He continued to thrust into me, his mouth at my ear, breathing harder and harder. His lips went down my neck, nibbling lightly until he was full-on biting me again. I could feel my blood trickling down my skin.

"Fuck!" I yelped. "You're hurting me, you asshole."

Dex sank his fingers into the hair at the top of my head and yanked it back sharply until I cried out again.

"What did you call me?" he growled. I tried to look at him, and I was sorry I did. Blood was smeared all over his face, his expression contorted into one of absolute hate, absolute soullessness.

This wasn't role-playing. This wasn't Dex.

Suddenly his fingers went around my throat. "I thought you always wanted it rough," he said. "Pretty young things always want it rough, always want their blood spilled."

His grip around my neck tightened, cutting off the air from my lungs. Panic coursed through me, and I felt like he was going to crush me to death.

I tried to cry out but the sound was lost beneath the relentless pressure of his fingers. My vision started to darken and blur at the corners, and I sluggishly tried to figure out what to do, what I could do to survive this.

I only had one thing.

I had to hurt him. Or I was going to die at his hand.

While he grinned down at me, his eyes darker than sin and filled with hate I didn't even know existed, I gathered all my strength and plowed my head up into his nose.

The headbutt was enough to surprise him, and in that moment, I punched my right fist into his head. He yelped, and then I jerked my knee toward his balls.

That was the final straw. He released me with an anguished cry, and I was able to roll out from under him. I immediately got to my feet and ran over to the desk, and picked up the heaviest object I could find—a lamp.

"Jesus, Perry," he said, trying to get to his knees with his eyes pinched shut, coughing up a lung. I could barely breathe myself, my windpipe feeling crushed and bruised, so I had no sympathy if I ruined his balls. "If you don't like it rough, just say so."

I adjusted my grip on the lamp, holding it out in front of

me like a weapon, breathing heavily in an attempt to get all the lost air back in my lungs.

He got to his feet, and without looking at me, hobbled over to the bathroom, shutting the door behind him, leaving me alone in the room to try and figure out what had happened.

It seemed like him now, but that had not been him. I knew Dex, knew him with my heart and soul, and that had not been him inside of me. It had not been his tongue, it had not been his touch. I looked into his eyes, and I didn't sense his beautiful soul. I sensed nothingness, foul and black and endless, a gateway to a world I prayed I'd never see. It had held me there, hypnotized and I'd been lucky enough to break free.

It hadn't been in my head. That had all been real.

I gingerly put the lamp back, slipped on a robe and grabbed my room key off the desk. I waited by the bathroom door for a second and heard the toilet flush. I wanted to be out of here before he came back out.

I quickly left the room and ran up the stairs straight to Maximus's. I pounded on the door, and when Maximus answered it, his eyes nearly fell out of his head.

"Dear Lord, Perry, what the hell happened to you?" he asked, and I pushed past him into the room, tears stinging my eyes. I tried to hold it together, but as soon as the door closed, I started crying. Maximus immediately put his arms around me, holding me for a minute before he stepped back to inspect me with a horrified eye.

"What happened?" he asked again. "Where is Dex? Is he okay?"

My lips twisted into a grimace. "I don't know. I kneed him in the balls pretty hard."

He raised a brow. "Did Dex do this to you?"

"He did. But it wasn't him. I know it wasn't." I sniffed and walked over to the mirror. I gasped at the sight of my reflection staring back. My throat was already showing pinkish purple finger marks on it, my neck was bleeding from several wounds, and the blood had smeared along my shoulders and collarbone. There was no way Dex could have done any of this.

I eyed Maximus in the mirror.

"I see," he said. "Where is he now?"

"He's in the bathroom. He seemed to be himself again, but he never really looked at me. I don't know what he thinks just happened. God, I hope he doesn't, he's going to hate himself."

"How did it start?" he asked.

I gave him a look. "Well, when a man and a woman love each other…"

"That's not funny," he said. "I'm being serious."

"So am I," I said, turning around to face him. "I don't know what happened. As soon as we were in the room, he started being really rough with me, more so than usual. Talking dirtier than usual. He was like an animal." I took in a deep breath. I couldn't get the fear out of me. I was so afraid he was going to really hurt me, kill me.

A strange look passed over his face, like he was considering something for the first time. "Perry," he said carefully, "this is going to sound odd, but do you remember when we … um, you and I … had …"

"Sex?"

He nodded. "Yeah. That. It kind of got weird there for a moment, do you remember?"

"Kind of," I said, not really wanting to remember that shit.

"Well, what do you remember?"

"Oh come on, you want details of what it was like to have sex with you?"

"I promise I'm going somewhere with this," he said, raising his palms to me. "You started to act in a similar way. Violent. Not yourself. Do you remember doing that, and if you do, what was going through your head at the time?"

I couldn't really remember. I'd swept that whole time period under the rug. But when I really thought about it, I recalled feeling like this incredible power had taken over me, like I'd suddenly become bloodthirsty. Like I hated Maximus and wanted to hurt him. I relished the hate, the desire to destroy and inflict pain. It was me and not me at the same time, and if Maximus hadn't stopped me, I didn't know what would have happened.

"It's happening to him," I said quietly. "Something is inside him, sharing his space."

Maximus nodded gravely. "That's what I think. But Dex is still there, just as you were still there. We're going to have tread lightly with this one." He didn't have to explain what he meant by that. Dex would never hurt me in a million years. If it was the real Dex I was going to return to downstairs, he was going to be hurt badly. Far more than he had hurt me.

But if it wasn't Dex, who was it?

"I don't know," Maximus said, and I realized he was picking up on my thoughts. "But it's not good."

"Are there ever any good tales about possession?" I pointed out. I sighed. "Is it Michael?"

He pursed his lips. "That's a bit of a stretch. As far as I know, a living person can't possess another living person. Even the Jacobs couldn't do anything like that, and we had an awful lot of power at our fingertips."

I didn't want to get off the subject but I couldn't help but suddenly ask, "What was that like?"

He cocked a brow. "Being a Jacob?"

I nodded.

"I can't really say. I mean, I don't have anything to compare it to. We're supposed to cycle in a way, keep living new lives with new memories, so the burden of immortality never really sets in, but you always remember something."

"Burden," I mused caustically.

"Well, it is a burden. All life should have an expiration date. To keep on living, it's not natural. To watch all your friends and family die again and again, there's nothing like it. It's an eternity of loneliness. When I realized I could give it up for Rose, I didn't hesitate. And no, I don't regret it."

"Especially now that you're back with Rose," I said.

"That helps," he said. "But as painful as life is sometimes, you have no idea what it's like to be able to relate to someone, to know you aren't alone. As a Jacob, I was alone and I was different. In some ways, I was condemned. Now, I'm just like you. I'm free."

"And you're not afraid of death?" I asked. "Because after all I've seen, I'm terrified of it."

"I am afraid of death," he admitted. "But not because I don't know what's on the other side. I do. I've been there. I'm afraid to leave Rose behind. To leave love behind. The idea that I can be taken from her and her from me ... you don't want immortality unless you both have it."

"Well, I won't have that problem," I said. The subject of death was making me a little uneasy. Everything was making me uneasy. I gingerly reached up and touched my neck, feeling the tender skin. Somehow, I had to get past the idea that Dex had done this. It hadn't been him. I couldn't be afraid of my own fiancé.

"Do you want me to walk you back to your room?" he asked, ever the Southern gentleman.

I shook my head. "No, it's okay. Believe me, if there's a problem, I'll come straight here."

"Be prepared," he said, as I got to my feet. "And alert. But remember it's still Dex. Until we know what's going on, it's still Dex."

I nodded and quickly left the room. I went down the staircase and was back outside our hotel room door. I took a deep breath and slid my card through. The light turned green and I went inside.

The room was black except for the bathroom light. I could see Dex asleep in bed, his face illuminated. He was snoring lightly, and his perfect face looked totally peaceful and almost childlike as he slept.

I quietly closed the door behind me and stood at the foot of the bed, debating whether to get in with him or sleep on the floor or in the bathtub.

But watching him sleep, I could barely imagine him doing what he had done, even though my neck and throat throbbed with a dull ache. I was going to marry the guy, and that meant for better or for worse.

Or for possessed, I guess.

Still, I picked up the corkscrew from above the mini bar and put it under my pillow.

You could never be too careful.

THAT NIGHT I dreamed that Dex had died. I woke up with tears in my eyes, cursing our mortality. I could still see the embers raining down from the sky.

## 10

DEX

I was falling.

Free falling, kind of like Tom Petty, if Tom Petty was singing about falling into the fiery pits of Hell.

Maybe he was, I don't know.

All I saw was the black, all I could grab was handfuls of nothing. All I felt was evil, waiting to sink its teeth into me, a presence at the very bottom. Soon it would have me, and I, I would be empty.

The sound of the television brought me out of the blackness. I groaned and tried to roll over, away from the sound of morning television, my head throbbing with shards of pain. This could have been Hell for all I knew.

I expected to be roused from my half-conscious state, for a familiar voice to chide me for sleeping in so late and not getting up.

What I got wasn't words, but it had that floaty, airy quality of a singular thought, plucked from elsewhere.

*I'm afraid of him.*

I opened my eyes to see the hazy morning sun of Manhattan filter in through the window, blinding me. It only revved my headache into high gear but managed to get me thinking.

Why did I feel like such utter shit? What happened last night? And where did Kelly Ripa get her crack cocaine from, because shit, did I need some of that.

My brain immediately brought me back to the phrase: *I'm afraid of him.*

Carefully, as if my head was comprised of nothing but glass, I sat up and looked around the room. The TV was on, and Perry was sitting on the chair in the corner of the room, watching me with steady eyes and a firm mouth.

I had done something wrong. Immediately, I knew that's what it was. The problem was, I didn't know what. The last thing I remembered was coming back to the hotel after the self-indulgent play. I remember being horny as fuck, slamming her up against the door, eager to get in her pants.

None of that was very unusual. But after that, my memory kind of tapered off. I hadn't had that much wine at dinner, and I just had a beer at the theatre, much to Daniel's disappointment. Still, I usually remembered having sex. Like, that was the one thing in life I *never* forgot.

And then, as I was staring dumbly at Perry, trying to piece back the night, I noticed her fingers caressing her throat, and suddenly my mind was flooded with unwanted images. I remembered her crying out in pain, the feel of her neck beneath my hands, so easy to crush. I remembered blood in my mouth, the need to eat her, devour her, consume her until there was nothing left. I remembered feeling nothing but hatred, pure and primeval, pouring out of me and directed at her.

I remembered her pleading for me to stop.

I remembered enough to make me feel like I'd just been kicked in the heart, in the gut, in my very soul. The shame flowing through me was enough to make a weaker man kill himself.

And I wasn't sure how strong I was.

"Perry," I said gently, hoping that my memories were lies.

But the blank look in her eyes, the kind she got when she'd been hurt too much, when she'd cried too much and couldn't take anymore, that's all I saw.

She lifted her hands away from her neck, and I saw the dark red fingerprints around her throat. I knew they were from me. I knew I had done that.

She looked away from me, staring at the carpet instead. Maybe she could sense it. Maybe she could read the pain on my face.

"Did I do that?" I asked softly, my voice cracking. "I did, didn't I?"

"Someone did," she said. "He looked a lot like you. Talked a lot like you. I could have sworn it was you. But I've never had to knee you in the balls before."

The sound of that brought back a sharp wince in my groin, as if my body was suddenly saying, "Oh yeah, that." Fuck, she could cut off my balls and I'd find it fitting if I did that to her. I'd deserve it.

I just didn't understand what happened. I didn't want to ask, but I had to.

"What happened?"

She gave me a smile that wasn't all there. "You don't remember."

I shook my head, wincing at the pain. "I don't remember anything. We came back here. I remember pressing you up against the door, and that was it. I ... have flashes of things but they don't make any sense. Was I drunk?"

She shook her head. "Or maybe you were."

No. I wasn't. Ignoring the pain in my head, I swung my

legs out of bed, surprised to find myself in a t-shirt and pajama pants, as if I had gone through the process of dressing for bedtime before I went to sleep. Not exactly the actions of a drunk.

I walked toward Perry, but she immediately flinched and moved back in her chair. She was trying so hard to hide the fear in her wide blue eyes, but it was clear on her face.

It felt like I'd been stabbed. Not just the fear, the fear of me, but the way she looked. It was very obvious that she'd been strangled. She also had gashes along her neck that were raised and swollen. Bites.

From *me*.

I remembered the taste of blood.

I fell straight down to my hands and knees, the carpet grinding into my skin. Fighting for breath, I clenched my eyes and fists, wanting to inflict pain on the man who had done this and realizing that it was me.

"Dex," Perry said softly, and I heard her come off the chair. I didn't want her near me when I didn't understand myself.

I could only shake my head and try to take in air. My breaths were ragged, my lungs felt shallow. As much as I tried, I felt like I was a just above this moment, feeling it but not really in it.

She placed her hand on my shoulder, and it seemed to ground me, tether me to the time and place. Perry prevented me from flying away. And what did I do to her?

I heard her sniff, as if taking in tears, and she crouched down beside me, not wanting anything from me but trying to bring me comfort. I opened my eyes and stared down at the white carpet, spying flecks of blood that stood out like red graffiti. What was that from? My nosebleed? Her neck?

How could so much blood have spilled in such a short amount of time?

"I am so sorry," I said, but it was barely a whisper. I couldn't even find my voice. It was such a pale substitute for what I was really feeling. I knew no matter what I did, I could never make it up, never take it back.

"I know," she said softly. "It wasn't you, Dex."

How could she be so good to me? "If it wasn't me, who was it?"

"I don't know," she said. "But I looked into your eyes and you weren't there. I don't know who was in your place, but I hope to God I never see them again. You tasted ... foreign." She trembled a bit over those last words. I wanted nothing more than to pull her into my arms and hold on to her, never let her go.

But now I was afraid. Afraid to see her flinch from my touch. Afraid that I would no longer be me.

But who was I?

"We have to go to the house today," I said. I raised my head and looked right at her. My beautiful woman. The wife I would spend my life with. She came all the way here for me. I needed to prove it wasn't for nothing. I needed answers. The answers were in those walls, I swore they were.

"Do you even know if your house is still standing?" she asked gently. She was treading so carefully around me. Each cautious tiptoe was like a dagger to my heart.

I pushed past the pain. "No, but it's a brownstone. Townhouse. No one tears that shit down in the city, especially not in this neighborhood." Besides, I knew it was there. I hadn't been there since I was a kid, but for some reason I knew. I could almost see it, like I'd been inside it recently.

"Are you certain you need to go there?" she asked. She had settled down into a cross-legged position, her hand still on my shoulder, as if to steady her or steady me. I wanted nothing more than to kiss the fear from her lips and take away everything that happened. But I was as scared of myself as she was.

I nodded. "I just ... I think I'll be able to move on. Or ... get some closure in some way."

"You don't think Michael is there?"

"He could be," I said. "I don't know. Maybe that's the closure I need."

Her eyes were glued to mine, growing grave and hard. "And you don't think you need to be afraid of him?"

I could see why she felt that way. I couldn't blame her. I shook my head. "I'm not afraid of him until I have a reason to be."

She stared at me for a few beats, and if I concentrated hard enough, I could hear her thoughts. Just pieces of them. I hated doing that, so I always pulled back the moment I heard her.

*You have all the reasons*, she thought.

And yet I couldn't quite agree. Not yet.

I sat back on my ass. "I think it's just your mom who wants to see it for nostalgia's sake."

"You're not going without us," she said quickly, as if she had readied herself for that.

I eyed her neck, and again felt like a hand had reached into my chest and ripped out my heart from the bottom. How was I even going to get on with my day knowing those marks were from my fingers and teeth?

"Baby," she said, and the purity of her voice brought me out of my spiral. "It wasn't you, okay? I'll be fine. Ada will lend me a scarf, no one will know."

"Ada knows?" I spat out, horrified that her little sister knew what happened to her.

"My parents won't though," she said.

"And Maximus?" I asked, my nerves on fire.

She was reluctant to meet my gaze. "I turned to him first."

I held her eyes with mine and let that sink in. She turned to him first. Another kick to my gut, a steel-toe going in deep.

I let out a puff of air, nearly doubling over again. I guess I deserved that.

"He has experience," she said.

I frowned at her. "With what?" I cried out. "Being your shoulder to cry on?" And yet I realized how right my question was the minute I said it, and how petty I was for even considering it.

"Yes," she replied. "But also..." She trailed off and looked away.

"What?" I put my hand over hers and tried to ignore the fact that she jumped slightly from my contact. "What is it? What else could it be?" I felt like I was turning into more of a madman, spurred on by jealousy that absolutely had no place here but here it was.

She gave me a frank look. "This isn't news to you. But, he has experience with certain things." I stared at her, dumbfounded. She went on with a sigh. "When I had sex with him, a similar thing happened."

Holy McFuck, I was going to vomit.

"Dex," she said quickly. "Get past the sex part and think about what I'm saying. When we slept together, I was possessed, and I did things to him that I would have never done sober."

"I hope you kneed him in the balls," I grumbled, trying to quell the jealousy that was trying to work its way through me. That was the last thing I needed to be reminded of.

"He didn't get off easy," she said. "And neither did I."

Crushing, crushing pain. I couldn't even look at her anymore. "I wish…"

"It's done," she said with finality. "But I'm still going to marry you because I know the real you. We're going to get past this. And if you need to visit the home you grew up in to do that, then you have my support. I'm going with you. We all are."

I nodded, even though I felt like she was flooding me with feelings I couldn't quite absorb. My brilliant, beautiful Perry had been through so much already, and yet here she still was, by my side while I was at my absolute worst. And considering I was Dex Foray, that was saying a lot.

An hour later, we were all standing outside the hotel, breathing in fumes of garbage and exhaust. Daniel and Ada had gone to get us coffees for the delightful journey back into my personal Hades.

Perry seemed to be handling everything well, despite the fact that she had a scarf peppered with giraffes tied tightly around her throat. But her mother only commented on what a lovely, elegant look it was. Ada and Maximus knew better, and it was hard to endure their glances. There wasn't a moment that went by when I wasn't beating myself up over it.

When we were all given a coffee, we took off down the street. I was in the lead, even though I didn't really remember where I lived. Still, it only took a few blocks before instincts kicked in, and I was remembering a route I used to walk a long time ago. It was weird to know that

Perry's mother might have walked the same route with Pippa.

Even though I had been close with Pippa as a boy, I didn't feel like I had the same kind of relationship with her as Perry did. Ironically, our relationship had been while she was alive, and Perry's had been after her death, yet theirs was always stronger. Pippa had never come to visit me after she left her position.

I'd be lying if I said that never bothered me. As overjoyed as I was that Perry found some love in her life, even if by the great beyond, growing up I had looked up to Pippa more than I looked my own mother. She was love while my parents were not.

*You were loved*, a voice rang throughout my head, ripe with bitterness.

I had no idea where it came from, but it was telling the truth. Pippa had loved me. And now, whether it was for me or Perry, she seemed to be gone forever.

As I walked down the street, my feet moving eagerly, I glanced beside me at Perry's mom. We were leading the pack. She had staunch determination on her face, her thin lips pressed together firmly, her brow furrowed in concentration. I wondered what was in it for her, what she was hoping to find. This was more than wanting a stroll down memory lane. She was being driven there much in the same way that I was.

But what were we being driven by?

It didn't take long before the road started to become familiar, and with that, the sense of urgency increased. I looked back at Perry. She was beside Maximus, both of their eyes trained on me, as if they expected me to turn around and look at them.

The sight of them together riled up my caveman center, but I ignored it and tried to give them a smile.

*You're all going to die*, the thought jabbed into my brain.

And then everything went black. Time jumped and skipped.

The next thing I knew, I was standing in front of my childhood home. It looked exactly as I remembered, even down to the potted palm in the front, still half-wilted, its bright green leaves peppered with brown rot. After hearing my father wax on about how magical Hawaii was, I convinced Pippa, and through her, my mom, to get a palm for the front porch. It never really grew and kind of stayed dormant in this hunched over, sickly state.

And it was still here, the same cracked pot and everything.

For some reason that made me smile. I looked back at everyone else, but I was surprised to see them staring at the house in concern and that Daniel was gone.

"Where did your dad go?" I asked Perry.

She gave me an odd look. "He decided to go to the Natural History Museum," she said, as if I was stupid.

I nodded, like I understood, but instead I was aware that time had skipped by me again. I looked around and counted Maximus, Ada, Perry, and Perry's mom. So there were five of us now.

*All of us believers*, I thought. If that counted for anything.

"This is it," Perry's mom said, staring up at the windows. "Looks just like I remembered."

I nodded. It did look just the same. It probably should have been a warning to me, since New York life changes so quickly, but it wasn't.

The house looked abandoned. The front door was even open a crack while the rest of the house seemed to retreat inside its dark windows. The neighbors, very close by along the sides, seemed to have a lot more life and vibrancy. Their buildings seemed to dance in the air.

This building looked dead.

"I guess no one has lived here for some time," Maximus said, and when I looked over at him, he was inspecting the pot that had held the palm tree. Now the tree was dry and curled around itself, dead to the world.

"I guess not," I said, blinking at the way the plant had changed.

"So, we've seen it," Ada said quickly. "Time to head back."

I looked at her and noted how damn scared she looked. She kept rubbing her hands along her arms, as if it weren't eighty degrees out and we were all sweating.

"Not yet," her mother said, and I turned to see her on the landing, opening the door to the house.

"Mom, no," Perry said, but her voice sounded like it was swallowed up by a nonexistent wind.

It was too late. She stepped inside and disappeared.

Well, fucking great. Like hell I was going to be shown up by my mother-in-law. This wasn't her damn house.

I ran up the brick stairs, my hand skirting the black iron railing, and followed her into the foyer.

I immediately felt a change in air pressure. I flexed my jaw, trying to get my ears to pop while I got my bearings.

I stood in the foyer and looked around. My body immediately calmed, like a wave of clarity came over me. I had done well. I don't know how, but I had done well by coming here, by bringing everyone.

The place was dark, all familiar shadows. A thick layer of dust coated the floor and stuck to the chandelier above. Everything was exactly how I remembered it, down to the furniture. Even the same paintings hung from the walls, including one I used to love, Renoir's *Les Dejeuner des Canotiers*. While Perry's mom walked forward, stepping cautiously down the hall, I ducked into the living room off to the side.

It had the most light, the windows large and tall, facing the street. There was a Christmas tree in the corner of the room, branches brittle but still green, strands of cobwebs strung up over the lights. Stranger than that, there were presents underneath it. Just a few, but they were there, still wrapped. Waiting.

I stared at that for a few moments. I could almost make out "Declan" on one of them. A strange droning, buzzing sound came from inside the package, and I had the sudden urge to go look at it, open it, but suddenly Perry was at my side.

"What the hell?" she said, breathing out. It froze in a cloud in front of her face. I hadn't even noticed it was that cold in here. "Whoever was here last must have left before Christmastime." She timidly walked across the room, to the mantle above the fireplace where Michael's trophies were displayed. "I can't believe they never came back for their stuff."

*I was here last,* I thought, as she peered at the closest trophy.

She looked at the next trophy, blinking hard. "These are all for Michael O'Shea," she said, her voice soft and confused. "I don't get it." She looked at me. "Dex, was your family the last ones in this house?"

"This is all our stuff. But I don't know, there must have been other people. That was so long ago.."

"Wow." I turned to see Maximus behind me, taking it all in. "You can feel that, right?"

"It's freezing," Ada said, stepping into the house, the last of us. "And it's giving me the willies." She went to close the door behind her, and Maximus shouted, "No, don't!"

But it was too late. The door closed. Not sure why that made me smile.

Ada gave Maximus an odd look then reached for the knob and yanked on it. The door opened right away, and I could see the relief on his face. It was like he expected us to be locked inside. Actually, I expected that, too. In some ways, I wanted it.

Now that I was here, I had no intention of leaving.

I was home.

"So this place is freaking you out, is it?" I said to Maximus with a smug smile.

His gaze on me was trained and careful. "There's definitely a feeling here." He looked at Perry. "You feel it? It's heavy, the air."

"Could be all the dust," Ada said, wrinkling her nose. She walked down the hall toward where her mother disappeared. As she passed the Renoir painting, something in the painting moved. It was barely noticeable. Ada didn't pick up on it, but the black eyes of the woman in the background, leaning on the railing, watched her move past.

Then the eyes were looking at me. I sucked in my breath until I felt a hand at my waist.

I jumped and whirled around to see Perry staring up at me, a hurt expression on her face.

"What is it?" she asked.

I shook my head and eyed the painting. It wasn't moving now. Suddenly I was glad that the front door had opened when Ada tried it. Why some part of me wanted to stay in here was beyond me. I felt like it was already starting to mess with my head.

*Don't tell them that*, a man's voice came into my thoughts.

I turned around, certain that it was Maximus right behind me, talking. But he was paused at the foot of the stairs, as if debating whether to go up or not. I wanted to tell him that was a bad idea. All of this was a bad idea. Whatever clarity I had moments ago was gone.

And yet, I felt compelled to keep exploring.

"Where did my mom and Ada go?" Perry asked suddenly, looking panicked.

"We're in the kitchen!" Ada's voice rang out from around the corner.

"Maybe we should all stick together," Maximus said, stepping away from the staircase. "I don't think splitting up is a good idea."

I laughed, despite myself. "It's not a haunted house, Scooby Doo."

He exchanged a look with Perry but didn't say anything. I was starting to hate all their little glances and unsaid words. Still, I followed them.

The kitchen looked exactly as I remembered. I mean, to a fault.

The table was made with settings for three people. One at the head—where Pippa would sit. The other two across from each other at mid-table. There was never a place for my father—he was never home—and there stopped being a place for my mother. She was just never sober enough.

Each setting had a red, white, and black graphic woven placemat, something Swedish that Pippa had picked out, a plate, a fork, and a knife. There were matching graphic napkins held together with a silver circle. Her place had a white glass. The other two had mugs.

One of the mugs said Michael. The other said Declan.

Perry's mother was standing over them in a daze. She slowly raised her head and looked right at me.

"I don't understand," she said. "Why are these still here?"

The answer wasn't in my eyes. I had nothing.

Perry and Maximus were equally silent, trying to make sense of it. Ada leaned over Michael's cup and peered in.

"Oh, gross!" she cried out, stumbling backward into her mom who held her up. She looked like she was going to vomit.

Curious, I walked over and looked for myself. It was filled to the brim with wriggling black insects. I stared at them for a moment, trying to figure out why that seemed familiar.

"What is it?" Perry asked. I heard her come up behind me.

I glanced at her over my shoulder and smiled. "Just Michael's daily tea."

She frowned, her face paling a bit. "Dex. What is going on here?"

I shrugged and walked over to the fridge. I opened the door.

A puff of dust blew out of it, and once it cleared, I could see a dead rat inside and black insects crawling out of it. "I guess they came from here."

"All right," Maximus said, irritation coloring his tone. "This is getting ridiculous. I think it's time to leave."

"It's always been time to leave," Ada said with disgust, walking around the table and heading to the hallway.

"No!" I suddenly yelled, the force of my voice surprising myself. Ada stopped in her tracks. Everyone stared at me in shock. "We're not leaving until I find what I'm looking for!"

"Dex," Perry said carefully. "I don't know what's going,

but someone is playing a cruel joke on you, on us. None of this shit should be here all these years later. Dex, we have to go. You're not yourself."

At that, Jingle Bell Rock came blaring out from the living room. Perry's mom screamed, jumping in the air.

I ran out of the kitchen and down the hall to the living room, my eyes briefly glancing at the Renoir lady. She had the head of a black goat.

I skidded to a stop at the entrance to the living room, and felt everyone crowd behind me. Perry sucked in her breath.

The Christmas tree was lit up, a mess of cobwebs and twinkling lights. The radio was blaring, and black candles were lit everywhere, inky droplets of wax gathering around their stems like they'd been burning for decades.

"The presents," I heard Perry whisper. Under the tree, the presents were leaking shiny red blood, soaking through the wrapping paper.

All of a sudden a few thumps resounded from the ceiling, making the light fixtures swing. The upstairs bathroom was above us.

We weren't alone in the house.

But then again, I already knew that.

It was time for me to come home.

I turned and quickly darted up the stairs, taking them two at a time, while Perry yelled for me to stop. But she was already too far away, and the world was turning a little too black.

## 11

PERRY

I didn't know what happened. One minute we were staring at the Christmas display in the living room, as if the house still had electricity under all that dust, the next minute Dex had pushed past me and started sprinting up the stairs.

"Dex!" I yelled at him, trying to grab at his shirt. What had Maximus just said about not splitting up?

"Damn it," Maximus cursed, and then went up the stairs after him. I was about to, but then I didn't feel quite right about leaving my mother and sister downstairs alone.

"I think you guys should leave," I told them, but their attention wasn't on me. It wasn't on Dex and Maximus who had gone up the stairs. It wasn't on the Christmas display and the presents of blood.

It was on the man standing by the window, slowly pulling the curtains shut. He was wearing a sharp suit, his back to us. There was something off about him. It was his hand, as he reached for the curtain.

It was a cloven hoof.

The curtains closed, shutting out the outside world,

making the world inside turn almost black. I widened my eyes, trying to see better, but the man was gone, disappearing into the shadows of the room

"Who the hell was that?" my mother asked, her voice soft and shaking. I looked at her and Ada. They both looked like they were going to faint.

I swallowed down the lump in my throat, my mouth feeling like it was filled with sawdust. I hadn't even noticed how fast my heart was racing until I felt it leap against my chest.

"I don't know," I croaked out. "I don't know, I don't know." I grabbed their hands and they both gasped from fright. I pulled them toward the front door. I didn't know what was going on, but this was not their fight. This was Dex's, and because it was his, it was also mine. But my mother and Ada, they had no reason to be here, no stake.

They had to go. It had been a mistake to bring them here in the first place.

I reached for the doorknob, ready to turn it and escape into the heat and sunshine that seemed like another world, but I cried out in pain instead. It was as hot as grabbing a stovetop and immediately seared my skin.

"Perry!" my mom shouted, reaching for my hand. I could barely open it, it was already raw and red, burning like hell. "We need to get ointment on it."

"We need to get out of here," I told her, trying to push past the pain. "It's fine. Let's go out the back." There had been a glass door leading from the kitchen into the small backyard, we had just been so enraptured by the place settings that I didn't get a good look at it.

We hurried to the kitchen and were surprised to see that the blinds in there had been pulled shut too, shuttering us in darkness. I walked straight to the backdoor and went to open it with my good hand, but Ada had already beat me to it, wrapping the end of a placemat around her palm as a precaution.

But the doorknob wouldn't turn, no matter how hard she tried. "Fuck!" she yelled.

I expected my mother to admonish her for her language, but she was looking back at the hallway. While Ada struggled, I turned and saw a little boy enter the kitchen, dressed in pajamas.

"What are you doing in my house?" he asked. He had to have been around seven years old, with sandy hair and big dark eyes. He had a sharp look about him and spoke like he was highly educated for his age.

My mother and I exchange a glance.

"Uh," I said, "you live here?"

Had we just been busted in someone else's house?

But as much as that seemed like it, that couldn't be it. The little boy narrowed his eyes at us and padded across the kitchen to the table where he sat down. "I'm not the only one here," he said. "I expected dinner to be ready." He clasped his hands in front of his plate and bowed his head as if he were saying grace.

My mother cleared her throat. "I think we have come in here by accident. Could you tell us the proper way out of here? The front door and this door don't seem to be working." Her voice was shaking but she was holding it together.

The boy kept his eyes closed and mumbled a few incomprehensible words under his breath before saying, "You can get out through my window. Upstairs. But don't go out my brother's, you'll fall to your death."

My chest tightened as the kid reached for Michael's mug and brought it toward himself.

"I wouldn't drink that," I told him. "Something has gone rotten in there."

He looked at me, and his eyes were completely black, like a shark's. My mom stiffened beside me, seeing it too.

"There's something rotten in the whole house, so long as the door stays open."

"What door?" Ada asked, sounding like she wished she hadn't opened her mouth.

He brought the mug to his lips and took a sip. Tiny black wood bugs fell from his lips, spilling onto the table where they squirmed. "You don't want to go through that door," he said. "I was brought there once." He wiped his lips with his pajama sleeve, leaving the bodies of insects behind. He looked like he wanted to continue but he shut his mouth.

This had to be a dream. This couldn't be happening. Nothing was making any sense at all, and the longer we stood in that kitchen, talking to a little boy in a house full of dust, the more the outside world seemed to darken beyond the blinds.

*This isn't a house*, I thought to myself. *This is nowhere. This is where we were led.*

The boy smiled at me. "I can hear your thoughts, you know." He said this with pride, and a wicked look came over his empty eyes. "You are opening the door wider, just by being here. That's what he told me."

"What who told you?" Ada asked.

"The man in the suit," he said simply. "The more you stay, the wider the door gets. He says you need to stay here with me."

"What is your name?" my mother asked in a harsh voice.

He turned the mug so we could read it. "Michael," he said, pointing at the name on the mug. "My brother is upstairs. We've been waiting a long time for him to come home."

"Why?" I whispered. I found myself clutching my mother's arm with my good hand.

Little Michael smiled at me. "Do you want me to show you?" He looked past me at Ada and my mother. "You'll have to come too. Then I'll show you how to get out."

I wanted to find Dex and Maximus. I wanted a way for Ada and my mom to leave. We really didn't have a choice.

"Okay," I said. "Can you promise no harm will come to any of us, including Dex?"

Despite his eyes, he looked crestfallen. "I would never hurt my brother. I wouldn't hurt any of you either." He got out of his chair and started toward the hallway. He said over his shoulder, "But the man in the suit..." He raised his finger to his lips. "Stay quiet so he won't know you're here."

But the man in the suit already knew we were here. That was the man in the living room. And when we crept down the darkened hallway, my eyes were drawn to the painting on the wall. What used to be a watercolor of people sitting around, talking and eating, was now a scene of utter destruction—dismembered bodies being engulfed by flames. I could almost hear their screams and feel the heat of the fire.

There was a laugh from the living room, and I could just see someone's long legs as they sat in a chair, the wall blocking me from the sight of their body. A glass of scotch was on the table beside them. Silent night was humming softly from the speakers, and the fireplace was now lit. The perfect scene on a cold winter's night. Even though I knew I would see a cloven hoof if he reached for his scotch, then maybe a face of unimaginable horror, I couldn't do anything but stare.

But little Michael reached for my hand, tugging it, his finger still at his lips. His eyes implored me to follow him and to not go into the living room.

He led us up the stairs, his ice cold hand in mine, and down the darkened hallway. All the doors we passed were closed, and I couldn't help but wonder which one Dex was behind. Everything was so quiet, so, so quiet, that it was hard to imagine anyone being up here at all. But both Dex and Maximus had to be, unless they both escaped the way Michael was about to show us.

At the end of the hallway there was one door open, and I got the impression that the inside of the house was a lot larger and longer than it should have been, as if it was existing in its own dimension.

"In here," Michael whispered, and pointed inside his room. We stepped in. There was a small lamp lit in the corner, casting the room in shadow. There were trophies and ribbons and pictures of cars and trucks on the walls. There was also a window that was slightly ajar, showcasing the brick wall of the neighbor's house.

I walked right over to it, and was shocked to see that it was now dark outside. In the span of an hour it had gone from eleven a.m. to eleven p.m. That couldn't be right. But regardless of how time was moving, there was a little ladder hanging outside of the window. Either Michael had an escape route growing up, or it was put here just for us.

I turned to say something to my mother and sister, but just saw Michael leaving the room, closing the door behind him. He never looked back at us.

"Mom," I whispered, turning to her. "Call dad."

She nodded and brought out her phone. The three of us huddled by the window while she tried to dial.

Ada was staring at me with a blank look in her eyes. "I'm dreaming, right? Totally dreaming. Totes."

My brows furrowed in sympathy. "I wish we were. All I know is this isn't a house and you guys need to get out of here right now."

"Damn," my mother swore, hanging up the phone. "No service at all. No nothing. The phone doesn't even work."

We quickly tried Ada's and mine, but the same thing happened. They were useless electronics.

There was a polite knock at the door and a shadow spilling out from under the frame. It looked far too large to be little Michael's. Shadowy fingers trailed down my spine.

I turned back to Ada and my mom, making sure they were looking at me. "Listen, you have to go now. I'll hold the ladder and make sure it's steady. But I don't think the kid was joking when he said this was the only way out. We don't know what's downstairs, but I know we all know it's not of this world." I made sure to look at my mother long and hard. "Mom, I know you see it. I know you can't explain this away, so don't even try."

To my surprise her eyes started watering, from sadness or from fear I didn't know. I had forgotten how terrifying all of this could be if you weren't used to it. Hell, I had never been in a situation like this before. Ghosts I could handle, but this was something so beyond my understanding that I didn't even know how to combat it or if it was even possible. It was larger, and deadlier, than anything I'd known.

She sniffed, and it occurred to me that I hadn't seen my mother cry in a long time. With a thin, shaking hand she wiped away a tear and said, "I'm sorry, Perry. For everything."

Oh, and now she was going to make me cry. Of all moments, she was choosing this one.

"Mom, it's okay," I said, my eyes imploring her to stay calm and focused. "I just need you to leave and go find Dad. Bring help, bring someone, but you have to get out of here *now*."

"I'm so sorry I didn't believe you," she said, her voice cracking, more tears spilling down her cheeks. In the shadows of the room they looked like rivers carving out her skin. "More than that, I am so sorry I didn't believe my mother."

I softened, feeling a pain in my gut. Pippa.

"I wish she were here right now," she whispered. "I would tell her so many things. I keep waiting for her to show up, but she hasn't."

"I know," I said gently, rubbing her back with the base of my palm. "I do too. But I think she's gone to a better place. It's what she wanted, and what we wanted for her."

The knock resounded again on the door. I didn't want to turn around and look. It was far too solid—and coming from a higher place on the door—to be Michael.

At least, not Michael as a kid.

"Guys," Ada said. "Seriously, let's go."

I nodded and ushered them to the window. Ada pulled up the bottom with ease, and it rose soundlessly. Even though the rope ladder was attached to two solid hooks, I still held the end while Ada climbed over the edge.

"Take care of Mom, okay?" I whispered to her.

She nodded and looked down beneath her. It wasn't a far drop, and unlike the garbage cans under another window, there was nothing beneath us but the brick path between this house and the neighbors. "You're coming right after, aren't you?"

I nodded. "Hell yes, I am. As soon as I get Dex and Maximus, we'll be right behind you."

Ada raised her brow, as if she didn't believe me. Or maybe it wasn't that, it was that it seemed impossible at this point. Then she dropped the five feet to the ground, landing on her two feet with ease.

"You're next," I whispered urgently to my mom.

"Perry," she said, pausing at the sill, "this doesn't make sense. You should go next. I'll find Dex."

I shook my head. "This isn't your battle, Mom. You shouldn't have even been here in the first place."

Her eyes grew frenzied. "And yet I came," she hissed, holding on to my shoulders. "I came here because I felt I needed to. Why was that? Why did I need to come here? What did I need to find, to see?"

"Maybe you needed to see that you're just like me," I said, full of hope and doubt at the same time. "Maybe you needed to see that you're not alone." She breathed out heavily and I continued, "Maybe you just missed your mother and wanted to see a part of her life."

She put her hand on my cheek. "I am sorry," she said. "I'll never doubt you again."

I debated whether this was the time to bring up the whole switching pills thing but decided against it. There was too much going on as it was. I didn't even know why a demon would bother knocking, but it was obviously waiting for me.

A loud, guttural cry interrupted our moment. It seemed to come from within the house, within the walls. The door to the hallway flew open, and I saw the silhouette of a beast standing on two legs, the same beast we saw in the hotel. It cried again, a horrible scream that smelled like death and sliced into your ears.

"Go!" I screamed at my mother, practically pushing her out of the window. She fumbled for a moment, and I thought she was going to fall, but the ladder began to swing with her weight. There was a second of uncertainty, and then I heard her land on the bricks below, followed by Ada's hushed cries.

The window shut behind her with a deafening clatter and I felt like my last tie with the real world had been severed.

Now I was facing a beast, a blackened shape of evil with eyes that glinted white. I could feel the frustration coming off of him, knowing it was all for me. Something had happened. I had ruined something.

That was good, at least. I smiled at the beast.

I expected the monster to start charging toward me. I expected to have to fight and to have to die.

But that didn't happen. The beast remained in the doorway, its head tilted to the side as if it were listening.

Then it screamed again, this one worse than the first. It ran off down the hall, turning into a pool of fluid smoke that slinked through the air, leaving hate behind.

I stood there, afraid to move, unsure of what to do. Then I turned around and frantically tried the window. It was sealed shut, like it had been glued, and the glass had been replaced with black ooze. I couldn't see my mother and Ada, and couldn't hear them either. They were out there, hopefully going for help, hopefully making it out into the city of New York.

And I was in here. So was Dex. So was Maximus.

So was Little Michael. So was a beast.

And I had a feeling, a million other horrible things.

I took in a deep breath, wishing I knew what was going on, what I was fighting, wishing I had some mode of defense. But I had nothing.

Well, almost nothing.

Once my heart rate slowed down enough for me to catch my breath, I closed my eyes and started to yell for help inside my head, all while trying to prevent my thoughts from being read by anyone else.

I yelled for Maximus. I yelled for Dex like I'd never yelled before.

And hoped they could hear me.

## 12

DEX

I woke up to a pounding at the door. It sounded like some giant sledgehammer was going to smash through it any minute, followed by the face of Jack Nicholson saying, "Here's Johnny!"

But that didn't happen. The pounding continued, as did a familiar voice.

"Declan, let me in!"

It was rough, ragged, slurring. It was my mother.

I opened my eyes and saw nothing but blackness at first. After a second, they adjusted to the glow coming from a nightlight in the corner of the room.

Holy McFuck, I was back inside my childhood bedroom. I was under the covers, my favorite flannel blankie that still smelled like the lemon detergent Pippa used to use, my legs hanging off the bed.

I slowly eased myself up, wondering why my head was pounding. How did I end up here?

Images of the day came piling into my brain all at once. Perry, Ada, Maximus, Perry's mom, dad. Daniel had left us. The rest of us went to the house. We went inside, and everything changed. Everything was black and patchy. My memories and thoughts didn't seem like my own.

And yet, now I was here, tripping balls, because how the hell do you end up in the past? Because I was in the same bed I slept in as a child, my collection of cassette tapes still in the corner, my fencing sword and nunchucks displayed on the wall, and my mother, my drunken mom, was pounding at the door, wanting to come in, wanting to terrorize me.

I had no reason to be afraid of her anymore. I was a grown man. I'd overcome my delinquent childhood.

But I was alive and she was dead. So there was that.

There was always that.

"Declan, open this door or I will cut you," she said. I'd forgotten how literal she was when she was drunk.

"Fuck the fuck off!" I yelled at her.

There was a pause, maybe she was in shock that her young son had used such profanity. Then it started again. The pounding. Her slurring. The doorknob rattled.

This was a house of horrors, one created especially for me. But I wasn't the only one in the house; I knew that. The last thing I remembered was running up the stairs, sure that Michael was there, hiding, and that I needed to see him. I had left Perry and everyone else down below, hopefully where it was safer, and there wasn't some annoying dead French woman trying to speak drunk to them.

I sat up and swung my legs over the side of the bed. I needed to go back downstairs. I needed to get everyone out of this house. I didn't even know what I had been thinking when I brought everyone here—clearly my thoughts had been compromised.

Then I remembered Perry's neck, the way her tender skin had submitted under my hands.

It wasn't just my thoughts. Everything about me had been compromised.

I got up and started for the door, prepared to see my mother again in her most violent form. The last time I saw her was in a dream, and it went well. She had been sober, coherent, even loving. It would be a shame to fuck that all up again.

I was halfway across my room when I heard a whisper. It was coming from the closet.

I turned and faced it, looking around my room for a baseball bat. I spotted one in the corner, a kid's version, and picked it up. It was better than nothing. I gripped it hard in my hands and took a step toward the closet.

The closet door slowly creaked open.

The whispering started again.

"You don't want to go in there," a voice said from behind me, and I whirled around.

Sitting on my bed was a man in a suit. Though I'd never seen him before, I also knew that I had.

I knew it was Michael.

My brother, all grown up.

He was staring up at me with an impish smile on his face. "You really don't remember?" he asked. "I thought we really bonded the last few days. I mean, literally, *bonded* to each other."

I stared at him, momentarily dumbfounded.

Then the bat dropped from my hands as all the memories came crawling back in.

I remembered him showing up in Portland. I remembered that god awful feeling that he was there to kill me. I remembered telling Ada to go and get Perry. Then he did something to her with just a flick of his eyes, and she was out cold.

And I, I couldn't do anything at all. He reached into my brain, into my soul, into my existence, and made me move, made me breathe, made me act.

He got me from Oregon to New York without me having a singular, autonomous thought. He controlled me from the inside out.

Then I came back just in time for him to inject himself again. This time, he was just along for the ride, taking over when he saw fit.

Like last night, when I'd nearly killed Perry. It had never been me. It had always been him.

"Very good, Declan," he said. "Then I guess you know that I was quite pleased you brought them here. You won me some favors."

I ground my teeth together. "I had no idea, and you know it."

He cocked his head. "Oh, you must have known that your reasons for coming here were not of the most unselfish nature. But that's you, isn't it? A selfish boy. So obsessed with your past and the love you thought you never had that you were willing to risk everyone's lives and happiness to come here. That wasn't me, you see. That was all you. That was just you being Dex Foray, a total, selfish asshole. Just being yourself."

I quickly bent down to pick up the bat again, but instead all I got was a snake—a black, writhing python that I immediately dropped, leaping backward out of the way.

Michael laughed then grew serious. "Of course, it would have been best if they had been able to stay longer. Your fiancé, her mother, her sister, your friend. If they hadn't been helped by your actual brother, the conniving little worm, we wouldn't even be having this little chat right now." He got off the bed, all elegant, like he was some fucking billionaire playboy. "Having them all here in this house, so close to the gates, enabled me to open the door just wide enough. They were easy to feed off of, all that energy, all that ability, all that fear. They got our foot in the door. But I'm afraid you're going to have to do the rest of the work."

I shook my head slowly. "I'm not doing anything for you," I said, my jaw stiff, my eyes trying to murder him. Now that I knew it wasn't my brother at all, all bets were off.

His smile was quick like lightning. "But you must. You know you must. You know you have no choice." He took a step toward me, the python slithering out of the way and toward the closet. I eyed the little sword I had on the wall. It was the real deal, and I had never been allowed to touch it, and could only practice with the longer, bendy ones, but my father bought it for me just the same.

It could kill a man if you aimed it at the right place.

"I always have a choice," I said. "As do you."

He snorted. "You don't understand a thing, do you? Ignorant human fool. But that's to be expected, I guess. You never were the sharpest tool in the shed. Declan, what I'm telling you isn't an option. I will make you bring them back here. I will make you do it again. I can even get a little bit of influence over on the mother—her brain is soft, her soul is easy to penetrate. She's new, you see. She doesn't know better. Dumb foreigner."

He sighed, looking down at the ground, as if in regret. I realized that the pounding on the door had stopped, and for once I actually wished my mother was on the other side of it. I would have asked for her incoherent help. "Yes, I will try again. And it will work. And I'll ensure the gates will never close, and they'll never make it out of here alive. They escaped once, but they won't do it again."

"They escaped because you're a fucking douchecanoe," I told him, edging slightly toward the sword.

His eyes narrowed into snakelike slits. "They escaped because they were lucky and foolish, and because young Michael showed them the way. This house should have never trapped his soul here like that. It shouldn't have worked that way."

"And what way does it work?" I asked, stepping even closer to the wall.

He sighed in annoyance. "I told you. The walls are thinner here. This isn't a place that even exists in the human world. It's a floating elevator between time and space and here and now. This is the closest gateway to hell that I know. And once they can all cross over to this side, no one will ever forget my name."

"Michael O'Shea," I said.

"That is not my name," he said, his voice growing guttural and severe, as if grated down with sandpaper. "You will die never knowing my name. But Perry ... I'll make sure she knows."

I stared at him, at the haze of hatred in his eyes. I wanted to call his bluff, but I knew that would be a lie. He already hurt her through me. I couldn't stand to think what he was going to do next.

"You could just leave her out of this," I said. "Last night, there was no reason for that, no reason at all."

He smiled, his teeth sharp. "Of course there is a reason, Declan. The reason is to hurt. To make others hurt. To have them wallow in pain. What greater hate is there in the world than to have someone suffer at the hands of someone they trusted? I loved seeing her agony, her fight for breath, that betrayal in her eyes as she thought it was you. I got off on it." He paused. "And I will again. More so. I'll keep her alive for just long enough, just to bring her here, then when the gates are fully open and my job here is done, I'll make sure she dies thinking that I'm you. At the very least, your face will be the last thing she sees."

The amount of anger flowing through me was probably enough to blast a hole into the wall with only my fist. But that was what he wanted. He wanted double the pain. He wanted to see it on my face before he saw it on hers.

"Oh," he said, "and by the way, you'll be fully conscious and unable to do a thing while I fuck her with a knife and slice her from cunt to chin. You'll have to watch it all, watch yourself do it all. Maybe then you won't feel so fucking smug." He took a step toward me. "Then, finally, I'll kill you. But not until then. You're useless to me dead, unfortunately."

And that was just as I thought.

Before he could make another move, I leaped to the wall and grabbed the sword off of the molding. My body remembered all my old stances, and I had the sword aimed at him, ready to strike.

He laughed, his head rolling back, his hand at his stomach as if to keep it all in. "Oh, Declan, you really are stupid, aren't you? All this time you spent in your life seeing ghosts and filming them, and you really think that stabbing me with a sword is going to do anything at all?"

I shook my head slowly from side to side. "No," I said. Then I smiled. "This sword is not for you."

I watched him blink at me in confusion for a moment. Then I turned the sword around and aimed it at the hollow of my throat. It was a place I knew could do damage. It was a place I knew would kill me. Even for all my strength, the blade in my throat would do the trick.

Before he could do anything but widen his eyes in

horrific realization, I brought the tip of the sword toward me, fast and swift.

It was almost an out-of-body experience as it pierced my throat. Perhaps I died sooner than I thought. It hurt, but not that much—just a short but intense jab of pain through my throat. Then the pain subsided, and I only felt the pressure of the blade and the sensation that I was drowning.

I was drowning, after all. Blood was pouring down my throat and into my lungs, filling them up, bit by bit. I immediately fell to my knees, sputtering. I wasn't trying to breathe, to make it worse, but your instinct to live is a strong fucking thing. I kept on trying to get air, even though the whole point was not to live but to die.

I had to die. If I died, I was useless to him. He couldn't possess me. He couldn't harm Perry. He couldn't bring her family here and try to open some fucking gates to hell. He couldn't do anything if I was dead.

And so, that was the plan. A split-second plan, but it was the only one I had. I had wanted to die once when I was in college, right after I was institutionalized. I wanted to throw everything away.

I was glad I didn't. No matter how hard it got, I was glad I kept going. I would have missed out on so much. It angered me, actually, that I thought I was doing the world a favor. Life, no matter how much it sucks—and believe me, being told you're crazy because you see ghosts sucks, growing up with a crazy, abusive drunk mom and a deadbeat dad sucks—it's still a *gift*. That's some cheesy Hallmark shit there, but it's the truth.

If I had ended it back then, I would have never met Perry. I would have never found my purpose in life. I would have never known pure joy and happiness. I would have never felt fulfilled. I would have never known what real love was. I would have never known the pleasure in having hope for the future. I would have never known any of that.

And so, killing myself in order to preserve some of that, it didn't seem like that crazy of an idea. Of course, dying sucks. Dying when you have so much to keep living for has to be the worst joke God has ever played on people.

But sometimes you have to do the shitty fucking things in life. Sometimes those things mean death. If this meant I could save Perry and everyone else, well, there wasn't much to consider. I mean, we're talking the gates of Hell here. We're talking about the love of my life.

That didn't mean, though, that when I fell to the ground and felt the blood pool around my head, that I didn't feel sorrow. I felt absolute sorrow. Because I just wanted to go back in time. I just wanted to be at Perry's parents' house in Portland, editing, happy as a pig in the shit because my woman just agreed to marry me. I wanted to go back to that and hang on to it and yell at myself for not breathing in every single second. I wanted to keep living that joy over and over and over again.

That's why I had asked her to marry me. I wanted joy, forever. I wanted her forever. I wanted all the wonderful things that life was giving me, and I wanted them over and over and over again. I wanted to live.

I just wanted to live.

And now, well that just wasn't in the cards. It wasn't a choice I could have made.

For the first time in my life, I did what was best for everyone.

I stepped into the sword. I stepped into the abyss.

I would miss Perry more than anything.

But the fact that this way, she would go on living, that was worth it for me.

I died with tears in my eyes.

I died with love in my heart.

I died knowing that, after everything I had been through, life was still good.

Life was still good.

**13**

PERRY

I don't know how long I just stood there for—seconds, minutes. I yelled and yelled and yelled inside my head, but I got no response—not from Maximus, not from Dex.

Finally, the bedside lamp flickered, and I felt a giant *whoosh* go through me, like something was powering down and I was being emptied. Tears sprung to my eyes for no reason, and it felt like my whole body was losing something. I fell to my knees for a moment, trying to breathe, trying to make sense of what was happening.

"Come with me." I heard a whisper.

I looked up and saw Little Michael standing by the door. He waved his hand at me, frantically, trying to get me to follow him.

I managed to get to my feet, feeling off-balance and hollow. He grabbed my hand and led me out into the hallway. I heard growling, snapping sounds coming from behind me, but he gave me a firm tug and hurried us along in the opposite direction.

"Don't turn around," he said. "Keep blocking yourself. He doesn't know you're here."

I was stunned. How did this boy know what I was trying to do? More than that, it was actually working?

Before I could ask him, he brought me into a room at the end of the hall. It was dark in here save for a light in the bathroom. There was a shadow underneath the door—someone was in there. But the boy paid it no attention. He closed the door to the hallway and pointed at the king-sized bed in the middle of the room.

"Go hide under it," he said.

"I have to find Dex," I told him. "Your brother."

He shook his head, looking saddened. It made my breath hitch.

"No, you don't want to find him," he said. "Go hide under the bed."

He tried to push me down until finally I dropped to my knees and slid underneath. Mattress stuffing hung down beneath the wooden slats, brushing against my face. He then crawled in beside me, but further back, until I could only see the glow of his eyes.

"Who are we hiding from?" I whispered.

He held my eyes but did not say anything.

The door to the bathroom creaked open, flooding the room with pale yellow light. I held my breath and heard the soft smack of footsteps on tile.

A foot slowly came into view, then another. White, laced with dark veins. I could only see up to the mid-calf, but I knew they belonged to a woman. A very dead woman.

This was a house of nightmares—Dex's nightmares to be more exact. I knew who this woman was, and I knew why Michael was hiding.

The feet turned toward me. Creepy, crawly bugs began

to slither down her legs and fall onto the carpet, as if she were brushing them off. They crawled right toward me, and I stiffened as their tiny legs got tangled in the lengths of my hair.

They were no scarier than the feet that had taken a step toward me.

She knew I was here. She knew we were under the bed.

She walked, slowly and with deliberation. Her pale toes flexed.

Dex's mother stopped at the foot of the bed, facing my direction.

I waited. One second stretched on and on.

She began to drop down to her knees.

One knee, then another.

One frail hand. Then the other. Both of her palms were covered in blood, and bugs crawled out of her broken nail beds.

The scraggly black ends of her wavy hair floated down into view.

I went rigid. Ready to run, to fight, to scream. I didn't want to see her, what would have been my mother-in-law had she still been alive.

Her white face appeared inches before me, and I was hit with a blast of cold, feral fear. Her lips were cracked and bleeding, maggots writhing in them. Her eyes were black, just as Michael's had been.

I expected to feel animosity slither off of her, just like the insects. I expected for her face to contort into fathomless anger, all directed at me. Wasn't that always the case with in-laws?

I did not expect her dead features to crumple, and for inky tears to fall out of her eyes, dripping onto the carpet.

"He shouldn't have come here," she said, her voice

metallic and weak, like listening to a lost transmission. "I tried to tell him, to warn him." She reached out and grabbed my hand, slick with cold blood. It grew translucent, until I could see the bones shining through. "It is too late."

I licked my lips, trying to speak, but nothing would come out.

*What was too late?*

She gave a shake of her head. "He shouldn't be with me. Not now. Too young. My baby is too young for this."

Was she talking about Michael? Mrs. Foray was making no sense, but at the same time, I didn't think she was drunk. She was sober, albeit dead.

"What is this place?" I finally managed to whisper.

"This is Hell," she said harshly. "My boys grew up in hell. They died here too."

My eyes bugged out. "Died?"

The light in the bathroom went out. Darkness descended upon us.

"Mrs. Foray," I cried out, gingerly reaching forward to touch where her hands and face should have been.

There was nothing.

"Michael?" I asked over my shoulder, scooting further back and trying to feel where he was. There was only carpet and empty space.

I was alone. The world was silent.

Almost.

A familiar scratching sound came from behind me, like something was brushing up against the wooden slats under the bed. It sounded like long, spindly legs, crawling my way.

The image of a cat-sized spider flashed through my brain.

I wasn't wasting any time. I quickly pulled myself out

from under the bed and stood up, trying to find the door out through the darkness.

*Perry! Dex!*

The sound was so faint I thought I was imagining it.

But it repeated once more. Maximus's voice, softer than the air and only inside my head. He was out there. But if he was calling for Dex, it meant he wasn't with him.

My heart felt like a block of ice. That sense of loss I had experienced earlier came back, tugging me down. I was afraid to know what it meant. Way too afraid.

*Where are you?!* I yelled. *Maximus? I'm upstairs in a bedroom. Where are you?*

But there was no reply. And the thing under the bed was starting to growl.

I stumbled forward, feeling for the door in the dark. I smacked right into it, stifling a cry, and quickly found the knob. I was certain it wouldn't turn, but it did, and I yanked it open.

The hallway was dim except for orange light that flickered in from one of the open doors. Heart in my throat, I walked down the hallway. I peered in the first door that had been Michael's room. It was dark inside, shaped like a cave. Fire danced in the distance. The dimensions of the house were gone.

Feeling eyes staring at me from the long, cold tunnel, I kept walking.

The next door was open a crack. A trail of blood led out from it, the red barely visible in the spotty light. I pushed the door open and peered inside. It was another kid's room; Dex's, I assumed.

In the faint glow of his nightlight, I could make out a wide stain of blood in the middle of the room. Immediately I knew it was from Dex. I just knew.

I whirled around the room, searching under the bed, in the closet. There was nothing, and like the other rooms, no way out through the window.

I wanted to tell myself not to panic, not to think the worst, not to lose it, but I couldn't. The only thing I could do was follow the trail of blood out of the room.

I followed it down the stairs, my footsteps quickening, past the living room where the Christmas lights were all off and the music was gone. The room was empty, and I grabbed one of the black candles that were still burning on the mantel. I continued to follow the blood, past the painting that was back to being Renoir again. I followed it past the kitchen table, which was still set for three, past numerous closed doors, and all the way to a narrow door at the end of the hall that was shut with a look of finality.

Trying the knob and finding resistance, I felt horror take me over. This was panic. This was desperation, and it had its claws in me. I put down the candle and threw myself against the door again and again, crying out from the pain, crying out Dex's name. The blood had gone under the door, and I knew it was him, I knew it was him.

I let out another yelp and kicked the door as hard as I could, conjuring up what little martial arts skills I had left. I had a brief flashback of being in my uncle's lighthouse in Oregon, the night I first met Dex. It was so long ago. Why couldn't I have held on to that moment for longer? Why does life move along so fast and lead us to places like this one?

The door gave way with a splintered groan, and I burst through it, nearly falling down a row of narrow cement stairs. They disappeared into the blackness. I picked up the candle and let it light the way. Surprisingly, it burned bright, and I was able to walk down, down, down. It felt like I was going stories and stories beneath the earth, the air growing colder and thicker.

Finally my feet hit the solid ground and I found myself in a large room. Bare walls, their bottom halves scorched black, no windows, no furniture, nothing except a trail of blood leading to the center of the room.

The blood led to Dex, lying lifeless on the floor, a sword sticking straight out of his throat.

I gasped, my chest squeezing into oblivion, and dropped the candle, but it did not go out. It burned so I could continue to see him.

I ran over to him, my limbs, my lungs, my heart shaking from the horror of what I was seeing.

It couldn't be.

But it was.

*It was.*

I dropped to the cold earth, my hands hovering above him, unsure of what to do, what to touch, how to help. I didn't think I could speak but I screamed, "Dex!" It ripped out of me, echoing off the walls.

Dex was lying there, eyes open to the ceiling, but there was no life in them and there was no ceiling, just black sky that pressed down on us. My hands found courage and my fingers felt along his chest, demanding a heartbeat.

He was still. His heart was silent.

I couldn't breathe. There was no air in the room. I had no lungs left. I was just a fist inside me, tightening and tightening. Even the tears were held back in my eyes, frozen in shock, unable to fall.

This couldn't be.

And it was.

I shook my head, my vision going dark and then light again. "Dex," I cried out pitifully. I touched his soft hair, his face, his beautiful brows and the way they curved over his eyes, the shiny glint of his ring. His dark brown eyes that I willed to blink, willed to look at me, but they didn't. They were empty, and he was dead beneath them.

I closed my own, trying to concentrate, to turn back time and make this all go away. But when I opened them again, I saw the same thing, my eyes focusing on the blood that had pooled out of his throat.

My heart launched itself in my chest, and suddenly I was gasping for air, trying to breathe, trying to live, and why, why was it all so pointless. I didn't want to live. I couldn't live without him. I couldn't, I couldn't.

I cried out, a long ragged sob that bordered on a scream. I slammed my fists into the ground then curled my fingers around Dex's shirt and held on to him like I could bring him back to life that way. I held so tight, so damn tight, as the waves of sorrow plowed through me, twisting my heart and soul into knots that could never be undone.

The pain was real, physical, tearing me apart, splitting me down the middle until everything inside me was falling out.

I put my head on his chest, wishing so hard to hear his heartbeat. I wished for him to sit up and look at me one last time. I wanted to hear him call me kiddo, I wanted to feel his hands on my skin, his lips on my face.

For everything that had happened, everything, I did not go into the day thinking he would die. I did not even know it was a possibility. We had gone through so fucking much together, cheated death a million times, dying wasn't a possibility.

But then there was my dream last night, seeing him in a grave, in the cold hard earth, and I screamed again, my mouth open and sobbing, cursing myself for not paying attention. Why didn't I see this coming? Why did I let Dex come here? Why did I let him out of my sight?

There was no way I could handle this, process this. I screamed, over and over again, sobs that were wrenched out of me, snapping my sanity like torn arteries. He was bleeding, I was bleeding too, from my heart, my poor, poor heart. How was it even still in my chest?

I bawled onto him for what seemed like hours, days. I cried and cried and kept going over everything in my head, everything I could have done differently. Why didn't I know, why didn't I know just how fucking easily he could be taken from me?

And each time I had to lift my head and look at him, because it just couldn't be true.

How could this be my life and the end of his?

Maybe this wasn't even him.

My pulse quickened with what I knew was false hope. I sat up and leaned over him.

"Dex," I whispered, gently pressing my fingers to his cheek. I lowered my lips to his and spoke against them. They were cold. "Dex, can you hear me? Are you in there somewhere?"

I listened to nothing. I pulled back, tears falling on his chest. I couldn't look at him like this. He couldn't die like this.

Wincing, I reached for the sword, wrapping my fingers around the cold steel. It was small, as if made for a child. Somehow it was in his throat. It didn't make any sense, none of this made any sense.

With one fluid motion, I pulled it out, gasping at what I had done. The wound was deep and open and quickly filled with more blood. It rose and spilled over the sides, following the path of the blood from before, over his neck and on to the ground.

Another sob escaped my throat. I had half-expected him to wake up, if not just from the pain. But he didn't stir.

He never would.

I reached over and ran my fingers down over his eyes until they were closed.

Now, at least, he looked at peace.

I prayed he was at peace.

Because one of us should at least be, and it wasn't me.

I felt like a heavy boot was pressing down on my chest, and it would never lift again. I would never be whole again.

I collapsed against him, the tears still coming, my breath still weak and ragged, as if it were dying with him.

No. No, no, no, no, no.

This wasn't the end.

I would never let it be the end.

With what strength I had left, I put my arms underneath his and pulled him up onto me, cradling him in my lap. I let his blood flow over me. I wanted to drown in it, to let it sink into every pore.

I was supposed to marry this man. I was supposed to be the mother of his children. I was supposed to live with him for as long as we could go, a bumpy journey, but one we would travel hand in hand.

Till death do us part.

I sobbed and squeezed him to me tightly.

Why did it have to part us so soon?

"Perry?"

I woke up slowly, my body protesting consciousness. For

one brilliant, beautiful moment I thought I was in Seattle, in our bedroom. I thought my life hadn't changed at all.

But when I opened my eyes and only saw flickering candlelight, I knew. When I felt the sticky, congealed blood on my hands, I knew. When I moved slightly and felt the dead weight of Dex's body on top of mine, I knew. My life had changed forever. There was no going back.

I lost the love of my life.

It was like losing life itself.

I sucked in a breath and looked to the corner of the room where the voice had come from. Standing at the foot of the stairs was Maximus, staring down at me in restrained horror.

"What happened?" he whispered, his voice cracking and barely audible.

I wanted to cry again, but it seemed like I had no tears left. I just felt this resolute emptiness, this hollowness where my heart should have been, where he should have been.

The loss threatened to take over again, to drown me, but Maximus crossed the room and crouched beside me, a hand on my shoulder, looking between Dex and me and trying to make sense of the situation. Good luck with that.

"Perry?" he said again, his brow furrowing as if he was going to cry too. "Please, what happened? Tell me what happened."

"Where were you?" I whispered weakly.

He shook his head, rubbing a hand over his face. "I don't know. I ... I went after Dex upstairs. He went into the bathroom and shut the door behind him. I knocked on the door, waited. After, I don't know, a minute, water started to come out from under the door. I knocked the door down but he wasn't in there. Then I heard him say my name, from behind me. I went down the hall and saw him standing in the room at the end. I went in after him. That door closed. It was dark. I thought I was in there for a minute, maybe two. I kept at the door but it wouldn't open. That's when I heard you screaming in my head. Then finally it opened by itself and I came out." He paused and closed his eyes. "I followed the blood. It brought me here."

I was too numb to even be shocked by the time skips. Time didn't really seem to exist in this house anyway. This house didn't even seem to exist.

"The same for me," I said blankly. Actually, I was leaving a lot out. But what was the point in saying anything? What was the point of anything anymore? Dex was gone, and I was left behind to carry on.

Death was torture for those who were left behind. I could only hope that Dex wasn't suffering like I was.

"Who did this?" he asked.

I attempted a shrug and failed. Dex was too heavy, but his weight felt real, reminding me that he had been real this whole time and not some beautiful dream.

"Michael, I guess," I said.

"No," Maximus said. I looked at him in faint surprise. "It wasn't him."

"Who then?"

"It was Dex," he said. "Dex did this to himself."

My heart clenched. "Why?" I said breathlessly. "Why would he do this?"

"To escape," Maximus said, settling down on the ground, legs splayed. His eyes never left Dex's body. "To save us."

"How?"

He swallowed hard. "If Michael happened to be in his body, and Dex killed himself, the spirit or the demon or whatever was in him would have died too."

"And if he wasn't in him?"

"He knew he would just be taken over again." Suddenly Maximus let out a roar, pure agony that shattered the room. He buried his face in his hands, and I was struck, feeling it deep, by how much he cared for him. But of course he did. He had originally been sent to be his guide, to watch over him. And now Dex was dead. He had failed. I had failed.

When he recovered, he looked up at me and said, "Whatever Dex did, it was to save you. Save me, save everyone. But above all, it was to save *you*."

"I didn't ask for that," I whispered.

"No, you didn't. But that's Dex. That man loves you so much. Sometimes it doesn't even seem possible. He gave up his life for you, and if he could, he would probably do it again." He sighed. "But you already know that, don't you? You love him the same way."

I found myself nodding. I would have done the same. I still would, if I could.

If I could.

What if I could?

I licked my lips, and for the first time in a while, felt a thread of strength returning. "Maximus," I said softly, urgently.

He slid his eyes to mine. Before he could say anything, we heard a thump from upstairs. The ceiling was once a fathomless black sky but now was just a ceiling with a broken light bulb hanging from it. It was swinging back and forth, casting moving shadows.

"Did you see anyone else in the house?" he asked, his eyes trained to the light.

Who didn't I see? Minutes ago I wouldn't have seen myself caring. I wouldn't have cared what happened to me.

But that was then and this was now, and now I had an idea.

"There may be spiders the size of cats," I said absently, my mind elsewhere.

He raised his brow.

"I saw them in the Veil, last time I was in there," I explained. "I think they snuck through."

"Or Michael let them in," he said. "This house is nothing but a portal."

I swallowed and nodded. "It's the gateway to Hell. Dex's mother told me so."

He narrowed his eyes. I managed a smile.

"Hey," I said. "Do you think Dex is gone? Or do you think he's just..." I waved my hand around the empty space in front of us. I knew I was acting delusional. "Just here."

"He's dead, Perry," he said hoarsely. His eyes flitted to Dex's body. The proof was literally in my arms, covering me in blood. Part of me had died with him.

Unless I could bring him back.

Maximus was staring at me, his expression cautious. He was hearing my thoughts.

"Darling," he said gently, "if you go into the Thin Veil, through this place, this close to the darkness we don't understand, there is a chance you're not coming back."

"Maybe I don't want to come back."

"But you do, Perry," he said. "You do. You want to come back with Dex. You don't want to live on the other side. What if Dex has already moved on? If he's not in the Thin Veil, you still may never see him again, and you'll be stuck there. Forever is a long time."

I thought about the man with the cockroach eyes, the severed woman, the spider cats I swore were upstairs. I thought about all of them and living with them for eternity, cursed to stumble through a monochrome universe for the rest of my life.

It was worth the risk.

"If I can go in and there's a chance I can find him and bring him back," I told him, "then I'm taking it."

He nodded solemnly. "I know. I just wished it wouldn't come to this. That's the problem with you two, I reckon. Death just seems like an obstacle sometimes. You have the false hope that you can get around anything. But Perry, some things you can't get around. Some things are final. Believe me, you don't want your poor sister to spend the rest of her days wanting to go back in there and fish you out."

That gave me pause. That was the last thing I wanted, for Ada to hunt through the Veil, looking for me, looking for Dex. I knew she'd do it, too. Her bravery surprised me more every day. But I wouldn't let that be an issue. I would make it out, and I would do so with Dex.

"Are you going to stop me?" I asked carefully, aware that the burly ginger could very well prevent me from doing anything.

He smiled. "What I really want is to pick you up and take you out of here. Giant bugs, or Michael, or worse are upstairs, and they want to take us with them."

"So why don't you?"

He ran a hand through his red hair. "Because I owe you more than that." He seemed to grin to himself. "And the crazy thing is, I wish I could join you."

Then his face fell. "I went to Hell once, you know, for someone that was very dear to me. And it worked. I brought his soul back to where it needed to be. I pray you never end up there. But I understand, I really do. There are some people you would do anything for. And I want you to know that for me, at this point in my life, it's Rose, you, and Dex. If I could take your place, Perry, and go in after him, I most certainly would. But that ship has sailed for me."

There was a thud at the door, making us both flinch. Maximus paled and quickly rose to his feet, running over to the staircase and glancing up at it.

"What is it?" I asked, feeling the urgency of the moment running through me. If something was coming for us, how the hell was I going to go into the Veil?

"I don't know," Maximus said. "But I reckon we don't have that much time to figure it out."

I looked at him, suddenly terrified. "How do I get back to here? Last time Ada had to pull me through. Can you?"

He shook his head. "I can't. I just don't have the skill anymore. But you can get back, I know you can." Another thud at the door. He looked over his shoulder and let out a shaky breath of air. "You're going to have to hurry though. I will stop them from getting to you, but I don't know for how long."

"No, you get yourself out of here!" I cried out. "Forget about me!"

He crouched down beside me, resting his hand on Dex's lifeless arm that had already started to stiffen with rigor mortis. It made my stomach turn. "I have to stay here. You can step into the Veil in your physical form and disappear, but Dex cannot. His body will be here. I don't even know if he will be strong enough to endure coming back—he's lost almost all his blood. But if anything happens to him, here, while you're in there, he's not coming back at all. You got that?"

I nodded and took a deep breath. "I got it."

"All righty," he said, holding his hands out for me. "Let me help you."

As carefully as I could, I lifted Dex's head off of me. Then I put my hands into Maximus's warm ones and let him pull me up to a standing position. He put his hand on my cheek and gave me a sad smile. "Well, little lady," he said with full-on drawl. "I'll do the best that I can. But for whatever reason, if I am not here when you get back … we'll meet again someday. I don't know when, but someday, some place, I'm sure."

My heart panged again. He leaned in forward and kissed me lightly on the lips before pulling back. He winked at me. "That was for Dex, too. Now turn around and go."

"Thank you," I whispered to him. He squeezed my hand and then made me twirl around so I was facing the blank space on the other side of me.

"Concentrate," he whispered. "Think about Dex."

And so I did. I ignored the bangs at the door, the sticky blood at my feet. I closed my eyes and thought of Dex. I thought about his smile, his laugh, the way he could make me melt just by looking at me. I thought about the love he had given me, and all the love I had left to give him.

I opened my eyes and let my gaze gloss over, fuzzy and out of focus. And just when the world seemed to be pulling back, I walked forward.

My ears screamed, my head felt ready to explode, and the wind that blew past me was cold as ice. But when I blinked a few times and let the world settle around me, I saw I was in the grey basement of a house. There was no Maximus. There was no Dex. There was only fog that hung around my ankles and floated up the stairs.

I was in the Veil.

I was this much closer to Dex.

And this much closer to Hell.

## 14

PERRY

While the house that Dex led us to had been a carnival of horrors on the inside, in the Veil, it looked normal.

Well, sorta.

There was this blanket of fog that clung to my legs, making it look like I was walking through a soupy cloud, and though everything was void of color, here it took on a shade of blue/black instead of grey.

It was cold though—very cold—and I had to fight the constant shiver that wanted to run through me. I had always imagined Hell would give off a bit of heat.

I walked up the stairs, pausing every other step and listening. I wondered if the giant spiders were on this side, or if they had all crossed over to the other. Either way, it was bad news.

As soon as I got to the top floor, I went straight for the kitchen to get a knife. I never knew when I'd need it, and this time I wasn't going to take any chances. Could I kill something that was already dead? Well, experience told me I could. I felt like every single ghost and paranormal beast we had encountered up until this point was preparing me for this. In comparison, that had all been a walk in the park.

The moment I pulled it out from its sheath on the counter, I felt a breath tickle the back of my neck. I whirled around, knife raised, but saw no one. I paused, listening. There was a loud *click click click* coming from the hallway, the sound of claws on a hardwood floor, only far louder than they should have been.

My pulse jumped in my veins.

I looked around the room. Here the blinds were up, showcasing the empty backyard. I was certain the door to the outside would work in this dimension. I began to head toward it, trying to stay light on my toes, lest I alert whatever it was out there.

But it was too late. Just as I reached the door, I felt a terrible, heavy presence at my back. I slowly turned my head to look. A dog had appeared in the hallway, standing still. It looked like a rottweiler. It was hard to tell. It had no head.

My eyes widened at the bloody stump, and though I was certain that there was no way it could see me, let alone smell or hear me, it adjusted its body so that it was facing me dead on.

I started wondering what kind of damage a headless dog could actually do when I focused on those claws. They were sharp, nearly curled under like a velociraptor's, and at least as long as my fingers. They had pieces of ragged tissue and skin attached to them—I didn't want to know how it got there.

I held the knife out, my hand shaking slightly. I didn't have time for this. I needed to find Dex before it was too late. But shame on me for even thinking this was going to be easy.

The dog lunged for me in silence, which was worse than if it barked or growled. I screamed and went for the door, nearly dropping the knife. So much for that idea.

Thankfully the door opened with one pull and, screaming as I went, I leaped out and slammed the door behind me, putting my weight up against it until I was sure it would hold. The dog jumped up, smearing its bloody stump on the window, its claws punching through, but somehow it stayed shut.

I whirled around and started running, trying to figure out where to go. I only made it a few strides into the backyard when I realized it wasn't a backyard at all. Though the world still had a blue tone and fog licked at my ankles, it was dispersing and faint washes of color were seeping back in.

I looked around, dumbfounded. I was surrounded by tall Douglas fir trees and cedar, a worn path in front of me snaking through overgrown salal bushes with their smooth green leaves and pinkish berries. A cold breeze buffeted me and carried the tangy smell of salt.

What the fuck?

My hair began to float around my face, carried by the wind, and I turned around to look back at the house.

It was gone.

Instead there were more tall trees, reaching for the grey sky, and below them was a bench surrounded by a rose garden.

On that bench was a girl, wearing an old-fashioned dress, her attention focused on her hands folded neatly in her lap. She was deathly pale, frail, and short. She was also very pretty.

My blood ran cold before she even looked up at me. When she did, I saw that half her face was rotting off.

Leprosy.

Mary.

Oh holy fuck.

"I knew you'd come back," Mary said in her sing-song voice. "You can never really escape."

I gripped the knife harder. "Where am I?" I asked.

"You're neither here, nor there."

"Have you seen my partner? Dex?" It was worth a shot.

She grinned at me with blackened teeth, and I wondered why I ever thought her pretty. "Have you seen my daughter, Madeline?" Her eyes darted over her shoulder. "There she is."

I turned around to see a little girl running down the path away from us.

"She'll take you to him," Mary said.

I didn't know if I trusted that. In fact, I totally did not trust this woman. After everything that happened on D'Arcy Island, I had no reason to. She was a murderer and a liar. And a fucking ghost.

But I also had no intentions of hanging around her. I turned and ran down the path after Madeline, all my D'Arcy Island flashbacks hitting me with each step I took. I remembered what happened here, and I'd be damned if I let them happen again.

Suddenly the path began to clear up and drop sharply to the left. I came to a stop and saw Madeline on a rocky beach below, running along it toward a lighthouse.

Not just any lighthouse. Of course not.

I sucked in my breath and watched as the burning sun in the grey/blue sky began to plunge toward the sea. In an instant, the sun was swallowed whole and the world around me was dark as night.

The lighthouse's light came on, illuminating a path just

for me. By the top, where the glass went around the giant bulb, I saw the bulky shadow of a man. It wasn't Dex, and yet I knew he'd be up there, somehow. If I were to find him, that's where he'd be. I was seeing what I was being told to see, the Veil bending to fit my memories. I was being manipulated for a reason.

Madeline's tiny body ran through the open door to the lighthouse and disappeared inside. I took one look behind me, afraid that Mary would appear and push me over the edge. But there was only blackness, the trees having come together so thick that they resembled a web of branches.

Only one way for me to go.

Using the silver light from the lighthouse, I picked my way down through the steep embankment, the fog clearing so I could see my feet. On the beach, the black ocean crashed close by, the sky feeling wildly heavy and oppressive. I looked up, taking in what I thought were stars but weren't stars at all.

They were eyes. Millions of eyes. All watching me from a black velvet sky.

I shuddered and averted my eyes. As I jogged over to the lighthouse, I could feel them watching my every move.

The minute I entered the familiar structure, the temperature dropped again, and I was met with the musty old smell of rotted wood and sea-rust. It was dark with several doors leading to rooms that shouldn't spatially exist. I glanced up the spiral staircase, hearing quick footsteps before they faded away. There were candles lit along the railing, illuminating the slick steps and the inky trails of kelp that slithered down them.

My throat felt like it had a piece of dry toast lodged in it. Every instinct told me not to go up the stairs, that I knew what was at the top, waiting for me as he had before. Old

Roddy had been banished from my world the moment the lighthouse blew up, but he existed here, in this realm so close to Hell.

This was his home.

I ignored the queasy butterflies in my stomach and began to ascend the stairs, careful not to slip. I'd face Old Roddy to get to Dex. I'd face anything.

As I climbed, I started to hear the sparse notes of a piano floating through the air. When I reached the first landing, I noted one of the doors was open and a faint glow was coming from the room. The trails of kelp went straight in there.

And so did I.

The room was large and bare, the walls covered in splashes of rust or blood. There was a grand piano in the middle, and from where I was I couldn't see if anyone was playing it. The notes were sad but dull at the same time, each one growing louder and filling the room with unease.

I carefully stepped toward it, prepared to be met with a gruesome sight.

But there was no one there.

I came closer and stared down at the keys, all cracked and broken. Though the music kept playing, there was no movement, except for a wasp that was slowly crawling down across, from F to G to A.

The sight of the wasp struck fear in the very heart of me, and I didn't even have to turn around to know there was someone behind me. I could feel *her*.

No, no, no, please not her.

The door creaked, like breaking bones, and shut with a loud click. Fog rolled between my legs, and the buzz of the wasp started to drown out the piano's haunting song. With my heart beating fast, vying for my throat, I turned around and saw...

Nothing. Just the closed door.

I let out a shaky breath, the handle of the knife starting to slip. I needed to get a hold of myself. For a moment there I was sure I was about to see someone I never wanted to see again. Wouldn't that have been—

"You can't have him," a voice said from behind me. Metallic, raspy, like buzzing wasp wings. Utterly, terrifyingly familiar.

I whipped around to see Abby standing in the corner of the room, her head askew at an unnatural angle, blood pouring down her arms and legs and pooling on the floor. Wasps crawled out of her mouth, pushing her lips aside.

This really was Hell, wasn't it? Filled with the ghosts of people I'd only been too happy to be rid of. And here, in this place, they were no less scary and no less dangerous. Abby had the power to keep me here. She was certainly going to make sure Dex didn't going anywhere.

Although, that meant he was here to begin with. A rocket of hope jolted through me, battling the fear.

"I can't have him," I repeated, surprised to find my voice. "That means he is here with you."

She smiled at me, the grin of a madwoman, a dead woman. More wasps came out of her mouth, heading straight for me where they circled around my head. A few came out of her nose and ears. One of her unblinking eyes pulsed and moved as a wasp squeezed between the eyeball and the socket. I was having a hard time not throwing up.

"He is upstairs. With them," she said. "They won't let him go. He's right where he belongs."

I raised my chin, staring at his grotesque ex-girlfriend with defiance. "I'll be the one who decides that," I said, feeling strength and conviction where I thought I would have none. I'd come this far, I guess. There was nothing left to lose, no reason not to believe I couldn't beat this.

Before I could even turn for the door though, Abby was flying across the room, her long, bony fingers wrapping around my neck like icicles. She threw me back, my head smacking against the door, and we tumbled to the ground. She smelled like rotten meat and blood and death, and I knew if I didn't act fast, she was going to kill me.

I somehow managed to roll out from under her, but she was fast, and as I struggled to get to my feet, my soles slipping on her greasy blood, she grabbed on to my ankles, her nails slicing into my skin.

I screamed and she yanked me back down on my stomach, pulling me toward her by my legs. The air started to swarm with wasps—first a few, then more, until their droning buzz was all I could hear. They landed on my arms, my back, my face, crawled into my hair, stinging me again and again. The pain was unbearable, and every time I screamed they made a go for my mouth.

Growls spewed from Abby's lips, and I felt the back of my shirt lift up, her ice cold nails trailing over my exposed skin near my spine. I felt like any second she was about to slice my back and pull my spine out with her bare hands. Panicking, I flailed my arms, trying to buck her off me, but she wouldn't budge. The wasps continued to assault me, and the blood around me was rising, moving, as if it were a living thing, wrapping sticky rivers around my arms and legs.

When I felt her mouth center over my spine, her teeth razing my vertebrae, I knew I was done for. She was going to tear me apart and eat me alive, sucking out my spinal fluid as an apéritif.

"Dex!" I screamed in vain, a wasp landing on my tongue.

I doubted he could hear me. It was a way to let him know that I tried.

I tried.

The sharp stab of her teeth sank into me, and I closed my eyes to the pain.

They were immediately blown back open.

A giant rush of wind, of fiery force, of power came blasting at me, causing Abby to fly backward, letting me go. I flattened against the ground, my eyes having a staring contest with the writhing blood on the floor, coming for my face. I was aware of Abby growling, screaming, and I lifted my head just enough to look over my shoulder, to see what was going on.

Abby was being dragged by her own ankles toward a black pit that had opened up where the door used to be, swirling in the air like a black hole, sucking all the wasps into it. I couldn't see what was dragging her, it was just this mess of shimmering light, a golden glow in this world of darkness, but the hole that it created was growing stronger and stronger.

I heard the piano screech, the keys rattling in a chaotic song, and I turned my head back to see it moving inch by inch, being sucked into the vacuum, just as my own body began to lift up into the air. I pressed my hands into the bloody ground, desperate to not be taken where Abby had been, but it was useless. The piano was sliding toward me, and I was pulled back too. I was going to be crushed.

Then, just as my body became airborne and I started to twist like I was going down a drain, the roar of sound stopped, and for one moment I was perfectly still in the air, floating. Then I dropped. I belly-flopped on the ground, hard, and all the air was squeezed from my body.

I gasped, trying to regain my breath and figure out my

next move. If I could just lay my head down and close my eyes for a while, I was sure that everything would be fine in the morning.

*Perry*, I heard a voice say. It came from behind me, and yet it came from everywhere. At first I wouldn't let myself believe in it, believe I could be hearing it.

But she spoke again, her voice drifting softly through my head like feathers. *Perry.*

I swallowed and gingerly turned over on my back.

The door had returned to normal, and in front of it was Pippa.

Pippa!

I couldn't believe my eyes, but there she was. She was faint, looking more like a hologram than anything real, but she was there, glowing wildly.

"You're here," I said before I lapsed into a coughing fit.

She nodded, giving me a sweet smile that was laced with worry. *Use your inside voice. Save your strength.*

I understood. *Okay. What are you doing here? I thought I'd never see you again.*

*I'm not really here*, she said, and when she caught the confused look on my face, she quickly elaborated. *I have moved on but ... I thought I could help. I can help. I can push through, make holes from where I am into this part of the Veil. I can take people, demons, away.*

*Where are you?*

*I am in death,* she said, but she said it with a smile. *Almost at peace.*

*Except for this whole thing.*

*There will be peace when I help you. I had warned you this would happen. I knew to expect it, even though I didn't want to believe it.*

Yes, well her warning was rather cryptic, but I didn't bring that up.

*Do you know where Dex is?* I asked as I got to my feet. *Please tell me you do*, I thought, *and this isn't all for nothing.*

She nodded. *He is upstairs, but he is not alone. This is your Hell, Perry, and it's his too, and the ones that brought him here will use what scares you to kill you, to keep you here. They know you are coming. They planned it this way.*

*Why?* I cried out. *Why do this? Why us?*

*Because sometimes ... there are energies that just want to destroy. They aren't picky. It all brings them pleasure and strength. And, of course, you're both very powerful, very unique. You're something they covet. They always have. Why do you think you both have seen so much while others haven't?*

*That means they have coveted you, too.*

I could have sworn she blushed, like it was a compliment. I suppose for her, there wasn't really much to fear anymore.

*They did, of course they did. And I still have some aspects they desire, but they know now they can't have them. In peace you can't be touched. But I can surely touch them.*

Her face fell, her eyes turning grave, and despite her serious expression, I was struck by how pretty she was. Unlike the last time I saw her, now she was looking younger and vibrant, even as she was transparent. Peace suited her.

*We must go*, she said. *And you must block your thoughts. No matter what you see, what things they have arranged, do not let them hear or sense your fear. I will take care of everything. All you have to do is get Dex and run for the door.*

*What door?*

*You'll know it when you see it. I'll create a distraction, and if I can destroy the demons, I'll do that as well.*

*Michael?*

*Michael is an angel's name*, she said sharply. *This is a demon. And if you don't do as I say, he will keep you here as he has kept Dex.*

Glowing and brilliant, she turned to the door and it opened before her. She stepped through it, floating a few inches above the ground like a radiant ghost.

*Wait!* I cried after her, and she quickly swiveled her head around to give me a look. *Sorry,* I thought, reminding myself to concentrate, to imagine walls up around my mind, blinders around my thoughts.

As I caught up to her and she began to ascend the stairs, I asked, *What happens after? When I get him out? Will he be okay?*

She didn't answer. We made it to the second level, a foyer of wriggling kelp strands, twisting around each other like snakes. I kept my eyes away from them; they were only there to scare me.

As we climbed up the next flight, she said, *He is stronger than you think. He should be okay.*

I didn't like the sound of "should." *And the demon? If you don't destroy him?*

*He will be weakened, that is for certain. I will do my best, what I can from where I am.*

*And if you can't?* I pressed. *Then what? What can I do to protect us on the other side?*

*Kill the body and the head will die,* she said after a moment. I was reminded of what Maximus said, his theory that if Michael had been inside of Dex while Dex killed himself, that would have killed Michael too. Of course, that didn't seem to be the case here.

*Are you ready?* she asked.

I wasn't. You couldn't be ready for something like this. But I nodded anyway.

We went up the stairs, her floating waves of gold a few feet in front of me. I stayed as far behind as I could without losing sight of her, and I worked on holding up those invisible walls.

When she disappeared around the last corner, I waited for a few breaths. There was a flash of light that made everything blot out into a blur of white and then an unearthly roar that shook up my blood. The walls of the lighthouse seemed to throb as it descended into chaos, and I took the opportunity to run up the rest of the way, unheard amidst the noise.

When I got to the landing, where the bulb was now blasting out rays of cold, stark light, I saw a flurry of gold and black swirling around it, and that black hole began to form in the middle. I could barely make out a beast, his blackened fur obscured by Pippa's fury. She was opening up the same door where she sent Abby, and if I wasn't careful, I was going to get sucked in.

And so was Dex.

I looked to the corner of the room and saw him lying there on the floor, face down in his own blood.

My heart skipped a beat and came crashing back hard. Dex.

I ran over to him, pushing through the wind, until I was almost at his side.

As if sensing me coming, he raised his head and looked at me. His face contorted in surprise and then sadness.

*Dex!* I cried out, and for that moment, I was so happy to see him that I didn't block it. I went down to grab him, but his eyes widened, and suddenly I was being jerked to the side, kelp wrapped around my waist.

The smell of rot and sea water filled my nose.

*Nice to have you again,* a decrepit voice said in my ear,

slimy kelp shooting around my throat and pressing against the wounds the demon had choked into me the night before.

I immediately swung my fist back, trying to knock a hole into what I knew would be the skeletal face of Old Roddy, but the kelp was too tight, and the helpless sense of déjà vu didn't help.

Choking for air, the world going black, I looked back to the ground, to Dex for help, but he was lying there lifeless again. Oh shit, oh god no. I was so close, so fucking close!

I kicked back at Old Roddy, fighting for life, determined to win against him again. But I just couldn't get the leverage, couldn't find the strength. So much of what had been done to me earlier was starting to take its toll.

Suddenly the wind from the vacuum that Pippa was creating kicked into high gear, spinning me and Old Roddy around and around like we were doing a dizzying waltz and pulling us to the middle of the room.

Just as I was losing the feeling in my hands and feet, the sense of evil permeating my bones and dragging me under, I was knocked out of Roddy's grip and flung to the floor. While the world spun and I continued to be dragged away by the vortex, I looked up and saw a flash of Dex, his hands wrapped around the kelp and pulling it around Roddy's neck, choking him. Dex's arms flexed, and with one big tug, he snapped the kelp so tight that Roddy's head went bouncing off and into the black hole.

The next thing I knew was Pippa's voice in my head, telling me to run, and Dex was at my side, hauling me to my feet.

"Fancy meeting you here, kiddo," he said. Blood had dried around his throat, but I still heard him as clear as day. The sense of awe and relief coming through was overpowering. Then he grabbed me and pulled me along, the both of us trying to make a run for the stairs. Unfortunately, the hole that Pippa was wielding was blocking the way as she tried to drag the beast who masqueraded as Michael into it.

"Only one way out!" Dex yelled over the noise, his eyes darting to the window. "Second times a charm, right?"

I could only nod. I had him. I could do anything.

We ran for the window, hand in hand, and jumped through it, the glass cracking all around us. Beneath us the darkness turned to rocks which turned to waves, and we were falling stories upon stories.

Just when I thought we were going to smash into the rocks, a wave swept up, lifting us away like cold, wet claws, dragging us out to sea. I floundered in the water, trying to stay afloat, trying to grab on to Dex, but the current was too strong. Then I felt his grip around my waist, and I was tugged up and onto shore, rough rocks beneath my skin and the waves crashing at my feet.

Dex pulled me up further until we were as far away from the shore as he could take us. As rocks turning to cool dune grass, he collapsed beside me.

I wanted to cry but I couldn't. Not yet. Not while we were still here. I rolled over, grappling for his touch—to feel him, to know I had him.

"I'm here, baby," he said with a sharp cough, grabbing my hand.

"Dex," I whimpered, holding on tight and rolling onto my side so I could stare at him, absorb the sight of him moving, seeming to be alive. Please god, let this work.

He tilted his head to look at me, his chest heaving up and down. "Is it just me, or is Hell a million versions of fucked up?"

A shaky smile broke my face. "It's not just you," I said,

moving closer to him. Pain shot its way through me in bursts but I pushed it aside until I was right up against him.

With some effort, he lifted his arm and let me rest my head on his chest. "Cuz if a shit ton of coffins holding Chinese lepers suddenly washed up here, I wouldn't be the least bit surprised."

So it had been the same for him.

"I can't believe I found you," I said, staring at him in wonder.

His smile faltered, his brows furrowing. "I can't believe you came to get me."

"Of course," I said, and that's all I could say. How could I even begin to explain what he was to me? I would go through Hell for him again and again.

I closed my eyes for a minute, hearing his heart beneath me. It was so steady, so beautiful. I wanted to luxuriate in this moment, in having my love back. I wanted to just breathe it all in. But we weren't in the clear yet. There wasn't a second in this world that we could take for granted. We didn't belong here.

As if to make a point, the lighthouse, which was only half a football field away, started to rock on its foundations, as if explosions were ripping it apart. The top of it went flying off, and the center of the light was now just a black hole, spinning violently while gold and black plumes of light battled for domination.

"We need to go," I said. "We need to find the door."

Dex sat up, carefully getting to his feet. "What door?"

He grabbed me by my arms and brought me to my feet just as the ground beneath us began to shake. From the lighthouse a crack formed along the earth, shooting toward us and splitting open.

We exchanged a glance. Fuck.

We turned and started running in the opposite direction, toward the trees. I glanced over my shoulder to see flames starting to reach up from the open fissure, and in the distance the lighthouse went down, swallowed whole. My eyes caught a stray beam of golden light as it escaped, jetting off into the ocean, and then I was tripping over a log and falling to the ground.

Dex hauled me up, pulling me along as I could feel the heat of Hell at my back, the flames racing faster and faster, the ground continuing to split and shake. The millions of eyes in the sky were now red embers falling to the ground and settling into ash and dust.

"Is this it?" Dex yelled as the earth in front of us carved up into a cliff. It was sheer, rising up for fifty feet, and impossible to climb.

I looked around for a door carved in the side, for anything, but there was nothing. Flaming embers landed on our arms, burning our skin, and we whirled around to see the ground completely torn open, a jagged, gaping wound of fire. Black beasts were starting to appear in the depths, their horns rising first, then their eyes.

We had seconds left.

I grabbed Dex's hand and kissed it hard, and we stared into each other's eyes, quick but deep. The look said it all. We were going down, and we were going together. We didn't win in the end, but together, we couldn't lose.

"I love you!" I yelled at him, the growl of the demons and the thunder of the flames growing louder.

"I love you!" he yelled back. "Always have, always will. Always."

I managed the saddest smile. He returned it.

We turned back to face our fate.

And the air in front of us shimmered and waved like a brilliant sea.

The door. The Veil.

To walk through it would mean we could fall right into Hell. But we were halfway there anyway. The flames licked at our feet.

I looked at Dex and squeezed his hand. He squeezed it back.

Together we stepped forward.

## 15

PERRY

I was burning alive. All I felt was the impossible pain of fire and numerous hands that grabbed at my ankles, calves, waist, and wrists. I must have screamed but when I opened my mouth, I only took in dust. The air around us began to warp and swirl, and all sound was sucked away.

Suddenly my brain was squeezed into painful oblivion, and my lungs and heart felt as if they were being wrung out like a dirty dishcloth. There was a loud pop, like the cork off a bottle of champagne, and I stumbled forward into the basement of Dex's old house.

The shimmer evaporated and everything bloomed into color. Dex was no longer at my side but at my feet, slowly blinking life into his physical body, one hand at his throat, face twisted with pain. I wanted to drop to my knees, to help him, but I couldn't.

We had landed in the middle of a battle. While I couldn't tell what had been going on from the other side, it was easy to see now.

I wished I couldn't.

There were giant spiders, at least a dozen of them, scattered throughout the room, some of them sliced in half, others just missing legs or heads.

And lying on his back at Dex's feet was the large body of Maximus. In one hand was Dex's sword. His other hand was missing. A slaughtered spider bleeding black goo was sprawled out on his chest.

Maximus's throat was absolutely ripped out, his head nearly severed.

I cried out and turned away as the contents of my stomach rushed out of me and onto the ground, unable to handle the sight of him dead.

I didn't know if Maximus would be here when we got back, but I had hoped he would be. He did his duty. He protected Dex until the end. And now Dex was alive and Maximus was dead.

I was tired of people dying. So fucking tired.

I heard a weak cough from beside me, and I quickly wiped my mouth and composed myself. This was not time to lose it, not now after everything. I had Dex back, and I had to keep it that way.

Dex was trying to sit up, having difficulty breathing. I could see the bubbles of blood coming out of the slice in his throat, though to my surprise, it looked better than when I had left him. Maybe he was already healing, like he had healed fast all those times before. Maybe we would be okay.

But Maximus was not, and now Dex was realizing what had happened. He let out a pitiful cry, his eyes glued to the horrific remains of the man who once was his best friend. My heart cracked for him. When I found out that Dex had sacrificed himself for me, it almost made his death more painful. Now he was grappling with that over Maximus. The guilt was heavy as sin.

"Shhh," I said, even though I could feel myself wanting to cry again. "He knew what he was doing." I hunched down beside Dex and tried to be there for him. I grabbed his hand, my eyes trained on his body instead of the other one.

Dex turned his head to look at me with hurt eyes, wincing as he did so. He couldn't speak, not yet, not with that throat, but I could hear him in my head.

*He died for me. You almost died for me.*

I gave him a quick, sympathetic smile. "You died for us. And now you're here. Dex, we have to go."

*We can't leave him.*

I gripped his hand harder. "Dex, you need to go to the hospital. This wound killed you before, there's no reason it shouldn't be able to do the same now."

*He died protecting me!* he yelled, and his eyes began to fill with tears.

I sniffed and tried to breathe in deep. "I know he did. But it's what he wanted."

*You think death is what any of us wants?* he said, his eyes blazing. *I fucking died for you, and I would do it again and again, but it's not what I want. It's not what he wanted. I want you forever. I want to live. He had Rose, Perry, just as I have you. To know he's losing that...*

He closed his eyes tight and a tear rolled down his cheek. I wanted to comfort him, to be there for him, to take all of this away. Lord knows I was just going through the same thing tenfold.

But I couldn't do anything until we were safe. And until we were out of that house, we weren't safe. I don't know what Pippa did to Michael in there. It worked, but who knew for how long? Who knew if he was gone for good? We couldn't stick around to find out. If we did, it had to be on our own turf, in our own world, not this crazy slice of hell.

I pulled lightly on his arm before straightening up, wiping tears away with my sleeve. "Please, Dex. Please, I can't handle this anymore. Let's just go. We have to go," I pleaded.

He shook his head and muttered, *I can't leave him here, he deserved more than this.* But he still let me help him to his feet. Neither of us wanted to leave him here. It wasn't right. He was our friend.

Ashes to ashes, dust to dust.

He nodded reluctantly, his hand rubbing lightly at his throat. I let go of his hand and headed for the stairs.

A spider launched itself out of the darkness, hitting me square in the chest and knocking me on my back.

I screamed as its claws sank into my side, its snapping pincers grazing my chest. I stuck my hands under its furry underbelly, trying to push it off of me, to keep its pincers from sinking into my skin.

*Perry!* Dex was bellowing, but I could barely hear him above my own cries that seemed to drown the whole room. The spider was too heavy, too strong, its legs vying for violent purchase on my torso. With each stab, I felt blood being drawn and my body growing weaker.

Just as the pincers snapped an inch from my face, old blood and gore being spat onto my cheek, there was a flurry of movement and the spider suddenly stiffened, letting out a horrible human-like scream.

The weight was lifted from my stomach, and I saw Dex standing over me, the sword in his hand. He took one glance at me to make sure I was all right, then went back to the spider that had been stabbed right through the middle. With skill I didn't know he possessed, Dex expertly sliced and diced it into many pieces.

"Arachnophobia, my ass," he said, spitting on the body

parts. I was stunned at the fact those words came out of his mouth. He anxiously felt along his throat again, and when he took his hand away, it was no longer covered in blood. He was literally healing before our eyes, much more rapidly than he ever had before. I guess going back into the Veil and coming out again only helped in this case.

He helped me to my feet, holding my arm tight. He put both hands on either side of my face and stared at me with feverish intensity, his eyes sparkling.

"We're going to make it out of here," he said, urgency in his voice. "We're going to go back to our lives. We're going to get married and live a long and happy life. Do you believe me?"

I nodded, my throat feeling thick with shock and sadness. "I believe you."

"I love you." He closed his eyes and ran his thumb over my lips, his breath deepening. "I love you, beyond death." His words reminded me of my dreams.

He kissed me quickly on the lips, and then, with a final, brutally forlorn glance at his friend, he took my hand and pulled me up the stairs into the rest of the house.

We went up them as fast as we could, but the minute we hit the hallway, everything started to change. The air became full of smoke, smelling of charred wood and burnt hair. The kitchen was on fire, flames shooting out of the room and into the hall.

A crackle came from behind us, and when we turned around to look down the stairs, we saw flames starting to spread where we had just been. The house was burning itself, and while it felt right for Maximus's body to be laid to rest in such a way, it also meant we would be next if we didn't get out of there. Fire was starting to come up the stairs.

"Come on," Dex yelled over the growing roar, and we started running down the hallway toward the front door. We were almost there when the Christmas tree in the living room keeled over, shooting wild flames into the space in front of us. Dex grabbed me and turned me away from the flames, using his body as a shield to make sure his back got the brunt of it.

He let out an agonizing cry as the flames licked him, but in moments I had my hand on the doorknob, and it was turning. Together we burst out of the house and into the dark of night. We stumbled down the stairs, running out into the street, Dex ripping off his burning shirt and throwing it to the ground.

We collapsed on the opposite sidewalk and turned around to watch the house go up in flames. People were already coming out of their houses to look, the flames now bursting through the first floor window, black smoke billowing into the sky.

No one was paying us any attention, not yet. We couldn't press our luck—I knew how this would look to a passerby.

I quickly got to my feet, and Dex followed. I ran my fingers over his side and back, inspecting him for burns but what redness there was, was vanishing by the second, turning a rosy shade of pink then disappearing. His throat seemed to be almost fully healed, like he'd never been stabbed at all, like he'd never died.

But we knew the truth. That would be something neither of us would ever forget.

"Let's go," he whispered to me, and I nodded. We slowly walked down the street, as if we had come to the house because we smelled something burning. While sirens went off in the distance, he was just another New Yorker, shirtless because of the early summer heat, and I was his hipster girlfriend in artfully dirty clothes. Luckily, my body didn't seem to have any of my wounds from the Veil anymore either, though the bloodstains were a bit harder to hide.

We walked calmly around the corner, then as soon as there was no one around, we both started running.

We ran all the way back to the hotel. I tried to call my mom along the way, but I didn't have my iPhone anymore. Hopefully this was the last time I'd lose a phone to something supernatural. I was getting really sick of giving Apple my money. They needed some sort of ghost warranty.

The thought nearly made me smile. But for the giddy joy that came from being alive, that came from skirting death, that came from being reunited with the only person who ever made me feel like it was okay to be Perry Palomino, there was still loss. Maximus had gone up with the house, and that was going to haunt the both of us for a very long time.

It seemed as if it took forever, but finally the lights of Broadway and the rush of cars appeared at the end of the street, the light at the end of a tunnel of brownstones. The hotel loomed a block away, and when we got close, I could see Ada pacing outside the building, talking to someone on her cell.

When she saw us, she burst into tears and started running toward us. She ran right into my arms and Dex held on to both of us. I didn't think I had any more tears left in me, but I did. I'd never been so happy to see her before.

Seconds later, my mom and dad came out of the building, and the crying happened all over again.

When we were finally done, Ada looked at us and asked, "Where is Maximus?"

I couldn't even say the words. To say them would make it real, would mean he was truly gone. I just couldn't.

I glanced at Dex, and the devastated expression on his face told Ada everything she needed to know. She put her hands to her mouth, her eyes wide.

"Oh no. Oh no. What happened?" she asked breathlessly. "Please, don't tell me..."

I looked over at my parents. While my mother looked just as shocked as Ada did, my father was watching us with one finely-tuned suspicious eye. I had to wonder what he knew. What had my mother and sister told him? What could he possibly believe?

But before I could say anything, he cleared his throat and said, "I think we all need to have a good long talk. I need to hear this story from you both, not just them," he said, jerking his head to Ada and his wife. "And then we'll see what our next steps are."

A fire truck roared down Broadway, bathing our faces in red light. Dex reached for my hand and squeezed it. Small comfort, but it was there. I was going to need it. For this and for everything we still had to go through.

## 16

PERRY

We all gathered in our hotel room. For the briefest, strangest moment, I thought we should ask Maximus if he wanted to join us. The realization that he couldn't made me break down in tears again.

Dex wasn't doing much better, but he put his arm around me and took the reins, trying to explain to my father exactly what happened from the start. Of course, my dad didn't understand and didn't want to. He kept interrupting the story with exasperated exhales and rolls of his eyes and the occasional, "Please, be serious now."

I thought my mom would have backpedaled and retreated to her old ways. I thought she would have ignored everything that happened. I thought she would have sided with my dad because that's what she'd always done, for as long as I could remember.

But she didn't. She even told my father to be quiet and just listen, and when Dex looked to me, her, and Ada for approval on the story, she nodded in agreement. I had to say,

I was proud of her. I would have never thought this would happen.

"And you said the house burned down?" my father asked incredulously when Dex started to wrap things up. Dex did have the insight to leave out the part about him dying and me having to go into the Thin Veil to get him. It wouldn't matter to him in the end. Everything was so unbelievable as it was.

Sirens wailed in the background, as if on cue. I jerked my head to the window where red lights swirled on the buildings. "Or it's currently burning down."

My father sighed and put his head in his hands, and slowly rocked back and forth in his seat. "You could be held for arson charges," he mumbled.

"We didn't do anything!" I spat out defensively.

"You broke into a house."

"It was abandoned, Daniel," my mother said, her tone just as harsh as his. Ada raised her eyebrows in surprise.

"Abandoned or not," he looked at Dex sharply, "and from the way you described it, it didn't sound abandoned at all, you can't just trespass. If they find any hint that you were there..."

"They won't," I told him.

"And how do you know that? You might have dropped some little clue. The NYPD is pretty smart, they can piece it together just like that." He snapped his fingers.

I sighed. I didn't know how I knew, I guess because I wasn't even sure how much of that house was real. I was certain that if we looked into the records, we'd find it totally empty and unlived in. The furniture, the Christmas tree, the appliances—those only existed to us, in whatever little hell we'd stumbled upon. Just like the lighthouse burned down on Uncle Al's property, this place would do the same, and there wouldn't be a trace of anything.

"I just know," I told him with finality.

"And your friend, your damn friend," he swore, suddenly getting to his feet. "You left him there?"

"The fire got him," I said, also glad that Dex skirted the cat-sized spider thing. "We couldn't..." And I couldn't finish the sentence.

My father walked over to the window, staring out at the cityscape. "No. No, I can't believe any of this. Maximus is going to walk in through that door at any moment."

"No!" Dex cried out, his voice rough and impassioned. "He *won't*." His eyes began to well up and he looked away. My heart kept breaking again and again. I held on to him tightly. My anchor that I almost lost. My anchor in this storm.

"Honey, please," my mom said, getting up and going to my father.

"No, no, no," he said, stepping away from her touch and keeping his gaze focused anywhere but on the people in this room. "You've all gone mad. You've been drugged. LSD. That's all there is to it. You all had a bad trip, and in a few days you're going to realize that. This trip has gone to shit. We need to get out of here immediately."

I couldn't argue with the last part, and I knew there was no point in arguing the rest. My dad, always staunchly religious and stubborn to a fault, used to dealing with faculty and theology students, would never ever see it our way. His beliefs only stretched so far.

He wasn't like us, and he never would be.

I suppose there had to be one clinically sane person in my family.

So that was that. I was certain my father was going to call

the cops on us anyway, because that was his duty as a citizen of this country, but my mother was sweet-talking him, and he seemed to at least calm down a bit.

He and my mother left, while Ada hovered anxiously near the door, flapping her arms from time to time like a nervous bird.

"Is that what really happened?" she asked us, her large eyes pleading for the truth and fearing it at the same time.

"What happened with you?" I asked, throwing it back to her, to something safer.

"Mom and I ran. I don't know where we went, we weren't even thinking. We ended up by Central Park, and finally I had the smarts to think about trying my phone. We called Dad. He was livid. We had been gone all day. Hours passed inside that house, not minutes."

"And what did you tell him?" I asked.

"I barely got a chance to say anything," Ada said, hugging herself. "Mom told him we needed his help, but when he wanted her to explain, she wouldn't. Well, actually she tried. I believe she said the house was pure evil, but that's when he totally shut her down." She gave me a curious look. "Mom knows, Perry. She *knows*."

Yes, she does. No thanks to me and my pill switching. I was going to have to come clean about that.

Suddenly she sucked in her breath and her jaw started to tremble. "Is he really gone?"

Dex looked at me, and together we shared an image of him lying, gored and motionless on the floors of Hell. He nodded, swallowing. "Yes. He's gone."

Her face crumpled for a moment, and I was about to get up and go to her, but she shot her arms straight out to the sides, like she was going to take flight and announced, "I'm okay. I'm okay." She blinked, gasping for breath, and then stilled. "You couldn't have gone back for him?"

I gave her a weak smile. "I thought about it. But the only reason why I could save Dex was because he's, well, you know. Special. Like I am. Like you are. Even more so. And his body, his physical body, it can handle things that most people can't. He could handle the return. Maximus ... he wouldn't have, even if he could cross over. I wish I could have though. I know he went to Hell for someone once. It would have been nice to return the favor."

She came over and sat down on the corner of the bed, running her hands over the pink and white embroidered quilt.

"What was dying like?" she asked quietly, as if she were ashamed to ask, afraid that Dex would get mad.

But he didn't. He gave her a soft, lopsided grin. "At first, it sucks. But I don't think that's death itself. That's just dying. That's knowing this is the end. Being scared. Being in pain. Being afraid to leave. That sucks balls." He paused and took in a deep breath, staring up at the ceiling. "But death, when it takes over, when you are gone ... it's not so bad. Think about staring into a summer sun, sliding down toward sunset. It's blinding and it's gold and you can't look away. It's a warm place."

"Did you see God?"

He let out a little laugh, something I didn't think either of us was capable of.

"God? No. I didn't see God, Little Fifteen. But if it makes sense to you, I know God saw me." He looked down at his hands and nodded to himself. "Maximus is in a good place. Unfortunately, that doesn't mean we are. The ones who are left behind."

After that, Ada left. I could tell she wanted to stay with

us, that she didn't want to go to a room with her parents. But she didn't have the courage to ask, and I didn't have the heart to ask her to stay.

I needed to be alone with Dex more than anything else in the world.

Once the door closed behind her, I got up and flipped the privacy lock on. I turned, leaning against the door, and stared at him.

I just stared at him. I needed to take him in, here, alive and sharing the same air as me.

Memories of his loss tried to crawl up my throat, tearing away my happiness. I wouldn't let it. He was here now and that's all that had to matter.

He stared right back at me, and I don't think I've ever seen him more handsome. I probably shouldn't have. He hadn't shaved for days, there were circles under his eyes, and he was as pale as a ghost. He looked like a man who had died and come back, to put it mildly.

But he was Dex Foray through and through, and life looked good on him. He was practically shining with it.

"While you're standing there staring at me," he said, "let me assure you that I'm alive."

"I know," I said, my voice soft, as if I would shatter this all if I spoke too loud. "I just need to look at you."

"Then keep looking, kiddo," he said. My heart may have melted like a pat of butter on hot bread. "Because I'm looking at you. I don't think I could ever stop."

But then he abruptly turned his head, and his gaze went to the window. He looked troubled. I couldn't blame him, but there was something about it that got my guts in a knot.

"Before things go any further," he said, his words careful, "there is something I need to talk to you about."

I stuck out my lower lip in thought. What was there to

talk about? But it didn't really matter. When faced with death, it seemed like nothing else could ever matter but having that person back. Everything else seemed trivial.

"I assure you, it's not trivial," he said, immediately chagrined. "Sorry, I didn't mean to hear that. But I did. It's important, Perry. It's something I should have told you a long time ago."

Suddenly, I didn't want to hear it, whatever it was. I crossed my arms, wishing he would shut up, wishing I could go back to just soaking up his company. "If you should have told me a long time ago, maybe it's best to just forget it."

"I can't," he said. "I don't want any secrets between us, not anymore. Not after that. Life is too fucking short, you know it."

Secrets? God, now he had my attention in the worst way. That knot in my gut tightened. I had no idea at all what he was going to say, but whatever it was, it was going to throw me for a loop.

"Please, Dex," I said. "Not now."

He finally turned his head to look at me. "I'm sorry. It will have to come up soon, before we are married. It's only fair."

"Then tell me in a few weeks," I pleaded. "You just *died*. You were just in Hell. I was too. Maximus is fucking *dead*. It can wait."

For a moment I thought he was going to relent. But would it have been so easy for me to just ignore it, to go on knowing there was something he was keeping from me? It would sneak back. It would make me second guess everything.

He didn't relent. "I'm just going to come out and say it. And fuck, I wish that big Ginger was here because I am sure he could explain it better than me. But, back when we were in New Orleans and I found out all about Maximus and what he had been to me ... I was given something else to grapple with. And the truth is, I'm still grappling with it, because I don't know what it means."

I raised a brow, feeling shaky. "Okay. Then what is it?"

He patted the space beside me. "Sit down." Then he held out his hand. "No, stay there. You can do less damage from far away. I don't trust your knee anywhere near my nuts anymore."

If the whole situation hadn't been so ludicrously important, terrible *and* sad, I would have laughed. As it was, I didn't. "Dex, what the hell is it? This isn't funny."

He sighed. "No, it's not." He rubbed at his forehead vigorously and said, "When I was in NOLA, Maximus and the fucking Mambo told me that you and I were doomed to be together."

I coughed, trying to speak and laugh at the same time. "Excuse me? Doomed?"

Of course, that made perfect sense considering the last twenty-four hours.

"Doomed," he repeated. "But especially so if you were to ever get pregnant."

Oh. *Oh.*

"What? What does that even mean?" I slowly stepped toward him.

He looked up at me, kneading his legs with his palms. "I don't know. I really don't. I don't even know if they know. They just said—well, Mambo Maryse said—that because I am the way I am and you are the way you are, a baby could be a problem. It kind of was before."

"Dex," I said sternly, "I had a miscarriage. The baby never became anything. That, that *demon*, took advantage of me because of my physical and emotional state. That's all."

He raised a brow. "Is that all? Even a miscarriage is horrible, Perry."

"You don't have to fucking tell me that," I snapped. I exhaled noisily, trying to calm down. "Sorry. I just...I don't care what people say."

He held my eyes. "They said it could bring harm to us or to others."

I shrugged. "Nope. No. Don't care, Dex. I really don't care. Is this something that you want? Do you want to have a child? Not right now, but at some point?"

He smiled, and it lit up his whole face. "Of course I do. Baby, I want that more than anything."

"Then who cares what people say," I said. I sat down beside him and grabbed his jittery hands. "Who cares what they think could happen? I'm not going to go through all of that—my dreams, my future life, and throw it away because of theories and speculations."

He kissed my shoulder and closed his eyes. "But what if it's true?"

"If it's true," I said, brushing his hair off his forehead, "and we have a child burdened with our so-called gifts, or we have the anti-Christ, then we'll deal with it. But only when it comes. Life is so fucking precious, Dex, we know this better than anyone now. We shouldn't throw it away on hearsay."

He looked up at me, strain coloring his face. "But what if it hurts you? What if you're the one who suffers? What if I lose you?"

"After all we've been through," I said, kissing him lightly on the cheek, "you should know that I will fight to stay with you, no matter what. Losing me will not be easy. Like it or not."

"You're not angry at me?" he asked. "For keeping it a secret, for not telling you?"

"Oh, I'm angry," I told him. "But this is getting suppressed for now. We've been through more than enough to have a fight over it right now." I paused. "I'm sure it will come out sometime after we are married."

"Typical Perry," he commented with a shake of his head. Then he grinned and cupped my face in his hands. "And that's why I love you."

Then he kissed me like he was a dying man all over again, gasping for the breath I held within me. Only I felt like I was dying too. His lips revitalized me. His touch kept me whole, kept me together. He let his fingers sink into my hair, stroking down the back of my head, holding on to the back of my neck. I loved it when he did that. Strong and meaningful, like he meant to protect me more than possess me. Like I was his but he was mine, and we would keep each other safe. I knew, deep in every part of me, how literal that was. We really would do anything for each other.

I stripped down to nothing in seconds and pulled his pants and shirt off just as quickly. We had gotten getting naked down to an art, all fast, smooth moves.

His lips trailed down my neck, and we lay back in the bed while he stroked me lightly with his fingers, my legs parting, wanting him, needing him. But there was too much distance. I needed to have all of him in me.

I sat up and, with one hand on his chest, held him down as I straddled him. I was already wet and throbbing and ready as I lifted up enough to guide him inside of me. I slowly rocked back and forth, building up hotter, faster, and making sure I rode him until he couldn't hold back anymore. I bit at his neck and earlobes and licked his chest, and when he asked me to bite harder, to make sure he was still alive, I did just that.

He sat up so that our legs were wrapped around each other, one arm around my waist, holding me to him. He brought his thumb to my clit and started rubbing me while I swiveled up and down on his cock, getting him in deeper and deeper.

I stared deep in his eyes as they changed from bright and manic to lustful and glazed. We never broke contact. We couldn't look away from each other until we came, and my thunderous orgasm made my eyes roll back. He filled me up, and I was overcome with his cries, feeling everything pulse inside me. I was whimpering, awash in emotions that seemed to gush from my heart, and then the whimpering turned into shaking, and I couldn't hold myself up anymore. I couldn't do anything but feel love.

So much love.

Afterward, I lay in his arms and we discussed our future. What we were going to do. The wedding seemed like a dream that would never come, but it was real. Maximus's death made every breath of life seem more precious. We needed to embrace it, plan for it, make the best of it.

"And then, after the wedding," he said, stroking my hair with gentle fingers, "what do you want to do?"

"Honeymoon," I said with a shrug. "Not sure where yet."

"But after the honeymoon," he said. "What is next for us? If Experiment in Terror is no more, what will we do with ourselves? We have enough money to figure things out up until the wedding, but after that..."

I stared up at the ceiling, feeling myself bob on that dreamy wave between sex and sleep. "We can do anything we want."

"We'll just know it when we see it," he supplied.

"I think so." I turned my head to look at him. "Doesn't that sound good? The freedom, the possibilities?"

He smiled softly. "There is nothing that sounds better."

"Of course, you're brilliant at what you do. Music, cinematography, editing. Whatever it is, it will have to involve that."

"And you?"

I shrugged. "I'll find myself. I'll figure it out. I have no doubts, not anymore."

"And the paranormal shit?"

I shuddered. It was too close, too much, too soon.

He went on. "I only bring it up because before you had mentioned helping people that way. You know, like a medium, like the Warrens, that couple in the seventies who cleared houses. Instead of chasing ghosts, you're helping people. I bet as time goes by, we could learn to communicate with the dead better."

I sighed and closed my eyes. I had brought that up before. I had always wanted to use my abilities to help people instead of hiding from them. They were never going away, the ghosts would never really stop.

"It would take time," he said, "over the years to learn how to speak to them without fear, to know what they want, instead of always running away. I'm not saying this should be our job, but if that's something you want to explore in the future, then I'm game."

I smiled and kissed his chest. "Thank you. I do like the idea of trying to use our skills to help, as scary as it all may be. But since this damn gift of ours isn't going away anytime soon, I think I'll file that away on the future to-do list." I made the motion of putting imaginary papers away. "*To do* in five years. Talk to ghosts instead of screaming at them.

Open a paranormal investigation branch. Wear fedoras and have a secretary named Babs."

"Can Babs be hot?"

"When *isn't* Babs hot?"

He grinned. "You know what, kiddo? I like our future. No, I love our future."

I laced my fingers into his and held on tight. "I love it, too."

I DREAMED AGAIN that Dex had died. But when I woke up, covered in sweat, I rolled over and grabbed a hold of his arm. He was alive. He murmured to me in his sleep, words that didn't make sense, as usual. In the faint light from the streets, I could see him smile too, as if he was trying to soothe me.

It worked. I nestled into the crook of his arm, and the dream never came back.

## 17

DEX

When I first saw the gangly douchefucker, I was in university, leaving my editing class, and he was being one nosey son of a bitch. He knew who I was, somehow, and he was eager to join my band Sin Sing Sinatra as a bassist. I guess I must have been incredibly stupid to not see how odd it was that Maximus just showed up in my life like that, but I had also been very good at the art of denial.

I was also good at the art of keeping people away from me. No one could get close, especially not giant gingers. But somehow, that guy, he got in. He became important in every aspect of my life. Looking back, I can see it was a ruse. At least, it started out that way. But somewhere along the line, Maximus stopped being a guide and started being a friend. I don't even think he got to give me guidance in any way except for what chicks to bang and what beer to drink.

And, until I banged his chick, that was the way it was for us. We were friends. Close friends. Maybe not so close that I would confide in him and tell him that I saw ghosts, and that he would confide in me and pretty much tell me he was a ghost. But other than that, we were close. He was the closest person to me.

When I lost him, when I was put away in the mental institute, it was bad. But I recovered. I had my own self to fix, and I had faith that he was getting on with his life somewhere. Well, actually, I hated him at that point and wished him a bad case of dick rot. How dare he desert me during my time of need?

Now, I can see why he did it. We were both to blame. Maximus let his pettiness and jealousy get the better of him, and I fucked him over, breaking our hard-earned bro code like it was police tape. Which was something I also liked to break a lot of at the time.

But now, now things were different. When Maximus came back into my life, sitting at that bar in Red Fox, he threw a wrench into the carefully orchestrated play I was holding. He was like Dorothy, pulling back that damn curtain and showing the world the man behind the show. I wanted Perry to keep thinking I was the all-powerful Oz. I didn't want someone from my past to come along and show her that I was nothing like who I was pretending to be.

That's what he did, though. On purpose, I'm sure, and also there are just some parts of you that are really fucking hard to hide. Perry eventually saw the real me. And she fell in love with the real me. And if it wasn't for Maximus exposing me for what I was, who I was, who knows if that would have happened.

There was a lot of wrong that Maximus did, but in the end, I couldn't fault him. For all of his shortcomings, he was never malicious. He was just an ex-immortal, struggling with the rest of us over what it meant to be human.

Now, Maximus was dead. Dead forever, dead for good, dead in the ways that the old him could never even have imagined. And though we'd never really grown that close again, though I'd come up with a million nicknames for his freckled ass and he'd done some shit that had royally pissed me off, losing him hurt.

More than that, it shocked me. I'd seen enough death in my day, but it never got easier. Maximus gave up his life so that Perry could get me back. In the end, he was a guardian. I just wished I had a chance to thank him for it.

But that's why we were standing along the East River, staring at the murky water as it slowly moved past. This was our chance to say goodbye.

I looked down the row of us, at Perry, holding my hand beside me, the wind making her hair move like a black silk flag, at Ada beside her, all bleached blonde innocence gone wrong, at their mother, who was standing so straight and strong, it was hard to believe she had gone through what she had with us, and of course her father, balding and portly, wearing a scowl on his face that said he'd rather be elsewhere and thought we were all still tripping on acid.

He could believe what he wanted. It made no difference to me.

Perry looked up at me. "Do you want to start it off?" she asked. She was holding a handful of yellow roses we purchased from a streetside vendor. Roses, for Rose. That was a phone call we hadn't wanted to make but Perry had the balls to do it that morning. Somehow she tracked her down by calling the bar she owned in New Orleans. The moment I heard Rose bawling over the speaker, I had to leave the room. I couldn't deal with the pain again.

I nodded and cleared my throat. Unlike everything I was just thinking, I was going to keep this short. Maximus would have probably appreciated it, and it would definitely prevent me from crying again.

"Maximus was a man of many faces," I said, feeling both honest and self-conscious. "Most of them aggravatingly handsome." I noticed Perry's dad looking at me oddly, and I shrugged. "It was annoying, actually, having his mug around me all the time. He could make me look bad just by showing up. He was always just so … much better than me. Better than everyone. And he didn't even try. He just was. He was strong, he was funny in his backward southern way, he was smart, again in his backward southern way."

"Is this a funeral or a roast?" Daniel asked, as if he cared.

I ignored him. "I can laugh about all of that, because it was true and that's the way he was to me. We made fun of each other constantly, because we could. He was a good man, you know. For all the shit we gave each other, he was loyal. Even when he wasn't, he still was. And he'd watch out for you. He cared. That was probably the thing that bugged me the most, and that's what stands out when I think about Ginger Balls."

Perry made a tsking sound beside me, her mouth turned down, but I couldn't help it. "What, it's true!" I protested. "He cared more than anyone. So I can give him a nickname in death. It doesn't mean he wasn't a heck of a guy, a heck of a friend. He was all of those and a bunch of other things that I can't even begin to be."

And now I started to choke up. I sucked in my breath, trying not to blink as the hammer chipped away at my chest. "He fought for so long to just be normal, normal like me. I wish I could have told him that normal didn't exist. He was fighting for something that wasn't real. But in that fight he found me as a friend, he found Perry as a friend, he found his girlfriend, Rose. He found her once, and he found her again. How fucking lucky is that? Well, that's Max for you.

And I know there was so much more to him. We just saw the tip of the iceberg and now the whole thing has gone to shit."

I sighed, hard. "I just wish he didn't have to do that for me. But I'm fucking grateful that he did. So fucking grateful." I squeezed Perry's hand then took a fistful of petals from the flowers she was holding and ripped them off the stem, throwing them into the river. Half of them floated in the breeze, landing at our feet. "Here's to you, big guy. Please, feel free to haunt me anytime."

Ada and her mother said "Amen," like it was the Lord's Prayer, while Perry was staring at me, perplexed, like it was the weirdest eulogy she'd ever heard. Or maybe it was the way I beheaded half the bouquet.

She stepped up to the bank next, gathering the few nice stems left in one hand. "Maximus, I don't have much to say. I ... I don't even know what to say. But, you came into my life for a reason, and I couldn't be more grateful."

"Don't say grateful," I said out of the side of my mouth, my hands clasped in front of me. "I just used grateful. Pick a different word."

She looked at me, aghast. "This isn't funny, Dex," she said.

I shot her a sad smile. "I know it's not. But I need it to be. Just for now, just to get through it."

She shook her head, not understanding, and went on. "So I wanted to thank you, Maximus, for being a friend. For being that guy I wanted to call when everything went wrong. For showing up and helping me. For looking out for Dex. Sometimes I was never quite sure about you, but I was always sure about you and Dex. You were friends, even when you weren't, and I want to thank you for that. I hope wherever you are, it's a warm place." She sniffed and wiped away a tear. "I hope that it's nice, and that you'll one day be with Rose again. I hope I'll see you too."

She closed her eyes and a wash of tears spilled down her cheeks as she threw her flowers in the river. I put my arm around her, holding her close to me.

Ada took the flowers next and gave half to her mother.

"Maximus," she said. "I'm gonna miss you. I never thought I'd find a ginger with a soul, but you proved that wrong." She kissed her fingers and then pressed them into the sky. "Peace out, ginger bro."

She threw her flowers in and so did Perry's mom, who said a simple, "Thank you," and that was that. Daniel, of course, was standing in a wide-legged stance, arms folded across his belly. The interesting thing was he was starting to sweat a little. There was a tinge of "Oh shit, maybe these bitches weren't tripping" on his brow, of course phrased in a theological way.

But ever the master of the house and of the smooth moves, he covered it up and said, "Well, now that that's all done, who is up for a visit to MOMA and then some lunch?"

Yes, because nothing tops off a funeral like looking at abstract art.

Ingrid put her arm around Ada and said, "I think that would be a good idea. Good way to keep busy. Right, Ada?"

Ada just shrugged. They could have suggested an all-expenses paid shopping spree and she still would have looked the same.

"What about you?" Daniel asked.

I looked to Perry, who was red-eyed and dabbing her cute little nose with a tissue. "Um," I said, "I think we'll pass on that."

"Wait," Perry said, turning to them. "Can we go eat first? Then you guys can go to MOMA."

"What are you going to do?" Ada asked, like she wanted an invite.

Actually, I had no idea what Perry had in mind, but I was suddenly hit by a crazy idea, brought on by all the sorrow and shit that was swirling around us.

She shrugged. "I think we just want to hang low," she said. "But if we all ate first, it would give us a chance to talk." She said that as she stared at her mom, sending signals that looked to be invisible but probably weren't. Interestingly, I tried to drop in on her thoughts, but I couldn't access them. Perry was learning how to aim and hide at the same time. There had to be a sexual analogy somewhere in there.

Her mom nodded, hearing her loud and clear. "Of course. That sounds good."

Daniel let out a puff of air, annoyed that no one was really listening to him anymore. *Good luck steering your brood of loons around*, I wanted to say to him. Especially as I would soon be included in that brood.

Poor guy.

WE HAD lunch at the café that was made famous in *When Harry Met Sally*. I couldn't remember the film all that well, but Perry's mom did a minor—and yet embarrassing—re-enactment of the "I'll have what she's having" scene and all that it involved. Thankfully the place had a fuckton of pie. Pie was awesome.

At some point during our meal, Perry and her mom both simultaneously excused themselves and went outside. Again, she must have been sending her telepathic messages that I couldn't pick up on. I knew what they were talking about, though. Perry was coming clean about switching her mother's pills on her.

I didn't know how I felt about that. I understand why Perry did it, but since I had been on the receiving end of that at one point, I also sympathized with her mother. There is nothing worse than seeing the carefully planned and crafted world you had created for yourself come tumbling down and you can't figure out why.

But judging by the way they were hugging out on the street, it seemed to go all right. I suppose after everything, her mom was just happy to be alive, and happy to have her daughter. I still wasn't too sure how she felt about her future son-in-law.

"So," her mother said as they came back inside, "we should get going." She clapped her hands together and smiled, and it was then that I realized she looked like she belonged in that god-awful Disney movie, *Frozen*. Not that she looked like a talking snowman, more like the blonde snow queen.

Beside me, Ada let out a small groan. I had been listening to Daniel talk about all the things wrong with New York and I hadn't been watching her. She got up to her feet and ran toward the bathroom, looking like she was about to barf.

"What's wrong with her?" Perry asked.

"I don't know," I said, eyeing Daniel. "She seemed fine."

"She probably had bad pie," he said.

I frowned. "There is no such thing as bad pie."

Minutes later she came back out, paler than normal but looking bright-eyed. "I'm okay," she said sheepishly. "Sorry, I just felt nauseous."

"It's all the stress, honey," her mom said. "We can go another time."

"No," she said, slinging her designer backpack on. "I'm all good. Totally. Let's go." She looked at us. "Are you guys sure you don't want to come?"

Perry nodded and offered her a kind look. "Thank you, but we'd rather be alone."

Ada nodded, understanding. "All right, me and the rents it is."

They left the restaurant, and after we got coffees to go, we followed.

"Think they'll be all right?" Perry asked as we stood outside the shop. The air was still stinky and as hot as a wet sauna, but I couldn't complain. I was alive.

"Don't see why not," I said, but even as I said it, it felt weird. Like I was jinxing things. But I didn't know how.

Perry appeared to be satisfied with that, though I knew she'd worry about it in the back of her brain. "So what do you want to do?"

She looked at me as if I was automatically going to suggest sex, but that, for once, wasn't what I had in mind. Not now, anyway.

"You were at the hall of records the other day, right?" I asked.

She cocked her head, appraising me. "Yeah. Why?"

"Did you find out anything about my father?"

"Your father? No. No, we searched for your mother." She paused. "Why?"

I tried to shrug it off like it was no big deal, but it really was. "No real reason. I guess, I just thought while I'm here, I'd try and track him down."

"Are you serious?"

I nodded. "I know it seems ridiculous considering he's a bastard that up and left me. And yeah, I kind of want to punch the guy in the teeth. But if he's here, I want to see him. And yes, possibly punch him in the teeth. At least step on his foot or leave flaming doggy-doo on his doorstep."

"Dex," she said in a warning tone, "are you sure about this? I mean, I know you have gone through the most traumatic event that anyone can go through, but I don't know if that means you should start contacting everyone you know."

I gave her a look, reminding myself to stay patient with her. "No offense, kiddo, but you don't understand. You have a dad. He's stuck by you, even though he can be a little Don Corleone at times. I never had that. No DeNiro, no Brando. I had nothing. If I have the chance to find him, get some closure, I want to take it."

She nodded and put her arms around my waist, pressing against me. "I understand. And I don't mean to be inconsiderate and shit. I just don't want you to get your hopes up. And I don't want you to get hurt. I will kill the next person who hurts you, I swear."

"I know you will, baby," I said, pulling her even closer and laying a hard kiss on the top of her head. "That's one of the many, crazy reasons why I love you."

It was hard to break the connection and warmth our lips were giving each other—something about the last few days made me feel like I was falling, tumbling, in love with her all over again.

She smiled up at me, sweet as sugar, and said, "You have my support, no matter what. If you want to go find him, then we'll try and find him." A devious glint came into her eyes. "Just don't forget I have ninja moves."

I held on to her hand, and together we walked down the street, heading to the nearest subway station.

"Hey," I said, "how did it go with your mom? I saw you guys hugging but wasn't too sure what that was about."

"You couldn't hear the thoughts I was sending?" she asked rather innocently.

I shook my head.

She grinned, pleased with herself. Then the ends of her smile turned down. After a pause she said, "I just told her the truth. About why she was seeing things. How I found her pills."

"Was she mad?"

"Yeah. She was. But more hurt, I think." Her eyes darted to me sheepishly. "Anyway, she understood. She said she was glad I did it. That it got her to see what she'd been missing. Obviously, none of what she's been seeing has been very pretty. I don't know if she can see everything we can. I mean, she can see major things. Everything that happened in the house, she knows it. But she hasn't been visited by any ghosts."

"Well, that's good."

"Yeah," she said, swinging our arms in the air for a few steps. "It's good. I just hope it doesn't get worse, you know? I don't wish our ... *problem* on anyone. I know my mom has kind of been horrible these last few years, but she's still my mom. I still love her."

I nodded. Oh, I knew how that went. No matter how badly they treat us, no matter how much we fear them, they are still our mothers. We love them despite all that. We hurt despite all that. It really fucking sucks.

"So," she continued, trying to keep her voice light. I could tell she was close to crying. I didn't mind if she did, she had a lot to let out. We both did. She cleared her throat. "I am really sorry I switched the pills, but I don't regret it. Does that make sense?" When I told her it did, she said, "For you, too. It made you move in a certain direction, made *us* move in a certain direction."

"It brought us together," I told her matter-of-factly.

"And I think it will do the same for my mom and me. She's already different around me, you know? I think … I think maybe she'll finally really get to be my mom. I'll feel like I have a mother that loves me. Not to say she didn't before, but you know how different it is when you *feel* it."

I did. And I only knew it for a brief moment, in that last dream my own mother was in. But it was enough.

After that, we walked like any couple in New York, stopping for hot dogs and complaining about the heat and stink while taking in the sights. Okay, maybe we were like any tourist couple in New York, but that was fine with me. Seattle was my home now—our home—and I was content to see this city briefly before saying goodbye. I couldn't say I ever wanted to return. My memories here only worsened. It wasn't just the place where my life went to shit … it's where my new life went to shit as well.

But we were going to come out of it, like a fucking Phoenix rising out of the ashes. Or at least like Phoenix in *X-Men*. She was hot as fuck and a badass motherfucker.

We didn't even make it as far as City Hall, though. We stopped into a trendy coffee shop for yet another hit of espresso since both of us were having trouble keeping our eyes open. I guess after being so close to death we wanted our hearts to beat into oblivion. Perry sat down at one of the iPads they had at their tables.

It only took her about five minutes of searching the net while I was in the bathroom taking a leak for her to locate my father.

When I got back to the table, she was wriggling in her seat like a puppy, like she was about to lead me to a boy trapped in a well.

"What is it, Lassie?" I asked.

"I found him," she said excitedly.

I don't know what expression came over my face. Probably fear.

"Timmy O' Toole?"

"No," she said, holding up a napkin with writing scribbled on it. "Your father. He's in Queens."

I tugged at my eyebrow ring. "Interesting. Are you sure?"

"Dex," she huffed out in annoyance, getting to her feet. "You're the one who wanted to hunt him down. Well, we hunted him. Or I did. He's in Queens. First, I found him in the paper for winning a regatta off of Long Island. Then I traced him through the online phone book. He looks, well, he looks like you, Dex. Or at least how you'll look when you're older. Do you want to see?"

I didn't think she could tell any better than I could about whether the guy looked like my father or not, but before I could say anything, she was pulling an article up on the iPad.

And there was a picture of Curtis O'Shea. My father. He hadn't even bothered to change his name.

I frowned, trying to feel something between me and the pixelated face staring from the screen. I don't know if I felt anything, though I had to say there was some resemblance between me and him. And more than that, well, it was him. I may have been a teenager when he left, but he was in his forties. Now he was in his sixties, and the aging process had been kind to him.

He had salt and pepper hair, but it was still thick, and he wore it parted on the side. His face looked saggy, but his eyes were dark and sharp, framed by impressive eyebrows. He could have given Jack Nicholson a run for his money.

It was my dad.

*My dad.*

I rubbed my lips together and looked away. Okay, maybe this wasn't a good idea right now.

"Hey," Perry said, hand on my forearm. "Let's just forget about it. You know he's alive. He's out there. And if you want to say hello one day, you have that option. But you don't owe him, or me, or yourself, anything."

I nodded and sighed. I knew all of that. "Let's do it."

She studied me for a moment, perhaps trying to figure out if I was in fact Dex Foray and not someone else. I couldn't blame her.

"Let's do it," I repeated, putting my hand on her shoulder and squeezing it. "Let's go meet my dad."

She gave me a small but supportive smile and nodded her head. We left without talking, the air heavy around us as we navigated the subway system that I still knew like the back of my hand. The closer we got to Queens the more she started to wriggle around again. It was so fucking cute. I would have banged her in the nearest disgusting washroom if we weren't about to find my father.

It wasn't long until we were walking down the street that she had mapped out for us. It was a nice neighborhood. Not as posh as the one on the Upper East Side, but it was one of the nicer ones in Queens and the townhouses and duplexes would have fetched a lot of money.

It was a workday so I wasn't completely sure if we'd find him at home, or if he even had a job. The newspaper article didn't say much except he had a boat and was an avid sailor. I know I wanted to find him, to see him, to make some sort of amends for things that weren't my fault, but I wasn't about to go hunt his saggy ass down at an office or anything like that. I would give, I would put in effort, but at a certain point I stopped. There were only a few people who I'd give all for and they weren't my father.

"This is it," Perry said as we stopped in front of a brownstone. In some ways it looked like the one I grew up in but for the most part it was different. The ceilings were shorter, giving the house a crouched appearance even with two levels and there seemed to be an expansive side yard. There were a bunch of flowers in the front, carefully arranged into terracotta pots. I wondered if my father had a green thumb – my memories pulled up that he did – or if he had remarried.

Shitballs, he might have had a whole new family, a new son, a new life.

"Maybe this was a mistake," I said to Perry just as the front door opened and a woman stepped out. She had grey hair piled into a bun and was wearing a Native American print poncho, jeans and Crocs.

"Are you Charles?" she asked in a very Katherine Hepburn accent, all nasally and raised chin.

"Uh, no," I said, looking at Perry for reassurance, as if she was going to tell me that I wasn't Charles. "We're looking for Curtis O'Shea, though." I said. Saying his name out loud kind of felt like saying Bettlejuice.

But as far as I knew, my father was not going to appear as Michael Keaton in a black and white suit. Though, knowing my family, I wouldn't hold anything past us.

"Oh," she said with a raised brow, looking us over. Well, she was wearing Crocs so she couldn't talk. "Who might you be? We aren't expecting anyone but Charles. He's our new nurse. Or caretaker, as Curtis insists we call him."

Nurse? I wondered what was wrong with him.

While I pondered that, Perry spoke for me. "We're... interested in his boat."

Okay, that wasn't exactly what I would have said but I went with it. It's not like we came up with coherent plan on the way here.

She nodded, her eyes lighting up. "Oh, goody. That's wonderful. Stay there and I'll go get him."

She disappeared into the house and as soon as she was out of earshot I turned to Perry.

"Interested in his boat?"

Her lip snarled defensively. "Well we couldn't quite say that you were his long lost son." She looked around her. "They are in a nice neighborhood, they have money. People always think the worst before they think the best."

She had a point and soon after, a man appeared at the door in a wheelchair, shadowed by the doorframe. The woman appeared beside him. "You can come up here. The ramp is at the side of the house but if this won't take long..."

I raised a palm. "That's fine," I said, smiling even though some small part of me, maybe my toe, felt bad for the fucker already. I grabbed Perry's hand and we walked up toward the front door.

And there, in a wheelchair, staring at me with begrudged curiosity, was my father. He didn't look as happy as the woman had seemed and I assumed that whatever business there was to be done about the boat, well it pleased her more than it did him.

"I'm Curtis," the man said and his Irish accent still lingered. It brought back a lot of memories. Most of them uncomfortable but some of them, a few of them, good.

Suddenly, I couldn't speak. I couldn't say anything at all. I was standing in front of my father, the man who had abandoned me all those years ago, left me with my mother and a nanny but with no wages to pay a nanny. He fucked off and he ruined everything – or at least he didn't help. Over the years I had come to realize that everyone was at fault, not just him. Still, even facing him in his wheelchair, all these years later, I couldn't help but think of him as a coward.

I vowed right there and then to never do that to my child, no matter if he saw ghosts, was as normal as apple pie, or happened to be the anti-Christ. There was love and there was pride and the former should always trump the latter.

"My name is Dex," I said, and I swear I saw his brow raise for a minute. He reminded me a lot of Gregory Peck, all overgrown black eyebrows and silver-coated hair. "This is Perry, my fiancé," I said, motioning to her. She smiled sweetly and I knew it warmed him over just a bit. Despite what she thought, she had that effect on people. She counteracted me in the best way.

"Very nice to meet you," he said with a sharp nod, though his eyes were focused on me. He looked like he was trying to jog his memory, perhaps trying to place my name or my face and was coming up empty. "So you're interested in buying Green Glass, is that it?"

That must have been the boat's name. I figured we only had a finite amount of time before we had to come clean.

"Could you answer a few questions about her?" I asked, without saying yes or no.

He nodded and his palms kneaded the armrest of his chair. "Why not?"

"I read in the paper that you won a regatta. Has the boat won anything else besides that?"

He grinned, just for a moment. He had nice teeth. I guess the rich could afford that. Then again, I had nice teeth because of the settlement he left me through my mother, so I shut that thought up.

"That was a good ol' fluke," he said. "My buddies and I, we're always racing off of Nantucket, Martha's, all the haunts. I decided to go for it, you know, have a laugh or two. I took my buddy on as my skipper since I can't do much with this damn arthritis and all. Somehow we won. But, if you paid attention to the ad, I never passed the ship off as a racing boat. We were just lucky."

"Arthritis?" I asked and his face immediately went sharp.

"Yes," he said defensively. "Plus I had an accident a few years ago. I don't let that stop me from doing things though."

"That lady," Perry said, "is she your wife?"

He nodded. "Aye. Margaret. Been married about…"

While he trailed off I said, "at least fifteen years."

He frowned but said, "That seems about right."

"Were you married before her?" Perry asked and now I knew we were getting down to brass tacks.

"How is this relevant to the boat?" he asked, brow raised in such a way that it made Perry flinch. Not because he looked scary, but because he looked a lot like me. We were down to the wire now. Time to come clean before they called the cops.

"So Green Glass is for sale," I mused, combing my hand through my hair, trying not to appear anxious but failing. Half of me wanted to just turn around and pretend this never happened but I knew I couldn't do that. I needed this closure in some shape or form. I never got it while my mother was alive, I needed it with my father, especially after I knew what had happened to Michael.

"Yes it is," he said, eyes narrowed. "But my marriages have nothing to do with it."

I nodded. "I understand. The truth is, we actually don't want to buy your boat, Mr. O'Shea. I mean, I love sailboats and everything but I just don't think I'd buy one here, on the east coast. We live on the west coast."

"So you're wasting my time," he said gruffly, his hands going to wheel himself away.

"Maybe," I said, "maybe not. It's not a waste of my time. You see, if I had a boat, I'd probably call it Fat Rabbit. Or, maybe not. Maybe I'd call it Michael." He stiffened slightly. "Or Regine." Now his jaw was clenched. "Or Declan. But it's pretty lame naming a boat after yourself. I'm not Donald Trump."

I kept my eyes on him the whole time and I recognized that acquiescence in them. The way his chin dropped a bit, his shoulder slumped slightly. His eyes took on this weight, as if I had just demanded the world from him. But that wasn't the case at all.

"You're Curtis O'Shea," I said. "You're my father. And I don't want anything from you. Even though you fucked right off when I needed you most, you still made sure I was taken care of. And I was. I did good for myself, at least I think so. So don't worry. I'm not here to cause trouble or law suits or whatever you east coasters do with your time. I just wanted to see you, that's all. And I wanted to know you were alive. I wanted you to know I was alive. Simple."

He stared at me in disbelief for the longest time. I thought he might have had a stroke. But eventually he pulled himself out of his tailspin and blinked at me. "Declan," he said and he sounded just as I remembered, only less mad.

"That's me." And suddenly I felt my heart crumbling into tiny little pieces. Shit. That was unexpected. I looked away, trying to keep the water behind my eyes.

There was a swath of silence between us and in it, my emotions were building. "It is you," he said after a moment. "My god."

"Well, I'm not god," I quipped. "But Perry calls me that sometimes."

She stared at me like she was going to murder me but I didn't care. I smiled at him. "Sorry, she's used to it by now. And what can I say, I guess I'm just being a nervous pervous here. Honestly, I don't mean anything by this, I don't want anything from you. I just wanted to say hello. We'll be on our way."

I took Perry by the elbow and turned her around but my father cleared his throat and said, "Wait."

We turned to look at him and he managed a weak smile. "Wait," he repeated. "Don't go. There's a lot to…explain. Talk about. Margaret doesn't know, you see." The minute he said that, his face recoiled in panic, as if he instantly regretted it.

But I shrugged. "Don't worry about it. We aren't here to tell her anything. If you want to keep on like you've been keeping on, I can do the same. I'm an old pro." I know it wasn't exactly polite, but I was throwing passive digs in there whenever I could.

He nodded quickly. "Thank you," he said. "I made some mistakes in my past." He smiled unsurely at me. "Not you, Declan. Not those kind of mistakes. Other kinds. There's a lot I would rather forget. But, not you. There hasn't been a day that I haven't thought about you." He paused and then added like an afterthought. "Or Michael."

For the first time, I was able to see my parents talk about Michael and his reality. My father said his name like he was scared. All this time I thought I was the one they didn't want. All this time I had beating myself up.

"When I heard about Regine," he said quietly, looking at the flowers along the stoop, "I wanted to reach out, to say something. But I was afraid. I didn't know how I'd handle you boys. I didn't know if I would ruin things."

I knew what he meant to say – he didn't know if he would get in shit for abandoning his family.

I swallowed my grudge, for now, and gave him a sharp nod. "I understand," I said. "Well, I turned out okay."

"And Michael?"

"That's probably a conversation for another time," I told him. I looked at Perry. "We should go."

She nodded and gave my father – *my father* – a cautious smile. "It was nice meeting you."

As she walked down the steps, he called after her. "Wait, Perry you said your name was?" She nodded and he looked at me. "When are you getting married? You said she was your fiancé?"

"I don't know," I told him. "Sooner rather than later, I think."

He appeared to think that through. The more I stared at him, the more I was pulled back in time, to the life I once I had, the life I never wanted back. I couldn't quite forgive my father for what he had done – I could, would, never think or act like him. But at the same time, he wasn't to blame for everything. My mother and Michael, they would have ended up the same, I was sure of it. I would still have seen ghosts. It was just life and the shitty hand she throws you sometimes.

But was I ready to have him back in my life, in some form? That remained to be seen. The fact that I could take it or leave it was a fucking good thing.

"I'll send you an invite," I told him. "It's up to you if you want to come. It will be West Coast though, Seattle area." Perry and I had discussed at least that much.

He seemed to be happy with that, his face relaxing. I gave him a nod, not about to call him dad or be intimate with him in any sort of way, and jogged down the steps to Perry.

"It was nice meeting you," my father called after us, like an afterthought.

In unison Perry and I raised our hands. I waited until we were out of sight from the house before I let the tears fall from my eyes. I didn't regret a thing we had done, but all these years of believing you don't have a father do a number on you. I cried for the loss I had suffered and the falsity that he was still alive and enjoying life, for the anger that propelled me and compelled me day to day. And, truth be told, I'd always wanted my dad to look at me like he was proud of me, and despite seeing him today, that still hadn't happened.

But I didn't cry for long. I'm macho like that. A couple of manly tears fell and then Perry snapped me out of it with a wet kiss.

"Donald Trump has a boat named after him?" she asked, trying to lighten the mood.

I shrugged. "I don't know, he must. The Trump."

"Maybe it's You're Fired."

"Bad Combover III."

And we went on our way back to Manhattan, thinking of names for Donald Trump's non-existent boat. In the back of my heart, I felt a bit more whole than I had that morning.

## 18

PERRY

"Do you want to take a carriage ride?" Dex asked as we crossed through Central Park. "I could feed the horse a can of beans like in *Seinfeld*."

"And why would that be a good idea?"

He shrugged. "It would be funny. Funny is a good idea."

It seemed that the more Dex could laugh about things, the better he was dealing with Maximus's death. Of course, it probably helped that the meeting with his father went better than expected. Well, *I* thought it went better than expected. Curtis O'Shea seemed to be an old man with many regrets who, in the end, would only benefit from knowing his son. I didn't expect them to start calling each other or anything like that, but it was a good step and a good start, even if it never went anywhere.

I sighed. Suddenly I was hit with a tightness in my chest and I shut my eyes with a gasp.

Dex quickly grabbed my hand, over-concerned about everything now. "What's wrong? What is it?"

I shook my head, not sure why it was so hard to breathe.

"I just need to sit down." I walked over to the nearest tree and slumped down onto the ground, my back against the trunk.

Dex crouched beside me, holding onto my hand still. "Perry. Do I need to get help?"

I shook my head. It felt like a panic attack more than anything but I didn't really have much to panic about. Perhaps it was grief catching up to me.

"I'm okay," I said, still gasping. "It's just a –"

I was about to say panic attack when I screamed. I just screamed. There was a man in a suit standing just a few yards away in the meadow, his back to me. The suit was crisp, dark and his hair darker. His hands were cloven hooves.

My world twisted into tunnel vision and at the end of the tunnel the man turned around. I saw his face, the indescribable face of evil and suddenly sharp black fingers were reaching inside my brain. I felt them behind my eyes, in my lungs, pulling at my veins and arteries. It was in my gut, black, penetrating me with depravity and the cries of the meek and tortured.

I wasn't alone in my head. I was in a battle for my soul. I would not let it in, I would not let it win.

With what I could, I closed my eyes and concentrated, putting those walls up, imagining barbed wire and shards of broken glass around me, keeping the thing out. I created a Fort Knox in my soul, hard and sharp and unbreakable.

*Something softer*, the demented, raspy voice said in my head, a voice that burned at me like battery acid.

And then it was gone. I felt it leave my body, as if I had been giving it too much resistance and it finally gave up. Wanting something *softer*.

"Perry, fucking talk to me!" Dex was in my face, slapping my cheek lightly. I blinked, staring up at him, concentrating on a bead of sweat that was threatening to fall from the tip of his nose. "Talk to me!"

"I'm okay," I managed to say, trying to sit up. He helped me, his grip tight, one hand behind my head, holding me gently. There were people passing by, staring at me in concern. I shot them a quick smile, just in case they were about to call an ambulance.

"Perry," he murmured, resting his forehead against mine. "I thought I lost you."

I swallowed, that feeling coming back. The evil. Such evil.

"No," I said. I pulled back and stared at him. "Did you see him? The beast in the suit?"

"No..." he looked around.

"He came inside my head. Just for a moment. He left, I pushed him out. He's going after something softer."

He frowned and placed his palm on his head. "I would know if he got in. Look at me, he hasn't."

I was looking at him and I knew he was right. He'd already had Dex and now Dex was tougher than ever before.

But others weren't as strong as us. Others were softer.

"Ada!" I suddenly yelled, springing to my feet. "My mother!"

Dex nodded, wearing horror on his face. "Call them!" He threw his hands up in the air. "Fuck, we need a phone."

He spotted a couple walking arm in arm a few yards away and ran over to them. When it looked like they were agreeing, I booked it over, shooting them a grateful look.

"Thank you," I said to them, "it's a bit of an emergency." I took the phone and dialed my mom's phone, knowing she was most likely to answer.

My dad answered instead. "Daniel Palomino," he said.

"Dad!" I yelled.

"Perry? Whose number is this?"

"Dad, where is mom and Ada?"

"They're with me, why? Do you want to talk to your mother?" His voice began to break up and I heard a loud grinding noise in the background

"Where are you?" I asked, feeling like time was falling through my fingers.

"We're just about to get on the subway," he said, the crackles getting louder.

"Where are you going?" There was nothing, then he said something I could barely make out. "Dad!" I yelled. "Where are you going? What station?!"

The static grew stronger but I finally heard him say, "Fifty-Third and fifth."

"Okay, get off at that station and do not going anywhere. Do you hear me?"

More crackles. I thought my heart was going to explode. "Here, talk to your mom," he said. And then the phone went dead.

"Mom!" I yelled. "Dad!"

There was nothing. Reception was dropped. Oh god, how I prayed it was just the reception.

I handed the phone back to the bewildered couple without glancing at them. I had to get to my family. I started running across the park, going as fast as my legs would carry me. I heard Dex yell my name, then apologize to the couple and take off after me.

He was fast as anything and when he caught up, he didn't ask questions. He knew. If the demon was still around, he was weak. That's what Pippa had said. But he was still a threat. He could take over someone else and never come out again. Someone softer with less defenses. Someone who believed. Someone like us – Ada or my mother.

Dex and I ran through the park. Since we had been at the bottom end, it was faster to run through the streets instead of taking the subway. I don't think I could have stay still on the subway long enough. I needed to move, feeling like I getting somewhere, doing something.

Oh, please, please, please, please don't let them get hurt. Let them stay strong. After everything, I couldn't handle another blow to my life. More than that, I would never forgive myself.

We ran and ran and ran. We bowled over overladen shoppers, bumped into surly pedestrians. We ran through red lights, cars swerving to avoid us, honking their horns. We passed by restaurants and cafes and souvenir stores and carts full of fake handbags. If there was thing that we were good at, it was running for our lives. This time it was to save lives.

And the entire city of Manhattan carried on, like nothing was at stake.

We finally reached the station at 53$^{rd}$ and 5$^{th}$, sweaty but not out of breath. I felt like I could have run forever. We scrambled down the stairs, running past artwork in the tiled mezzanine and looked around. They weren't here. Maybe they were down below.

I fumbled for coins in my pockets, practically throwing them at the ticket booth person and then ran on through the turnstiles. Dex took me by the hand and we flew down the stairs to the upper level platform, going against the river of bodies coming back up.

Down below there was barely anyone waiting for the

train since the last one was just pulling away.

But there, at the other end, were my parents hunched over my sister who was lying on the ground, convulsing. A few bystanders were gathered around, one of them looking like they were trying to help.

"Shit!" I yelled and I took off down the platform, Dex at my side.

When we got there, I could see her face had a blue-ish tinge and her eyes had rolled back in her head. She was shaking, a man with glasses and a beard was trying to keep her head up and supported while my mother and father knelt beside her, trying to understand. My mother was crying.

"What happened?" I screeched, falling to my knees in front of them.

My father could only shake his head. "I don't know, we got off the train and then she screamed and just collapsed a few seconds ago, holding onto her head."

My mother looked right at me, her eyes wild. "She said there was something in her head. That 'it' was in her head!"

My mouth felt like I had a wad of glue in it as I realized how true the horror was.

*It happened to me*, I told my mom in my head. *I fought it off. I knew it was coming for you next. We tried to get here in time.*

My mother nodded and looked up at Dex before turning back to Ada.

"What do we do?" my mother asked the man who was helping them.

He grimaced. "It's a seizure. She should pull through, we just have to keep her comfortable and secure." He talked like a doctor and nodded at another man who was running up the stairs. "My partner has gone to get help, call where there's reception."

My mom looked back at me. *What do we really do?*

I could only hear what Pippa had told me. Kill the body and the head will die. There was no way that was happening to her. It didn't matter what the demon did once inside, what he'd make her do, no one was going to hurt my sister.

*Your grandmother said that?* My mom thought.

I gave her a pained look. *Maximus said something along those lines too, but don't worry mom, no one is going to lay a hand on her. We'll take her to see an exorcist, we'll contact my friend Bird, we'll make this work, we'll fight this. If I have to go into the Veil again, I will.*

"No!" my mother cried out loud. "It shouldn't be you, it shouldn't be anyone! You girls are my girls and you have too much to live for, to have to deal with this, it's not fair!"

My father stared at her, worried by her sudden outburst.

And suddenly I was struck with the most dreadful feeling, like some other, heavier shoe was about to drop at any second. Heavier than what was happening to my little sister as she lay on the ground, writhing, battling something deep within her.

Dex must have felt it too. He was behind me, grabbing hold of my waist, as if to hold me back from something.

Ada suddenly sat straight up, looking straight at me with pure black eyes. We all saw it, all sucked in our breath, as she started laughing, a sharp, raspy laugh that wasn't human.

My sister was gone. The demon in her place was alive.

"Damn you!" my mother bellowed, grabbing Ada by the shoulders and shaking her. "Damn you, damn you!"

My father grabbed her, trying to pull her off but my mother wouldn't let go. "Damn you!" She screamed.

And at that moment, Ada smiled, pure evil, and my mom suddenly flew backward as if shoved by invisible hands. Ada's eyes turned back to blue and she collapsed back to the ground.

I whirled around, about to help my mom up but when she looked at me she wasn't her anymore. And then she was. And then she wasn't. Her eyes alternated between obsidian and azure, her mouth between a grin and a cry.

I didn't know what to do. I felt completely and utterly helpless, hopeless. I could only watch. My father stumbled to his feet to try and help her, while Ada slowly eased herself up, holding her head in pain.

My mother hit my father, sending him flying a few feet and in that moment I think he finally realized it wasn't his wife. I think everyone realized that, even the man who was comforting Ada.

My mother turned to face me and I stared right back at those shark-like eyes, at a grin that wanted to eat me alive. A grin that said, "I won."

I was barely aware of what else was going on around me. I know the platform was growing crowded with people watching, some of them filming it on their phones. I knew that a voice was on the loudspeakers. I knew a train was approaching, not stopping at this station, not slowing down, shaking the walls and filling our ears.

All that mattered was that the demon had won.

*It hasn't*, my mom's voice came through loud and clear and for one brief instance I saw her eyes go back to normal and fill with tears.

Before I knew what was going on, my mother turned and ran for the edge of the platform, toward the tracks.

I remember screaming. I remember trying to run after her, my arms outstretched, trying to reach her. I remember Dex holding me back while my heart was ripped out of me.

My mother jumped down into the train tracks.

One second later a passing train came through.

The whole platform seemed to scream. The wail of brakes came a moment after but what was the point in stopping. She'd already been killed. She was already gone.

And the demon was gone with her.

She just gave her life for her family.

And I had just lost my mom.

While I remembered the moments leading up to it, I barely remembered a thing afterward, just flashes here and there. I guess I was in shock. Police, EMTs, the place was crawling with them as Dex and the bearded man - a doctor after all – tried to explain what had just happened. Dex let the doctor do most of the talking, because he was the sane one here. We all knew what happened, but it wouldn't make any sense coming from us.

Ada had cried and screamed, violently, and my father retreated into himself. He was acting almost normal, falling back on denial. It got him through it but I could see the pain. There was going to be so much pain. My poor fucking dad. He didn't understand any of this and yet this was his reality. It was my reality. His wife had just died in a horrific way and in his eyes, her actions were one of madness.

But I knew the truth. So did Ada. So did Dex. My mother gave it all up so that it wouldn't take us. So that it would finally be gone. But of all the sacrifices that I'd seen in the last few days, this was one I understood and because of that, it hurt the most.

My mother and I had never been close. She'd always been cool and closed-off to me. She always looked down on me but I later realized it was only because she feared who I was. She feared that I was like her mother and, she knew, that she was the same as us. She was just better at hiding it, at pretending it didn't exist.

But it did exist. And there wasn't anything more noble than embracing that fact and using it the way she did.

What the fuck did I know though, about nobility? About sacrifice. We could all appreciate what someone gives up, the lengths that someone will go to for another. It touches us, makes us feel loved. But in the end, the sacrifice hurts. Because they did it for us and we may not be so deserving.

I certainly wasn't the best daughter. I never even came close. I was bossy and bitchy, I was weird and demented. I was fat and drank and colored my hair a million Technicolor shades. I stayed out late in high school and skipped classes, I burned shit down, I was sent to a shrink, medicated, I hated life, hated myself, hated her, hated everyone. I did drugs and distanced myself from my family as much as I could. I had no self-esteem and I blamed everyone for everything.

My mother tried to do right, I know she did. But she just didn't know how. Like Dex's parents were afraid of him, my mother was afraid of me and where there is fear you can't feel love. It doesn't mean they didn't love us, because they did. It just wasn't shown so easily. It was fought for and I appreciated every time my mother fought to show me just how she felt. They were few and far between, at least I thought so. But when I looked back, I could see them there. It was like watching a movie for the second time and picking up on things you missed. It was there – it just needed to be found.

Grief is this thing, a hand of water that reaches into your lungs, and drowns you.

I drowned in my grief, as did everyone around me. If it wasn't for Dex, lifting me out of it, and in time, lifting everyone else out, I don't know what I would have done.

He may have not given his life again, but he saved me all the same.

## 19

DEX

"Stay with me."

I must have said those words a million times. Just holding onto Perry, trying to bring her to me, into this world we shared but was so brutally shattered.

Some days she couldn't even get out of her bed. So I let her be. Most of the time, I joined her, just holding on, feeling her skin, her warmth, her assurance that she was still alive even though her mind was a million miles away.

Other times, I had to get up. I had to be part of the world. There were more people hurting than just her, people she cared about. I had to make sure Ada was keeping up on her studies. She didn't have to go back to school – it was June and her grade was graduating anyway. She was allowed to pass but her teachers thought it was best that she still learn what she missed, to prepare for the next year.

So I became the despondent schoolteacher, trying to distract her if nothing else. It didn't always work, but sometimes it did. Poor little girl. While Perry was struggling, I knew her heart, knew her strength. Perry would pull out, in time. At least, I had faith she would.

But Ada, I didn't know about her. She was feisty and bull-headed as shit but in this sorrow, she wasn't herself. She was just this walking blonde numb thing that roamed the house, silent. She was a ghost.

And then there was Daniel. He was the trickiest of all, mainly because he wasn't my father. Not that my own father would have been any easier, but it felt like I had no authority over him. It wasn't my right to tell him to eat or to shower, and so I didn't. But I had some pull with the neighbors. One down the street, Debbie, whom insisted we call her DeeBee, became the Palomino's guardian angel. She had no problems bossing her way into their life and making sure their ship was being run.

But most of all, I focused just on Perry. Just on bringing her back to life. Everything else was just put on hold. I talked to Rebecca every other day, made sure Fat Rabbit was being taken care of, that they were both all right. I talked to Dean and to Seb. I talked to Jimmy and finally got the chance to tell him Experiment in Terror was over for good. There was a lot of yelling but I think he understood. He had no choice.

I even talked to my real father. He contacted me, finding me the same I found him. We talked twice and both times it was awkward. He asked about the wedding again and I wasn't sure if he was hinting for an invitation. I was truthful with him – I wasn't sure there was even going to be a wedding.

It was everything I wanted, a chance to start a new family. But it had to have come from Perry. She had to be the one to tell me. She had to want to move on. There's nothing harder than trying to celebrate something – no matter how happy it makes you – when there is just so much fucking sorrow around you. Sorrow clouds everything grey, even the sunshine.

Her mother did have a lovely funeral, if you could use such a word to describe such an event. I guess you can't. I've never done very well at funerals – having to say goodbye to an old friend a week before was hard enough. But somehow we all got through it. We all said goodbye. There was closure.

At least for Ada and Perry there was some sort of closure. They knew what had happened, they knew what their mother had done for them. But their father was another story. In his eyes – and what matched the reports of the other witnesses – was that she went crazy with grief over Ada and had leapt in front of the train. It didn't matter that the doctor who was trying to help them had made a note of the way that Ada and her mother were acting, their eyes turning black, the things they said, their inhuman strength. None of that mattered. It was so easy to sweep it away. I was used to it, the way people can turn a blind eye to the unexplained. I had done the same once. It was easier that way.

The truth hurts.

But the truth also saves.

It saved me. And, in time, it saved Perry.

One day, about a month after New York, she woke up in the morning and gazed at me with these beautifully clear eyes.

"I had a dream," she said and though her round eyes began to water, she didn't cry. "Pippa and my mother were in it."

I smiled and brushed her hair off her face. "Tell me about it."

"Well," she said, sitting up. I made sure the pillow was fluffed behind her. "We were by a waterfall. It looked like the Pacific Northwest and also like the Veil. Like, it had that one color. But it wasn't grey, it was gold. Everything was gold, like autumn leaves. And the three of us were just watching the water go over the edge. I guess I knew they were about to jump." She sighed, blinking, composing herself. "And they both hugged me and kissed me and told me to take care of myself, to take care of Ada, to take care of my dad to take care of you. They said they loved me and I would see them again one day. Then they let go of me and together they jumped over the edge. I remembered looking over and seeing the whole waterfall turn to sparkles, like fairy dust. And that was it."

I had no idea my own eyes filling with tears as she said this, I had to quickly wipe them before they fell.

"Baby," I whispered. "That's beautiful."

She managed a smile. "It was. And you know what, I think it was real. I think it was more than a dream. I just…I feel like they're okay, both of them. They have each other. They're happy." She put her hand to her heart. "I feel it here. Right in here."

And somehow, I felt it too.

After that, Perry seemed to pull herself out of her depression. The grief was still there, it still smothered her from time to time, but she was putting one foot in front of the other and managing to go on. For a few weeks, we both took reins of the household, and with the help of DeeBee, made sure everyone was going to be okay.

Finally it was time for us to go home. To our home.

"Well, here's to the groom to be," Dean said, raising his beer in the air.

"Here's to my best man," I said, knocking my bottle against the bottom of his, ensuring that a rush of foam would be surging to the top.

"You're such a dick, Dex," he whined after he tried to slurp up the beer that spilled over.

I gave him a one-shoulder shrug. "I don't mind being called a dick. Why not highlight my best feature, right?"

He narrowed his eyes at me. "You're an asshole too, you know."

I grinned. "Tight as a whistle."

He grimaced. "Please tell me Perry and Rebecca will be here soon because I don't know if I can handle another moment of bro night."

"They'll be here," I assured him, leaning back in my seat. We were in one of my favorite bars on $2^{nd}$ Ave. Perry and Rebecca had gone and done girly shit so I decided to get together with Dean and meet up with them later. Now that Dean had officially accepted as best man and Rebecca had accepted as a bridesmaid, it felt right to have a little soiree.

I gave him a wry look. "So, you getting any preggo sex?"

He rolled his eyes. "Dude, she's still a lesbian."

"A lesbian you put your dick in. Your super sperm got her pregnant. I don't think it's that far-fetched to think that you may still be hitting that."

"Hitting that?" he scoffed.

"Sorry. Fucking that vagina with your dick. Better?"

"Dex you need to get more idioms. Join us in the future, will you?"

"Can't happen, my friend. I'm getting married. Didn't you hear? That means that Perry accepts me as I am, faults and all. It also means I don't have to ever change." I took a swig of my beer and burped. "Isn't that brilliant?"

"For you, maybe." He shook his head in mock sorrow. "Poor Perry."

Thankfully, Dean's baby mama and my wife-to-be showed up before our conversation could disintegrate along with the contents of our drinks.

"Were you guys talking about us?" Perry asked, settling into the booth, a round Rebecca going beside Dean. The first thing I noticed was the stiff way Perry sat down. It was almost like she was trying to match Rebecca.

"What's wrong?" I asked her.

She immediately looked at Rebecca.

"I told you he would know," Rebecca said in her smart accent, though she looked awfully relieved to be sitting down. Next to Dean. No preggo sex, my ass. He was totally hitting that. Sorry, *fucking* her *vagina*. God.

"What, what?" I asked.

Perry breathed out of her nose in a huff and then said, "Okay, promise not to get mad."

I frowned as she lifted up her shirt and exposed a black patch of plastic on her ribcage, the kind tattoo artists use.

"You got a tattoo?" I asked.

She nodded. "It's not of you though." She peeled back a corner and I saw a detailed blue and black waterfall with the names Maximus, Pippa and Mom on it. It was actually quite awesome. "You're not mad?" she asked.

I shook my head, taking it in and feeling a bit of sorrow at the sight of Maximus. "Of course not. It's beautiful. And painful looking. That must have hurt."

She nodded.

I went on, "Why did you think I'd be mad?"

She tilted her head to the side in thought. "I don't know, I guess cuz Maximus was on there too. And I'd only just got the anchor for you."

"Kiddo," I said, pulling her close to me and kissing her temple. "First of all, you can get a million tattoos, I don't care. And second of all, I think your mom and Pippa would love it. And Maximus, well, his ego would love it too. But he deserves it, you know, after what he did for us. I think it's wonderful, really."

And I did. It made my insides seem all warm and fluttery, though that could have been the beer and shots of Jameson.

She smiled. "OK, good. I just wanted to honor everyone, you know."

I nodded. I knew.

I gave her another kiss and ordered Perry her favorite beer and Rebecca a club soda with lime. After our drinks came, the four of us raised our glasses to another.

"Here's to living the good life," I said, making sure to look them all in the eye. "And if not the good life, then just life in general. Here is to living life."

We all clinked glasses and bottles, Dean getting mine good this time, my beer flowing over.

I grinned at him, grinned at Rebecca, grinned at Perry.

Life was good.

And it was only going to get better.

## EPILOGUE

PERRY

"On a scale of one to eleven," Ada said as she stuck her hand into a crinkly bag of chips and popped them into her mouth, "how nervous are you?"

"Judging by how you're driving me nuts by crinkling that damn bag and your loud chewing," I said, taking the bag from her and sliding it down the table, away from us, "I'm going to say I'm at an eleven."

"Hey," she said with a frown, staring at the chips. "I'm hungry. It's not fair everyone else gets to eat before we do."

"Well, that's the price you pay for being part of the bridal party."

"Plus having to wear a hideous dress," she added. "Don't forget that."

I managed to glare at her. The dress I picked out for her and Rebecca was simple and beautiful and she knew it. It was knee-length and strapless, a fitted cherry red color that flared out from the waist. With her red lipstick and updo, she looked gorgeous and far older than sixteen.

But she was still a brat. Loving her didn't change that.

She sighed and sat back in her chair. I wondered how

she could possibly be so bored when I was anything but. I was freaking the fuck out and half-expected everyone to be freaking out with me.

We were sequestered away in a waiting room just above the hotel ballroom where the reception would take place. Outside the window, guests were filing into the area where the ceremony was set up. It was truly stunning, I had to admit that, with rows of white chairs leading up to a quaint gazebo where the officiant was waiting.

Dex was nowhere to be seen. That didn't surprise me, but I knew that if I did see him, standing there, waiting for me, a lot of my anxiety would disappear. I hadn't seen him for days because of the ways things ended up and I felt like I was shouldering this wedding all on my own. It had turned into a circus of sorts and I wanted nothing more than to ignore all these people – even though they were family and friends – and go be alone with Dex for a long time. Our own private world was the only place I could truly breathe.

Most people thought Dex and I were crazy for having a partially outdoor wedding in Washington, in October of all times, but though the sky was grey, it looked like the rain was holding off and I could see a few glimpses of bright blue sky punch through. There was a chill in the air, thanks to our location in the mountains, but the ceremony wouldn't take long and I had this beautiful lacy shawl to protect me from the elements.

True to us, we ended up booking the Salish Lodge, overlooking Snoqualmie Falls. It was an absolutely beautiful setting, with the air coated in a fine mist from the roar of the waterfall and the autumnal yellow and gold peppered forest rising up on all sides. But really, we booked it because it's The Great Northern Hotel from *Twin Peaks*. I mean, come on. David Lynch, Agent Cooper, Log Lady and Killer Bob – totally *us*.

"How long is Rebecca going to be?" Ada asked. After the officiant had paid me a visit and went over the last minute details of the ceremony, I had sent Rebecca to go get my father, who would be walking me down the aisle, plus Dean and Seb, Dex's best men.

"I don't know," I said, getting out of my chair, careful not to get my dress caught. It was off-white, long and lacey with a button-up back. I'd found it in a vintage store in Portland – I was never even sure if it was supposed to be a wedding dress or not – but it was too perfect for words. It showed off my waist, hips and boobs, yet still looked elegant and demure, almost like I was some sort of fragile fairy. I wore my hair down, in long twisting waves, while Rebecca had fixed in a few sparkling clear jewels into my hair to complete the ethereal look.

"I'm going to go touch up my makeup," I told her, grabbing my purse off the table and sliding the bag of chips back toward her. I already had a shitload of makeup on my face but I needed something, anything, to do, than to sit here and wait.

After I stealthily made it to the bathroom, paranoid I'd run into people, or Dex, I touched up my pink lipstick and tried to take in a few deep breaths. I didn't know why I was so nervous. It had nothing to do with marrying Dex whatsoever. I definitely didn't like crowds or people or being the certain of attention. And I guess I just figured something would go horribly wrong.

New York seemed long ago but not long enough. The memories still haunted me and they were made worse today. Maximus would have been one of Dex's groomsman. My mother had always wanted me to get married. Neither of them would be here. Maybe in spirit – always in spirit – just as I knew Pippa would be. But the fact that they were both taken from us left me with a hollow pain in my chest that hadn't gone away.

For the longest time, I wasn't even sure if I wanted to get married. Though I wanted to spend my life with Dex, it didn't seem right, or even fair, to do something that would make me happy. My mother was dead and though we had never been close, she'd always been my mom. She would have liked this wedding – okay, she would have nit-picked the shit out of it – but she would have been here and she would have been happy for me.

It just didn't seem right to celebrate anything. But it was my dad who insisted we go through with the ceremony, because it's what my mother would have wanted and it's what he wanted. He needed this, to feel his friends and family around him, to see his daughter on her happiest day of her life. Ada needed it. And maybe I needed it too.

I blinked back the few tears that teased at my eyes and stared at myself in the mirror. I wasn't sure if it was the makeup artist or what, but I really did looking like a glowing, blushing bride. I just wanted more than anything to cry tears of love, not tears of loss.

I sighed and gave myself the once over then opened the door to the hallway.

Dex was standing right there, back to me, and I could only give out a faint shriek before he turned around and saw me.

"No!" I yelled at him, horrified, as if I'd been caught naked by someone.

His eyes widened. "Fuck me."

I turned around to head back into the bathroom but he

quickly reached out and grabbed my arm, bringing me to him.

I stared up at him, still shocked and worried that he had seen me before the wedding, but also soothed by his touch and revved by his look. My god he looked fucking handsome as anything, wearing a tuxedo and bowtie that complemented his athletic body and made him the sexiest James Bond ever. He was as close to clean-shaven as he could be, which still meant some masculine stubble, and had taken out his eyebrow ring. But his face looked clear, deadly handsome, and his eyes, his beautiful dark eyes – they were watering.

Oh no, not good.

"Perry," he whispered, his voice cracking. "You look beautiful. So damn beautiful. I think my heart is on the floor."

I gulped, now regretting my wish for happy tears. They wanted to barge on out and ruin my makeup. "You're not supposed to see me, Dex!" I said in an angry hush. "It's bad luck to see the bride before the ceremony."

His mouth quirked up. "Is that right? Listen, kiddo, the two of us have had all the bad luck in the world. I say bring it fucking on."

"I'm serious," I said.

He grabbed both my hands and kissed me softly on the forehead. "So am I," he mumbled against my skin.

I closed my eyes and fell into his touch. Immediately the ache in my heart was soothed, my nerves stopped fizzing. His lips brought me peace and warmth.

"Can we just stay like this and skip the ceremony?" I said into his chest. I could feel his heart beating steadily beneath his suit.

"Nah," he said. "We'd have a herd of angry people out

there and I really don't want your father to punch me again, especially now that your uncle is here. Don't tell me that they aren't part of the mafia because you and I both know that they have some sneaky shit going on."

"And now you're being welcomed into the family," I said, doing my best Brando impression. I lifted my head and stared up at him. "Do you really think I look beautiful?"

He smiled so warmly I felt it in my toes. "Perry, you are so fucking beautiful, you're making me want to cry. I don't think I've ever seen a sight on earth more beautiful than you right now."

I smiled softly as a single tear leaked out.

"And seriously, if I wasn't so scared of your father, I'd take you into that bathroom and fuck you good and hard against the wall, cuz my god, your breasts right now..."

Dex rarely looked impressed and always walked around with a smart-ass smirk on his face. It was part of his appeal. But now he was impressed. He was floored.

I stepped out of his grasp and punched him lightly in the side. "Hey, it's not my fault they're always the focal point."

"I ain't complaining," he said, raising his hands in mock surrender. "You still look very tasteful." He smirked and added, "Tastefully fuckable."

I gave him a wry look. "Well, so do you." I took a step closer to him, starting to seriously ponder the whole sex in the bathroom thing and would that really be a big no-no before the ceremony?

"Bollocks!" Rebecca's voice came shattering through us. "What the hell are you guys doing?"

We both turned to see Rebecca marching toward us with an uneasy Dean and Seb in tow. Dean looked very handsome in his suit. Seb, with his long hair and stoner expression, looked like Pauly Shore going to a business meeting. Oh well, can't win them all.

"It's my fault," Dex said quickly before Rebecca could get close enough to hit him. "I was wandering around and saw her."

"Why the bloody hell are you wandering around?" she asked him before looking to me for an explanation. I shrugged. Even though she was six months pregnant, you could barely tell, and she'd become more intimidating as the baby grew.

"Well what the bloody hell is taking you guys so long?" Dex asked, imitating her accent. "The ceremony dude is standing at the front doing nothing and everyone else is just sitting there. I don't want to go stand in front of everyone for an hour, looking like a total douchenugget with him."

She was unimpressed. "That's what happens in a wedding." She grabbed his shoulders and spun him around and away from me. "Now go back and forget the fact that you ever saw Perry beforehand."

"Just look at her, babe. That will be impossible," he said over his shoulder, moving with swagger. He gave the thumbs up to Dean and Seb as he walked past them and disappeared around the corner.

She shook her head angrily, the angles of her dark bob swinging against her face and took me by the arm. "I can't believe him. What an idiot."

I nodded my head in agreement but the fact was, even though it was against "the rules" to see him beforehand, our brief encounter had given me strength. My anxiety about everything had pretty much vanished.

I took in a deep breath and let her lead me back into the waiting room where Ada was dumping out the rest of the chips in her mouth. I wondered when her bad eating habits would catch up with her, then pushed the envy out of my head. We were different people and though I worked out steadily and went all "paleo' for a few months to fit in my dress, I would always be a curvy girl and finally I was proud of it.

The reaction I got from Dex only cemented that.

"Now are we ready?" Ada asked as Dean closed the door behind us, lest Dex wander past again.

"I think so," I said. I looked at the four of them, red dresses, black suits, all looking the best I had ever seen them (even Seb, though that wasn't saying much). Here we were, my sister, my best friend, Dex's best friends, and one unborn baby, all together in one room, celebrating the journey of Dex and me.

"Oh no, she's going to cry," Rebecca said, and suddenly a tissue was whipped out from her clutch and shoved in my fingers.

I gave her a mock glare but still dabbed underneath my eyes like a pre-emptive strike. "I'm not going to cry," I told her. I took in a deep breath and looked at all of them. "I just wanted to thank you guys so much for being here on this day. It means a lot to me and it means a lot to Dex. He doesn't have any family now, except for his dad and it's doubtful he'll show up, so I know you mean the world to him."

"Oh fuck," Seb muttered in a half-sob, quickly wiping at his eyes. "Don't worry, it's my allergies."

I couldn't help but smile. Even Seb was feeling emotional. "Anyway, thank you all so very much."

"I'd cheers to that," Ada said. "But we won't be allowed to eat or drink anything until you get this circus rolling." She gave me a pointed look.

"Okay, okay," I said, crumbling up the tissue and tossing it away. "Let's go get me fucking married then!"

"Huzzah!" Dean cheered.

"All right, everyone pair with your partner," I told them as if were in kindergarten.

Though Dean was Rebecca's baby daddy and the two had grown extremely close – albeit not in a romantic way – Dean was Dex's best man, which meant he'd be walking down the aisle with my maid of honor, Ada. Seb and Rebecca would go next. Then it would be me and my dad.

Just as I started to wonder where he was, there was a knock at the door.

Rebecca answered it and my dad stepped in.

His normally grim face immediately crumpled at the sight of me.

"Oh, my little girl," he said, his voice started to choke up as he came toward me with open arms.

"Aw, crap," Seb mumbled behind us, fighting back tears again.

"Hi dad," I said softly as he enveloped me into his arms while being careful not to smudge my hair and face.

He pulled back and brushed my hair off my face, staring at me admiringly, eyes shiny with pride. "You look like a woman, Perry. A beautiful, striking, radiant woman."

"Thank you," I said, always a bit shy when my father paid me compliments. He didn't do it very often, so it was always a shock.

"Your mother would have been so proud of you," he whispered and now I heard someone else sniffling in the group. We were all going to leave here as sobbing wrecks if this continued.

Somehow I kept it together and gave him a melancholy smile. "I think wherever she is, she knows."

"You're right," he said, his voice shaking slightly. "She does. Your grandmother, too."

My heart pinched but I refused to push the sadness away. It was okay to be sad. And it was okay to be happy too. Because my mother and my grandmother, whether they were in the Thin Veil or had moved on, I could feel them watching me, I could sense their joy. There was some comfort in that, some peace, and some acceptance that it would make them happy if I was happy.

He grabbed my hand and squeezed it. "Are you ready to become Mrs. Dex Foray?"

I nodded. "I always have been."

I linked my arm through his and we stepped out into the hallway and waited for Dean and Ada to go ahead, followed by Seb and Rebecca. We walked down the stairs to the doors which opened out into the yard and waited for the cue. My father and I stayed out of sight of the guests, tucked around the corner.

As soon as the first notes of the music started – a pretty piano piece – Rebecca and Seb went out, walking down the aisle. Then Dean and Ada, Ada giving my dad and I an exaggerated smile before they walked off.

I counted the beats in my head, waiting for the music to get louder, lusher, and when it did, it was time.

My dad kissed me on the head and whispered. "Let's go."

We turned the corner and I was met with a rush of emotions. Everyone I knew in the world was standing up, staring at me, smiles on their faces, cameras out, whispering to each other about how pretty I looked. But as I walked past them, none of that mattered. I wasn't aware of anything except the man at the end of the aisle, the man I was walking toward.

My eyes were glued to Dex's as his were glued to mine. I

beamed at him – he grinned right back. Though I had just seen him earlier, he still managed to take my breath away. He was the most handsome man I'd ever seen and it hit me in the gut, a wonderful blow, to know he was going to be mine forever.

Everything rushed past me in a blur and suddenly I was in front of the officiant and Dex, my father handing me off to him and placing my hands in his.

"Do you, Daniel Palomino, give your daughter Perry away to this man, Dex Foray?" the officiant asked.

My father nodded, smiling at Dex for what seemed like the first time ever. "That I do." Then he quickly pulled Dex into a tight embrace. I looked behind me at Rebecca and Ada and they both looked like they wanted to cry. My god, who knew weddings were such a tearjerker.

There were a few claps and my father went and sat down in the front row next to my uncle Al and his sons, Matt and Tony, all of them looking content, Fat Rabbit wriggling in Tony's arms, his tongue hanging out. Uncle Al winked at me before I turned back to Dex and the officiant.

The man started speaking, a deep but jovial voice that immediately put Dex and I at ease. That said, I was holding onto Dex's hands for dear life, as if I'd disappear if I let go. When I wasn't listening to the officiant, I was staring at Dex, as deep as I could, and nothing else out there mattered.

I wished it hadn't all passed by in a blur, but it did. We said our vows. Dex looked teary-eyed. When I looked at my father, I got teary-eyed. When it came time to put the rings on each other's fingers, Dex dropped mine and it rolled under the gazebo. Thank god for Matt and his long alien-like arms who managed to reach under and pull it out.

He gave it back to Dex who blew on it and then, after a shrug to the crowd, proceeded to put the sparkling diamond band on my finger. It settled next to my vintage engagement ring perfectly.

Then came the kiss. Dex put his hands behind my neck and head and pulled me in close and tight. The kiss was deep, sweet, and hot. And more than that, it meant something. It meant everything. This was just the start. After everything, this was just the start.

I couldn't wait to begin.

After we signed all the right papers and were pronounced husband and wife, we joined hands and walked down the aisle. I made note to look at every single person that I passed, to take them in, to appreciate what they were in my life and to silently thank them for coming.

To my surprise I found myself looking into the eye of Curtis O'Shea, his wife Margaret sitting beside him in the back row. I smiled at him, just in case Dex didn't see him, to let him know it meant something for him to come.

We were immediately whisked off to have photographs taken. Our photographer was a goof, which was great since we were too. After our sessions were done with ourselves, my dad and my uncle and cousins got involved, as did the bridal party. I briefly brought it up to Dex that I had seen his father. It was his call if he wanted to involve him.

Of course it was all too soon and too much for Dex to include him in something like this, but Dex at least seemed happy about his presence. Baby steps, it was all about the baby steps.

The reception was an absolute blast. There were roast-like speeches done by Dean and Rebecca and my uncle told one that had people laughing until they were crying. Then, people actually were crying. My dad got up and said his speech. By the end, when he'd finished telling me how proud my mother would be of me, he broke down in tears. Everyone in the house followed.

But it was okay, because the tears meant she was loved and wouldn't be forgotten. I leaned into Dex while holding Ada's hand under the table. We all felt her there, even if we couldn't see her. We felt loved and we felt pride. It was beautiful.

When that was over and we stuffed ourselves with food, it was time for the first dance. Only our first dance was a bit different.

Dex led me out to the dance floor and whirled me around, no sound. Then he grinned at me and went over to the DJ, who handed him a wireless microphone. After a moment, the music, a slow but familiar piano melody, started playing.

"What the hell?" I whispered to him. "I thought we were dancing to Led Zeppelin?"

He kept on grinning. "Not a chance," he said and then the music came in louder. It was none other than Herb Alpert's "This Guy's In Love With You" but covered by Faith No More. He removed his jacket and whirled it somewhere into the crowd of people, someone crying out as if they were smacked in the face with it. I hoped there wouldn't be a potential lawsuit.

He put his arm around me and he microphone up to his mouth.

"They say this guy's," he sang deeply with a wide, cocky grin, "this guy's in love with you."

I was instantly transported back to Seattle, when he and I weren't even dating yet, at the Christmas party for Shownet. Rebecca had been there, Dean and Seb, too. Dex had delivered the most amazing karaoke rendition of this song, something that knocked me on my ass and made me realize just how much I had fallen for him and what I would go through to get him.

Now it was pretty much doing the same thing. But this time, he was singing it to me, no mistake, and dancing at the same time. Our first dance and I was being serenaded.

He leaned back, eyes closed in passion, and belted out, "I need your love. I want your love." He looked at me, deep in the eyes and sang with perfection, the kind of powerful, confident voice that soared to the heavens, "Say you're in love with this guy."

I could only grin right back him. My heart had melted somewhere inside me and I was just this pile of newly married goo. I'd never felt more swoony in my life and I was swooning all for him. My husband.

Needless to say, it was hard to keep my hands off of him for the rest of the reception. Somewhere between The Chicken Dance and Billy Joel, we fucked off to the bathroom for a little fun. Unfortunately, the bathrooms were occupied and when we finally found a corner of the hotel where I could ride him up against the wall, we were interrupted by Ada, who was a bit drunk and looking for some guy called Jay.

The sex had to wait. I suppose it made it more special that way, though in my mind it was hard to get more special than being fucked in a wedding gown. I mean, there are only so many times you can have that happen.

So we went back to reception and watched as the guests grew tired and retreated to their rooms or their very long drive back to Seattle. Dex even managed to talk to his dad and stepmother for about a half hour while I was doing makeshift beer pong with Tony and Matt while Fatty Rab dozed at our feet. It was nice, just knowing that despite everything and everyone we had lost, we still had our families and were about to start a new one.

When there was just ten drunks milling around on the dance floor to all the bad songs, Dex and I quickly left, like we were fleeing the scene of a crime. It was late and we were unbelievably tired and if we were going to consummate this marriage, we had to do it now.

We went up to our suite – gorgeous and spacious – and he carried me through the door in his arms before depositing me on the bed

"Well, well, well," he said, grabbing under my dress and pulling me towards the edge of the frame. "This is the first time I get to sleep with Mrs. Dex Foray. She's sexier than I had imagined."

"You better believe it," I told him, spreading my legs wider. I was wearing sky blue lace panties. My borrowed was the sparkle pins in my hair, the old was my engagement ring and the new was my dress. I had at least made some kind of an effort.

I'd also gotten a full-on bikini wax. There was that too.

Dex pulled off my underwear with his teeth and then moaned with admiration.

"I think I'm going to like married life a lot," he murmured before his tongue snaked up the inside of my thighs.

"Me too," I said, my hips automatically arching for his tongue.

He didn't disappoint. He never did.

We fucked, made love, had sex as husband and wife. It felt better than I could have ever thought. Our relationship was consummated. Things were reborn. They were given life and new beginnings. We were given hope for the future.

And afterward, while I lay there in his arms, me his wife

and he my husband, I realized I didn't know what the future held. But I knew it held Dex.

And that was more than good enough for me.

That was everything.

The End

## WHAT'S NEXT?

You wouldn't think there would be anything next, right?

Well, you're wrong.

Yes, the EIT series has come to a bittersweet end.

But what if I told you that there is a spinoff, staring Ada, set a few years from now, where you would get to see a lot of a happily married Dex and Perry, and the mysterious figure Ada met at their wedding?

That book is called VEILED.

Just click here to read on.

*Death.*

*It's something that Ada Palomino has always known so well, having grown up in a house of horrors, surrounded by a family plagued by ghosts and demons and things that go bump in the night.*

*But after the sudden and tragic death of her mother two years ago, death has never felt so personal.*

*Or so close.*

*Now eighteen, Ada is trying to move on with her life and the last month of summer holds nothing but sunshine and promises with her first year at a Portland design school just around the bend.*

*That is until her increasingly violent and realistic dreams, dreams of other worlds, of portals and veils where her mother is tortured and souls bleed for mercy, start to blend into reality. Ada has to lean on her older sister, Perry, to try and make sense of it all but even then, she's never felt more alone.*

*Then there's Jay. Tall, handsome and deeply mysterious, Jay would be just another stranger, a familiar face on the bus, if it wasn't for the fact that Ada has met him before.*

*Every night.*

*In every single dream.*

*And the more that Ada is drawn to him in both worlds, the more she's in danger of losing everything.*

*Including her heart.*

*And her very soul.*

If you want to connect with me, you can always find me

on Instagram (where I post travel photos, fashion, teasers, etc, IG IS MY LIFE and the easiest place to find me online)

-> or in my Facebook Group (we're a fun bunch and would love to have you join)

-> Otherwise, feel free to signup for my mailing list (it comes once a month) and Bookbub alerts!

## ACKNOWLEDGMENTS

I can't even...

Ah, but wouldn't that be the cop-out – to say it's too difficult to thank everyone who has helped and inspired me on this journey so I won't.

But I will.

The idea for Experiment in Terror came during a drive through the rural landscape of Ontario. Kind of an odd place for it since I had never been to Ontario before that (LIVE AND DIE ON THE WEST COAST!) but while I was staring outside the window of my ex-boyfriend's family's car I started dreaming about Perry Palomino.

Yes, that's right. My girl Perry, she came first. Ada came second. Dex...he eventually came around. Anyway, I started thinking about the books I used to love reading...Baby-Sitters Club, Nancy Drew, Fear Street. I wanted to take that emotional connection that you feel to certain characters as you follow them through a series but I wanted to put it in a dark and scary setting. Something modern and new that I could keep going for a while, with the same romantic and sexual tension as The X-Files.

I'm not really sure when Dex came into the picture as "Dex" but at some point I stopped thinking about EIT as a series (or let's face it, a book – Darkhouse) I would one day write and I decided to write it. I needed an enigmatic young man (back then, Dex was totally inspired by my love of musician Mike Patton) as the love interest as so Dex was born. And then I put it all together by committing to writing every single day for a month. Six weeks later, the first draft of Darkhouse was born. See, I was always able to write fast :P

Of course the first draft totally sucked balls and barely resembles the book you read today (and even that book needs a lot of work but whatever, it was my first book ever and I'm still proud of it). Thankfully, after that learning curve of a book, I really became efficient at the writing process and I never had to do that first draft overhaul ever again.

Red Fox took me about a year to write because I was doing music journalism stuff and only wrote on occasion. I remember at the time voicing my thoughts to someone I knew "what if they call the show Experiment in Terror, after the Fantomas song Experiment in Terror?" and he said, "No, that sucks, don't bring down Fantomas by doing that" and I did it anyway. Ha! Whatever. The drummer for Fantomas, Dave Lombardo (also was in Slayer, obviously) has read both Darkhouse and Red Fox and he loves the name (and the books!), so fuck you. Also Dave Lombardo is awesome. I have a very distinct memory of giving him a paperback copy of Red Fox and he and his son started singing the damn Tomahawk song that I named the book after. One of the coolest moments ever! I'll never forget it, it was like the art that I created and the art I admired all came together.

Where was I? Oh yeah. Have you noticed the musical

them in the EIT series? Darkhouse's original name was From Out of Nowhere, a Faith No More song, but I later changed it to a non-song title. But Red Fox is the aforementioned Tomahawk song, Dead Sky Morning was inspired by a Team Sleep song (Kool-Aid Party). Lying Season is a B-side Alice in Chains song. On Demon Wings is from Bohren and Der Club of Gore. Into the Hollow is a Queen of the Stone Age song (and obviously, Josh Homme was the inspiration for our favorite ginger), Come Alive is Foo Fighters and Ashes to Ashes is, finally, Faith No More. Dust to Dust is not named after anything – just like Darkhouse. Full circle and all that.

But enough music talk. I can't properly explain the publishing journey, from when I first released Darkhouse on May 13$^{th}$, 2011, to now, releasing Dust to Dust on July 29$^{th}$, 2014. Hell, it's not even being released by me in the UK, it's being done by Piaktus, an imprint of Little Brown. It's got a freakin' publisher! It's been three years of pain and sorrow and happiness and joy. EIT was life-changing to me, it truly was. It still isn't the most popular series – most readers don't know who Dex Foray is and I think that should be rectified – but it was the series that put me on the "map" as an author, getting people to appreciate me and my work and gave me the skill that I later translated into other books. To put simply, EIT made me better in every way.

And for that, I have to thank a lot of people. Some were only there in the beginning, some were only there in the end. But they all matter.

In no freaking particular order, each of these people either read and loved the books or helped with the books – Scott MacKenzie, Kelly St-Laurent, my parents Tuuli and Sven, Kara Malinczak, Najla Qamber, Kass Healy, Mollie Caselli, Talar K, Nadia Yotis, Alex St-Laurent, Tami McColgan, Megan Caffery, Wendy Kennedy, Amanda Sanderson, Stephanie Brown, Megan Simpson, Jamie Sager Hall, Tressa Sager, Marj Mariano, Jen Hall, Amy Harmon, RL Griffin, Megan Ward O'Connell, Brenna Weidner, Rebecca Espinoza, Andrea Thompson, Rhiannon Frater, Dave Lombardo, Marc Paschke, Odette Gauthier, Wendy MacKenzie, Autumn Hull, Laura Helseth, Michelle Duncan, Nina Decker, Sandra Cortez, Bret Taylor, Lindsay Bayne, Robin Stranahan, Maryse Courtier Black, Sundae Colletti, Paula Novack, Kirsten Papi, Sherry Osterhout Durst, Joanna Wylde, Carey Heywood, Lori Parker, Carmen Jenner, Brandon Lemmons, Kelli Brown, Andrew Barber, Laura MacKenzie, Ali Hymer, Nadine Colling, all the people on Goodreads with "Dex" in their name, Sarah Chauncy, Mike Shearer, Kayla Veres, Bill Gould, Lucia Valovčíková, Amy Bartol, Scott Waxman, Latoya Smith, Amanda Polito, Rachel Sharp, Kimberly Cheeseman, Janice Pia, Emily Franke, LH Cosway, Taylor Haggerty, Farley Chase, Conner Galway, all them Twitter peeps who embraced me from the start, Jenny Bragdon, Sarah and Scott Trudeau, Robyn Summers, Lea Marika, Paula Roper, Chelcie Holguin, Rachel Hartman, Niki Jefford, Jill McIntosh, Dale De Ruiter, Matt Sardof, Crystal Chapman, Candice Roach, Kira Knappet, Linda Knappet, Tara Sivec, Barbie Fucking Messner, Lisa Chamberlain, Lisa Chamberlin, Barbara Lopez, Kristin Thompson, Heidi Hines, Tray Davis, Krystle Zion, Bob Hele, Chelsea M. Cameron, Erin Griffin, Shawna Vitale and many, many more! Basically, if you love Perry and Dex...THANK YOU!

Finally...is this the end of Experiment in Terror? For reals?

Yes. Sorry. The show is done. The series is over.

Does that mean we'll never see Dex and Perry again?

I have no plans to continue their story – though I will be continuing Ada's in a shorter series and you will see them there from time to time – but I also "never say never." If I do choose to revisit Dex and Perry one day, it will probably be a single book, set further in the future for this duo, and for you and I, I'm talking about 2016 and beyond. So nothing to get too excited about because my mind is a fickle beast and who knows if God allows me to still be writing that far ahead. But, just so as you know, the world is full of possibilities.

But for now, this is where you and I and Dex and Perry say goodbye.

May they haunt you in your dreams and everyday life as they do in mine.

<3

If you've enjoyed this book, please send me an email, I'd love to hear from you and maybe answer any unanswered questions (please note that I can't always get back to everyone because I am a scatterbrain, but I do read every email): authorkarinahalle@gmail.com

## ABOUT THE AUTHOR

Karina Halle, a former screenwriter, travel writer and music journalist, is the *New York Times*, *Wall Street Journal*, and *USA Today* bestselling author of *The Pact, A Nordic King*, and *Sins & Needles*, as well as over fifty other wild and romantic reads. She, her husband, and their adopted pit bull live in a rain forest on an island off British Columbia, where they operate a B&B that's perfect for writers' retreats. In the winter, you can often find them in California or on their beloved island of Kauai, soaking up as much sun (and getting as much inspiration) as possible. For more information, visit

www.authorkarinahalle.com

## ALSO BY KARINA HALLE

*Contemporary Romances*

Love, in English

Love, in Spanish

Where Sea Meets Sky (from Atria Books)

Racing the Sun (from Atria Books)

The Pact

The Offer

The Play

Winter Wishes

The Lie

The Debt

Smut

Heat Wave

Before I Ever Met You

After All

Rocked Up

Wild Card (North Ridge #1)

Maverick (North Ridge #2)

Hot Shot (North Ridge #3)

Bad at Love

The Swedish Prince

The Wild Heir

A Nordic King

Nothing Personal

My Life in Shambles

Discretion

Disarm

Disavow

The Royal Rogue

The Forbidden Man

*Romantic Suspense Novels by Karina Halle*
Sins and Needles (The Artists Trilogy #1)

On Every Street (An Artists Trilogy Novella #0.5)

Shooting Scars (The Artists Trilogy #2)

Bold Tricks (The Artists Trilogy #3)

Dirty Angels (Dirty Angels #1)

Dirty Deeds (Dirty Angels #2)

Dirty Promises (Dirty Angels #3)

Black Hearts (Sins Duet #1)

Dirty Souls (Sins Duet #2)

*Horror Romance*

Darkhouse (EIT #1)

Red Fox (EIT #2)

The Benson (EIT #2.5)

Dead Sky Morning (EIT #3)

Lying Season (EIT #4)

On Demon Wings (EIT #5)

Old Blood (EIT #5.5)

The Dex-Files (EIT #5.7)

Into the Hollow (EIT #6)

And With Madness Comes the Light (EIT #6.5)

Come Alive (EIT #7)

Ashes to Ashes (EIT #8)

Dust to Dust (EIT #9)

The Devil's Duology

Donners of the Dead

Veiled

Made in United States
North Haven, CT
11 April 2025

67869057R00178